Escape from Russia

Escape from Russia

Jane Boruszewski

PENNYWYSE PRESS
TUCSON, ARIZONA

Published in the United States of America by:

Pennywyse Press
3710 East Edison
Tucson AZ 85716

Names, characters, places, and incidents, unless otherwise specifically noted, are either the product of the author's imagination or are used fictitiously.

Library of Congress Control Number: 2010920549

Book and Cover Design by Leila Joiner
Title page art © Irene Dishaw
Cover photograph: Sunset © Kamchatka

ISBN 978-1-935437-15-4
ISBN 1-935437-15-1

Printed in the United States of America on Acid-Free Paper

To my family,
with love

Chapter One

Her parents were born in the part of Poland occupied for over one hundred years by Austria, but Frania came into the world after the country regained its precious freedom at the end of World War I. She grew into a lovely teenager in Eastern Poland. Her people and the land were her love and life, all of which changed completely one devastating day.

"Frania, Marysia, don't sneak out the window like this, please," pleaded Aniela, sitting up in bed on her straw mattress, the eiderdown covers pulled tight around her.

"The boys are waiting outside." Frania tossed her head, and her light brown hair shimmered in the light of the kerosene lamp. "And I'm going."

"If Tata finds out, he'll beat you both again."

Frania's blue eyes flashed with anger. "Let him. He can kill me if he wants, but I'm not staying home tonight."

"I like to dance, too," Aniela said. "But Tata—"

"You, dancing?" Frania laughed. She leaned closer to Aniela. "You're so plain no one would ask you."

"Stop that!" Marysia broke her silence. "Aniela's not bad looking. She has blond hair like Mama's."

"And pimples from wall to wall, and she's skinny as a stick. She's just like Mama. They're both afraid of Tata. He doesn't want us girls to get in trouble, so he takes the easy way out. He locks us up at night like prisoners. What's worse, Mama lets him."

"You're right—he's mean." Marysia smoothed out her dark hair and examined her pretty face in the small mirror on the wall.

"Do you hear the band playing at Wroble's house, Aniela?" Frania teased her younger sister. "Come on to the party with us."

Aniela shook her head and threw herself down on her pillow. She pulled the covers up to her chin and whispered, "I can't. You two go. But, please, don't get caught tonight."

The two sisters climbed through the window into the dark. Marysia ran right into the waiting arms of Marek. Frania pushed Julek away when he tried to embrace her.

"What's wrong with you lately?" said Julek. "You don't like me to kiss you anymore. And if you do let me kiss you, it feels like you're pretending I'm someone else."

"Don't be silly, Julek," Frania said. She was glad he couldn't see her blush in the semi-darkness. "Marysia." She poked her sister. "Break it up with Marek. Let's go to the party. I want to dance, dance, dance."

Dressed in a snowy-white blouse, her brown pleated skirt reaching to her knees, Frania danced and danced that evening. While the music played, she swirled about and smiled at her partners, but she refused to go out necking with them. Often, she would close her eyes and sigh deeply, for a strange longing had lodged in her young heart. If only *he* had come to the dance. If only he would. But, of course, he wouldn't, because he was of a better class. God, was this what they called love? Why did it hurt so not to see him here? Did he like her? She hoped he did. Why else would he be smiling and coming out of the school whenever he saw her passing by? She loved him dearly because he was different from all the others. He was educated, mature, and he didn't look at her the way the village boys did.

Suddenly, she saw him, tall and blond, standing in the doorway. A ring of school children was fast forming about him.

She was waltzing with Julek. "I have a bad headache," she said to him, then pouted like a child. "Could we sit out the rest of the dance?"

"What?" he said. "I've never seen you stop dancing while there's music playing."

"Do you mind?" she said and stopped in the middle of the floor.

She left him no choice, but walked off with him following close behind. They passed near a group chatting by the door. She glanced at the newcomer and saw him looking at her. A warm tingle rushed along her spine.

The band—two violinists, a drummer, and an accordionist—took a short rest. Many couples rushed to occupy the benches that leaned against the whitewashed walls. Holy pictures stared down accusingly at the human sinners.

Some of the young people paired off and wandered outside.

Frania chattered on about nothing to Julek and the other teenagers sitting nearby, but all the time, out of the corner of her eye, she watched the young man by the door. She was afraid he might disappear any moment. Soon the musicians returned, and the room filled with the beat of her favorite polka. Julek pulled at her hand, but she wouldn't budge. Again, she complained of a headache.

Then she saw him standing in front of her, bowing slightly like a real gentleman. As if in a dream, Frania went into his arms and seemed to float around the room. He was saying something, and she was answering, but all the time she wondered how would it be if he were to kiss her right there on the dance floor, in front of everyone. Too soon, the polka ended, and he walked her back to the bench where Julek still sat waiting.

"Please sit by me," she said to her new escort, her voice soft and quavering.

"Thank you. I will." He smiled at her and again bowed, as if she were a princess.

"I'm glad you came to the party, Mister…"

"Call me Andrzej."

"A…Andrzej," she said shyly.

"That sounds much better." He smiled, and she saw his eyes were focused on her exposed knees. "I'm happy to be here, Frania."

"Andrzej," she repeated and smiled at him, dimples in her rosy cheeks.

"It's stuffy and noisy in here," he said. "Would you like to go outside for some fresh air, Frania?"

"Yes, yes," she said, but then she lowered her eyes to the floor. Suddenly, she realized how eager she had sounded.

Ignoring Julek and heedless of curious eyes watching them, Frania left the crowded room with Andrzej. The night was young. Moonlight cast long blue shadows on the yard and the garden where tulips bloomed.

"We've talked together many times," he began, when they were seated on a small bench under the linden tree, "but you still haven't told me much about yourself."

She shrugged her shoulders, not knowing what to say. She could hear other couples giggling in the depths of the garden.

"You live in the white wooden house with the slate roof," he said.

"That's right," she said. Her teeth began to chatter. It was early in the spring, and the air still held the sharp edge of winter's chill.

"There are acacia, linden, cherry, apple trees growing all around your homestead. The white picket fence surrounds it all. Am I correct?"

She nodded, wishing she could stop shivering.

"You have four sisters. Right?"

"Yes."

"Your family must work hard to keep the farm so well kept. It's a charming place."

"Thank you, Andrzej," she said, her teeth clicking like chattering insects.

"You are cold, Frania." He took off his suit jacket and bent to put it over her shoulders. "Why didn't you tell me? I don't want you to catch cold."

She said nothing, but sat looking at the ground. She wished she were one of those city girls with soft hands and a delicate face. Andrzej would like her better then, and he would try to kiss her.

"Did you graduate from the seven-year grammar school here in the village?" he asked, holding both her hands and trying to warm them in his.

"Yes, I did." She ached to be in his arms.

"Do you like to read?"

"Yes, I do!" She suddenly was excited. "But books are hard to get."

"Would you like me to lend you some?"

"Oh, please do, Andrzej," she said, her eyes on his face.

"Books are good for you, Frania. They educate you."

"I know," she said, losing interest now in books, for she was listening to the giggles coming from behind a nearby lilac. The giggling stopped. Then she heard loud smacking as lips met in a long, passionate kiss.

"Are you with me, Frania?"

"What?" She turned to look at him. At this magic moment the moonlight slipped through the branches to lay a silver streak on Andrzej's handsome head. He was the prince of her dreams.

"Would you be interested in hearing something about me?"

She nodded, not really listening. She only wanted him to put his arms about her.

"I was born in Jaroslaw. My parents own a small brick house and grocery store in the suburbs."

"Grocery store?" she said. "That's wonderful."

"Ummm, yes. It's rather nice to have a business of your own. But getting back to me—I'm an only child and perhaps a spoiled one."

"I always wanted to be an only child. How does it feel not to have any brothers or sisters taking love and attention away from you?"

"It has its advantages and disadvantages."

"Oh?"

"I had as much pampering as I could stand—altogether too much fussing and smothering—and I loved it all. But I wished I had a brother to share things with while I was growing up."

"You were lonely?"

He was silent for a moment. "I never thought about it until I went to school."

"You graduated from a teaching school," she said.

"Yes, and then I came to your village to teach. I'm glad I did." He moved closer and put his arm about her shoulders.

She shivered with sudden joy.

"Because how else would I have met you, Frania?" he whispered in her ear. "You are so pretty."

She felt her heart melting as if it were made of burning wax.

"Do you like me just a little, Frania?" He pulled her so close to him she could hear his heart beat.

"I do," she said softly.

He turned her face to his and began kissing her hair, her forehead, her chin.

She closed her eyes. Oh, God. How good and sweet it was to be in his embrace, but when was he going to kiss her lips?

A man's voice, ugly with rage, sounded near the gate, and they broke apart.

"That's my father." Frania shuddered and pushed Andrzej away.

"Your father?"

"I have to run before he finds me here." She shrugged off Andrzej's jacket and leaped to her feet.

Later that night, Frania cried into her pillow. The beating she had received from her father did not hurt as much as her humiliation in front of Andrzej and the other young people. What could Andrzej think of the man who stormed into Wroble's home and tore Marysia from Marek's arms while the two were dancing? He practically dragged his daughter off by her hair. When he found out that Frania had also gone to the party, he whipped her, too. But at least she was home by then, not where the others could see her. Now she was sure Andrzej wouldn't want to see her ever again, because of her cruel father.

"I hate him," Frania said, sobbing in her bedroom.

"Hush," Aniela said, looking over her shoulder toward the door. "You're making too much noise. Haven't you had enough whipping for tonight?"

"Oh, hush up yourself, Aniela. You're such a scaredy cat. I don't care if he beats me again. I want to die."

"Why doesn't he go back to America, for the fourth time, and stay there for good!" cried Marysia. She pounded the pillow with her fists.

"I hope he goes and soon," moaned Frania. "When he's home, he acts like a dictator."

"Tata's trips cost money," said Marysia. "He has to work in the American factories just to pay his fare."

"And while he's gone, the rest of us have to work hard to keep the farm going."

"Tata is what Mama calls him: a man with a restless soul. He has to travel in order to survive," muttered Aniela.

Frania thought of the last such trip and shuddered. Her father had only been gone a few months when something horrible happened. One evening, her mother went out to milk the cows in the barn. Frania began to worry because she stayed out much longer than usual. She was about to go out looking when her mother appeared on the threshold. Her dress was torn, her face and neck scratched, and her hair hung loose about her face. She was shaking so she could hardly stand.

"Mama! What...what happened to you?" Frania cried.

"Nothing, child, nothing," her mother said, but Frania heard her sobbing until very late that night.

Nine months later, Frania's mother gave birth to a son. He was tiny and had red hair. All of the other children were blond or dark. Mama cried every time she looked at her newborn lying in the cradle. Neighbors didn't bother to hide the way they looked down on this unfortunate baby, brought into an unkind world through no fault of his own.

"Bastard," Frania heard them say, and she hated the word.

She never forgot the day her father returned home. Her mother hid in the hay in the silo the minute she heard of his coming. Without a word to anyone, he glanced at the infant and swore hard. Right away, he went looking for his woman. And when he found her, he beat her so badly that he put her in bed for a week.

Whenever Frania looked at her unwanted half brother, she pitied him. When he died at the age of two, she thought it must be for the best.

When she was born, things were very different. Or so she was told. Frania was not only the first-born, but also a girl. All the uncles and aunts— she had many of them—had sons. They envied Frania's parents for having a blue-eyed baby daughter. But soon their envy turned to love for the little one. The relatives fought over who was to play with her next.

Frania fell asleep thinking of how she had been spoiled, too, just like Andrzej.

The next morning, breakfast was gloomy, although the day was bright and sunny. Everyone was mad at everyone else, and Mama just wouldn't stop sniffling. They all dressed in their Sunday clothes and went to church in the neighboring village. While the smaller children skipped ahead of the parents, the older ones lagged purposely behind, but they all strolled along the road that ran across the countryside. The land, freshly awakened, was budding and blooming. Tender crops of wheat, rye, oats, barley, and blue-eyed flax lifted their heads toward the clear sky. Cattle grazed in green pastures. Spread over the horizon were villages identical in structure. Each had two rows of wooden houses, most with thatched roofs. A dirt road ran between. Barns were either joined to the dwellings or stood a little apart. Linden, acacia, and fruit trees shaded the buildings. Vegetable and flower gardens filled the front yards.

Frania, Marysia, and Aniela walked close beside each other. Marysia kept her dark eyes downcast, and now and then she silently touched the blue mark on her cheek. Frania, too, had bruises under her clothing, but all she felt was the aching of her heart. Then she thought of Andrzej's embrace, and a sweetness rushed through her bloodstream.

Chapter Two

THE SUN MOVED ACROSS THE SKY, FLOODING THE EARTH WITH LIGHT. The whole countryside shimmered in joy brought on by the presence of May. Life-giving rays poured down on villages, fields, and the river to the south. Through treetops the golden streaks fell on rooftops and danced on flower petals in the gardens and meadows.

When Frania saw the sun inching down toward the woods in the west, she said to Aniela, "It's time to go home." Both sisters had been working in the flax field since sunrise. On their knees or squatting, they hand-picked weeds and piled them in heaps along the furrows separating the rows of flax.

"Good," said Aniela. "Mama and Marysia left for home an hour ago."

"Well, they do have work there," sighed Frania, straightening her bent body. She stretched her arms up, up toward the sky.

Aniela stood up, too. "Why do we have to work so hard? I'm only thirteen."

"Yes, field work is hard," said Frania, "but I love it. I wouldn't know what to do with myself if I had to stay indoors in this warm weather."

"I see smoke coming out of our chimney," sang out Aniela, and she pointed north.

"Ach, Mama is making supper, and I'm starved. Let's go, go, go!"

"Shouldn't we wait for Tata?"

"No. He'll come when he's done hoeing the last row of potatoes, and not a minute sooner."

"He always works the hardest," said Aniela.

"He should, to make up for the time he spends in America."

"Maybe you're right." Aniela walked with her eyes to the ground.

"You know I am. The last time he was away, we almost killed ourselves helping Mama harvest the crops."

"Yes, I remember."

"I was only fifteen then," said Frania. "But never mind that now. Let's run—run home. Catch me if you can, my sister!" She leaped forward with the grace of a hare.

Aniela soon caught up with Frania and passed her, but then Frania passed Aniela and left her far behind. She imagined her father and the fields were chasing her. They wanted to catch her and hold her back. But she was fast—too fast for them. Yes, she was. It was fun to be running like this!

"Slow down, Frania," Aniela cried out.

Fits of giggles overwhelmed Frania, and she slowed to a stroll. Laughter shook her body.

"What's so funny?" asked Aniela. She had not only caught up with Frania, but caught her giggles, too.

"I'm just so happy to be alive and breathing all this sweet air."

"I'm happy, too."

"I wonder what Mama is making for us to eat."

"Chicken stew."

"How do you know?"

"She told me before leaving the field."

"I love chicken stew."

Aniela sighed. "I'd rather have potato dumplings with bacon."

"You and your dumplings," said Frania, slowing her steps even more. She saw how lovely the land looked when the sun's rays lay slantwise across it. Shadows stretched long and dark blue in the low parts, while bright green and gold adorned the high spots. She looked toward the west windows of her home and saw them blazing with fire. But she smiled, knowing it was only the sunlight trying to fool her.

Then her face grew sad. "How could God create such a wonderful earth, but make men so mean?"

"They are not all bad," said Aniela.

"Maybe not," said Frania, thinking of that magic moment in Wroble's garden. She touched her forehead and her chin where Andrzej had kissed her, then whispered, "Have to forget him."

"Forget who?" asked Aniela.

"No one." Then a little too loud, Frania said, "Do you think Marysia is done yet with the altar in the garden?"

"She should be. Her three friends were coming to help."

"People are coming for prayers after sundown."

"Yes, they are. But you know what?" Aniela began to skip along the road. "Tomorrow will be our turn to leave the field early."

"That's right," said Frania. "But we'll decorate the statue of Holy Mother with something other than lilac."

"What would that be?"

"We'll use field flowers with different colors and scents."

"I like that idea, Frania!"

The girls came to the gate of their homestead and stepped into a yard filled with dark shadows and faint streaks of light. The air was permeated with the scent of lilac and linden blossoms mixed with the aroma of their mother's cooking.

May—the most beautiful month of the year in Poland—was devoted to Saint Mary, with the Mother of God chosen as their spiritual queen. Prayers to Her were held throughout the month inside the churches and outdoors in the fields and gardens.

That evening, after the meal, Frania and her family went out to the garden. By now it was crowded with villagers of both sexes, all ages. In the light of kerosene lamps the people knelt on the dewy grass to say rosary before the statue of St. Mary placed on a small shelf that was nailed to a linden tree and flanked by huge bouquets of lilacs.

The worshippers envisioned their prayers turning into silver birds that flew straight up to Heaven. They believed those birds would reach St. Mary sitting on a throne beside her son, Jesus, and chirp messages to Her from the garden. They prayed even harder tonight than usual for the well-being of their country, needing consolation in their fear of unfriendly neighbors. Germany and Russia were forever attacking Poland

and enslaving her children. They had already erased Poland from the map one time and kept it off for over one hundred years. Barely twenty years had passed since the Poles regained their freedom after World War I. Now they heard that Hitler was turning Germany into a military power. The people were frightened. Would he try to take over Poland again? If so, when?

The rosary ended. Everyone stood up and began to sing:

"Praise, O you meadows spotted with flowers, the mountains and valleys all green, praise the Mistress of the universe..." This was always the first song to follow the evening rosary in the garden and was Frania's favorite.

After the devotion, children scattered among the bushes to play hide-and-seek. Teenagers flirted in the moonlight, while the grownups stood around in groups, talking.

To avoid trouble later on, Frania kept within sight of her father, whose voice bellowed above all the others. "Bully," she said under her breath as she glanced at his tall, dark figure.

"What? What did you say, Frania?" asked Julek. He was just one of the boys competing for her attention this evening.

"I said it's a gorgeous night, isn't it?"

"Yes, yes. It is," he agreed.

She was so tired of him always wanting to please her. "Excuse me, Julek," Frania said. "I have to find my sister, Marysia, and tell her something very important."

Frania hid behind the biggest lilac bush and stood all alone staring up at the silver moon. Round like an old man's face, it looked lonely and cold, a distant object floating on the vast ocean of the sky. It hurt to see such solitude. The sound of voices nearby brought her back down to earth. She saw her mother talking to Aunt Hanka, her mother's younger sister, who lived next door. Hanka, Frania's favorite aunt, had lost three of her first children to a mysterious illness. They all had died at the age of six months.

At the third funeral, Hanka tried to jump into the grave with her baby.

"I'm not a woman; I'm some kind of a freak," she cried out. "Please, let me die. Don't hold me back. Please!"

Frania's mother had embraced her mourning sister. "Hanka, don't blame yourself for something that's not your fault."

"But it is. It's all my fault! I'm cursed with something evil."

"No. You are not cursed."

"Easy for you to talk, my sister. Your children are all alive and well."

"Don't despair anymore, Hanka. I...I will give you one of my girls."

"You will? Which one?"

"Do you want my little Jania?"

"Oh, yes, yes. I want her very much."

But it was impossible for the mother to part with her baby. Every time she looked at Jania crawling at her feet, she would pick her up, cuddle her and start to cry. Then Hanka became pregnant again. The new life stirring inside of her kept her from asking her sister to hand over the child, Jania. Thus, months passed, and Jania stayed home where she belonged.

Hanka gave birth to another son, whom she named Jozek. His large dark eyes looked straight at the world as if to say, "I will survive." His parents watched him closely and shuddered each time he cried or whimpered. When he was six months old, he contracted the illness that had taken his siblings.

There was no doubt in anyone's mind that the baby would die, and Frania's mother was certain Hanka would not survive Jozek's death. One evening, Frania spied her mother kneeling down on the floor by her bed, making a bargain with God. She begged the Almighty to save her nephew at any cost.

"Please, oh Lord," she said to the big holy picture hanging on the wall, "take any child of mine you like, but spare the life of Jozek for my sister's sake."

Call it a miracle or merely coincidence, but Frania's mother's prayers were answered. The tiny nephew got well and soon started to gain weight. But a bargain was a bargain, especially one made with God himself. Two weeks later, Jania was bedridden. She had no fever, complained of no pain. She simply couldn't eat. Each time food was forced upon her, she threw up. One night, she died peacefully without disturbing anyone.

In the garden, Jozek, now almost six years old, suddenly bumped into Frania and woke her from her daydream.

"I got you," he yelled out, clasping his chubby hands about her hips and lifting his face up to hers. After him ran two of his younger sisters. One was just a toddler.

Under different circumstances, Frania would have grabbed Jozek's shirt collar and pushed him away, but the memories of his dead brothers put her in a tolerant mood. She smiled at the boy and patted his head.

Spring rushed away. In the summer there was even more work to do on the farm. Frania knew that Andrzej was going away for school vacation. Would he try to see her before he left?

One day he surprised her by sending one of his pupils with a note:

> Dear Frania,
>   You're beautiful. I can't get you out of my mind and my heart. Please meet me by the river on Sunday at 2:00 p.m.
>   Andrzej

"Tell your teacher I said 'Yes,'" she said to the boy.

Frania told Marysia about her secret rendezvous to be. After lunch on Sunday, Marysia brushed Frania's hair until it shone and braided it in two pigtails. Dressed in her freshly washed and ironed white blouse and blue skirt, Frania slipped out of the house while her father was taking his once-a-week nap.

Along the dirt road flanked by whispering wheat, she skipped and hopped, humming the melody of the polka she had danced to with Andrzej at the party. She even smiled at a frog that happened under her feet and was careful not to step on it. Above her head a lark twittered, and she waved up at it. She didn't mind the hot sun. She didn't even resent Tata, who would surely beat her if he found her out.

In the shade of an aspen, she saw Andrzej waiting for her. He started to walk toward her the minute she came into his view.

"I'm so happy you've come, Frania," he said, stopping in front of her. He held a brown package under his arm.

"You wanted to see me?" she said, trying to stay calm, while her heart pounded in her chest.

"I've brought you books."

"Books?" she exclaimed and took them from him. Hugging the package to her breast, she said, "I'll read them on Sundays and in the evenings."

"Read, Frania. Read all you can. Reading educates a person." He took hold of her free hand and steered her to a secluded spot where bushes grew thick. He asked her to sit down on the grass with him. They were facing the river. "I hope my meeting you like this won't cause problems for you with your father."

She blushed in shame, remembering Tata's crude behavior at the dance.

"I just wanted to say goodbye," Andrzej said.

"Goodbye?" She let the package slip from her grasp. It fell to the ground.

"I'm going home for two months."

"So soon? Don't go, Andrzej."

He seized her hand for the second time. But now he held it tight in both of his and said in a low voice that brought goose bumps to her arms, "I'll return to teach here in the fall."

She smiled.

In a very tender voice he said, "You do care for me."

She nodded and looked away toward the woods on the opposite bank of the river, but did not see them. In the treetops, birds chirped joyfully, but her heart ached. If only he would tell her he loved her. If only he would stay with her and not go away.

Andrzej moved closer to her and put his arm about her. "My dearest Frania, my sweet and innocent girl," he whispered in her ear.

Frania closed her eyes and leaned toward him like a plant turning toward the sun.

"Andrzej," she said, shivering.

He tightened his arm about her. "Frania, Frania, Frania."

Her heart flooded. She ached for his lips to touch hers.

But he pushed her away gently and, with a fingertip on her chin, turned her face to his. "Let me gaze into your eyes. Open your eyes, Frania."

"Do you like me, Andrzej?" she said, her voice weak and trembling.

"Do I?" He moved his fingers to her half-opened mouth, tracing the outline of it. "You, young lady, have gotten deep into my soul."

Lady? He called her a lady! Frania smiled, showing her white even teeth and the dimples in her cheeks.

What happened next, happened quickly. His arms held her tight, and his cheek pressed hard against hers. His breath was warm. Then his lips found hers. Finally!

Frania experienced a moment totally wonderful, sweet and elating. With it she started to spin as if she were riding a merry-go-round. The sky went satin blue, and the sun was a bright, golden center around which she moved, its warmth melting her heart. The earth shook a bit under her as it rotated. With it came perfumed greenery full of birds that sang and insects that buzzed and hummed. With it came crops ripening in the summer heat. Frania was like a flower unfolding to Andrzej's love.

"Be careful, my daughter, when you're out with boys." Frania heard her mother's words echoing in her head. She had said them to Frania just two weeks earlier. "Many boys will want you in bed, but only the one who truly loves you will save you for the wedding night." Frania remembered Mama's advice now when Andrzej had her flat on her back and was pinning her to the ground, his kisses hot and demanding.

"No!" she cried out when he began unbuttoning her blouse.

But he didn't stop.

"Let me go!" she said and tried to push him away, but he didn't budge.

"Andrzej, stop!"

"Frania, please, I need to make love."

"I will hate you for the rest of my life," she said and doubled her effort to get free.

Finally, he let go of her blouse, rolled off her and lay beside her, breathing hard.

"It's not that I don't love you, Andrzej," she said, working quickly to button her blouse, "but—but I don't want to get pregnant."

"I'm sorry," he said and sat up.

"I'm sorry, too. I didn't think we would get this far on our first date," she said.

"We are attracted to each other. Will you ever forgive me for losing my head?"

With her arms embracing her knees, she rocked back and forth in embarrassment. "Was I to be your first girl?" she asked, blushing. She turned to look at his profile.

He shook his head.

"Oh," she said, jealousy kicking at her heart. "How many girls have you have, Andrzej?" she heard herself say. She didn't really want to hear his answer.

"Not too many."

"Oh," she said, while she rocked and rocked. "My mother never explained the facts of life to me. I used to think storks brought babies."

"My mother told me God threw infants into rivers to be fished out by mothers," he said and grinned.

"Did you believe her?"

"No. I knew even then that babies would drown before mothers got to them, but I never argued with her. You just can't disbelieve your mother, I guess."

"I was seven when I found out about lovemaking." Frania kept her head bent, looking down at the grass. "A girl, two years older, described to me what couples did in bed."

"And you were shocked?"

Frania nodded and glanced at Andrzej. She was glad to see him unchanged after what had just happened. He remained handsome and dear to her heart.

"At that time, what did you think of sex?"

"I…I thought it was degrading to humans and refused to even admit that my parents ever did such a thing. Until I heard them one night. Right then, I vowed to myself I would never let a boy touch me that way, ever."

"When you got older you changed your mind, though, didn't you?"

"Yes, I did. To my surprise, I started liking boys. That's why Mama warned me about getting in trouble."

"She's a wise woman, your mother. But did she tell you not to tease young men too much?"

"What?" said Frania.

"How serious are you about Julek?"

"He...he likes me, and I'm fond of him, but I don't love him."

Andrzej smiled, then his face turned sober. "Have you ever made love?" he asked.

"No. Never. I'm saving myself for my husband."

"I see. You're very practical, Frania."

"Thank you," she said, not quite knowing how to take his last words.

Before they separated that afternoon, Andrzej kissed Frania one more time, but it was a gentle kiss he gave her. She wanted him to say he would see her in the fall, but he did not.

When Frania's seventeenth birthday came the following month, her father decided his oldest daughter was ready to get married—perhaps even a bit too old. A young man from a well-to-do family would be courting her, she was informed. He lived in the neighboring village.

"His name is Bolek, Frania, and you're going to see him on Saturday," her father told her.

"What? You're an old-fashioned man, Tata. Women today choose their own sweethearts!"

"You had better be nice to the boy," he said, his voice threatening.

"I don't want to see him or anyone else you pick for me," she cried out.

He grabbed her arm and squeezed it hard. "You know I don't like bratty children, even if they are big enough to go on their own."

Frania's mother rushed in, pleading with her daughter. "Dearest, please don't say no."

"I'm sorry, Mama, but I don't want to hear a word about that—that Bolek," said Frania, trying to pull away from her father's grip. "I'll not court with him, and that's that!"

"Oh, yes, you will," her father roared. He pushed Frania so violently that she fell to the floor.

"Please, don't hit her," begged her mother. Then she turned to Frania. "You don't want your younger sister, Marysia, to get a husband first, do you?"

"I don't care who gets married first."

"What would people say?"

"Let them say what they want." Frania struggled to her feet.

"But Frania, Bolek is a decent young man, and I know he'll make you a good husband."

"Like yours? I don't want to hear another word about him, Mama."

"Oh, yes, you will hear and listen," bellowed her father, stepping closer to Frania. He rolled his hand into a fist and poised it over her face. "Don't talk back to your parents," he said, his teeth grinding.

Frania's anger rose above her fear and made her shout even louder. "You can kill me, Tata, but you can't change my mind about Bolek."

He uncurled his fist. Shaking his finger at her, he said, "You're going to do what you're told, even if I have to break your neck, girl."

"Please, oh, please," her mother cried. "Say 'yes' Frania. Say 'yes.'"

Frania hated to see her mother shaking, but she could not give in to her father. "There's someone I love," she said, her voice trembling.

"What? Who?"

"Julek?" asked her mother.

"No."

"Who then?" said her father.

"Andrzej."

"The teacher?" He paused, then started to laugh. "Forget him, you foolish daughter."

"Why?"

"He'll never marry a farm girl."

"But he will. You'll see."

"Have you been seeing him behind my back?"

Frania nodded, bracing herself to be hit.

"Are you pregnant?"

"How can you say such a thing to me, Tata?" said Frania, tears flooding her eyes. These words hurt worse than his blows.

"Are you or aren't you? Answer me!"

"No. I'm not!"

"That's good," he said and seemed calmer. "But, as I said, forget the teacher."

"But I love him. And he loves me, too, I'm sure of that."

"Nonsense, Frania. Stop dreaming."

She said nothing more. For awhile she stared at her father, then walked away, her head lowered to her chest. For now, she would let him think she was going along with the marital plans he had made for her.

The day Bolek came visiting, Frania hid in the woods by the river. She sat high up in an old willow and read one of the books Andrzej had given her: *W Pustyni I Puszczy* (*In Desert and in Jungle*) by Henry Sienkiewicz. The novel, about two European children kidnapped by Moslems and brought into Africa, fascinated her.

"Frania! Frania!" She heard her father calling her.

"So Bolek came," she whispered, lifting her eyes from the book. "So soon?" She blinked as if she had just awakened, placed a marker between the pages and shut the book in her lap.

"Come home, girl. Come home right now!"

She looked in the direction of the voice, but all she saw was the green lace shielding her. "Hee hee. Try to find me, Tata, you brute."

"Where are you, Frania?" It was Aniela calling her now.

"Hee hee." It was fun to hide behind the foliage cascading down about her like a curtain. The willow was like a dear friend protecting her from her father. Feeling safe, she went back to reading and, when she got to the page on which the children escaped from their kidnappers, she wiped a grateful tear from her eyes. She, too, would escape, she hoped, if only from a loveless marriage.

Once again she closed the book, then sighed. "Andrzej, Andrzej." Down there on the slope he had kissed her for the first time. They almost made love that day. Maybe she shouldn't have stopped him. Maybe, afterward, he would have asked her to be his wife.

A small wind brushed through the treetop. It flirted with the leaves and made them dance and whisper secrets. She heard the leaves say, "Hold on, Frania, and fight for your freedom to choose."

"I will. I will," she answered them.

She didn't come down until darkness enveloped the river, and a strange grunting below frightened her. When she returned home, she saw that the window of her bedroom was open, and she sighed with relief. Marysia was such a thoughtful sister.

The next morning Bolek's name wasn't even mentioned, and she was surprised. He must have done or said something to displease her father. On Monday, a note was delivered to her from Bolek. She tore it into tiny pieces right in front of her father, but he said nothing.

After that, more suitors were brought to her, but she kept refusing even to talk to them. She cried, she shouted, she threatened to run away or kill herself. In reality she was stalling for time, praying and hoping that Andrzej would come rescue her.

And one day, he did indeed arrive at the village and drop by in the midst of one of their fights.

"Andrzej, you are here!" she cried, running to his outspread arms. "My father wants to marry me off to anyone who will have me."

"Sweet Frania," he said.

"What do you want, Mister?" her father said, staring at Andrzej.

Andrzej stared back, stammering out his name and holding Frania in his embrace.

"I love only you, Andrzej." She clung to him like a child to its mother.

"Are you here to make trouble?"

"No, no. I wanted to see your daughter."

"See her? What for?"

Frania was shaking against Andrzej now.

"May I court her?"

"Court? For what?"

"To marry, of course."

"Marry?"

"Yes. I would like to take Frania for my wife."

The older man's mouth fell open. After a pause, he said, "Do you really want my oldest daughter?"

"I do."

ᗡ

They were married on a sunny day in early fall, and to Frania it was the happiest day of her life.

"My lovely bride," Andrzej said into her ear as they danced together round and round the room, the largest one in her parents' house. It had been emptied of furniture and decorated with paper streamers and bells for the wedding reception.

"My beloved," she said. "You're such an elegant dancer."

"And you're a beautiful lady."

Whenever he called her lady, her chest swelled with pride.

"How does it feel to be Mrs. Poziomek?"

"Fine. Just fine," she said, glancing at her in-laws waltzing across the room. They had come from Jaroslav yesterday. Her father-in-law was tall and had gentle manners, like Andrzej, and a charming smile. His wife was short and stocky. There was something about the woman Frania didn't like.

"You look so appetizing in this national costume, I could lick you all over and eat you."

"Stop that, Andrzej," she said and blushed, but not really minding what he said.

"You live in the district of Lwow. Why did you pick the costume of Krakow for yourself and your bridesmaids?"

"Because I think this one is the most beautiful of them all."

"It is a gorgeous outfit. Where did you buy it?"

"Buy it? Marysia and I made them all by ourselves."

"You did?"

She nodded, smiling.

"You're very clever with your hands, aren't you?"

"I guess I am."

"From now on, I will teach you how to use your mind, as well."

"Yes, you can teach me."

The actual wedding ceremony took only a few minutes in the church, but the reception lasted three full days. The whole village was invited. The guests waltzed, polkaed, and marched to the band's music. They consumed plates and plates of chicken with homemade cheese, bread, and sweet pastry. They drank home-brewed wine and whiskey.

Then it came time to say goodbye to her family. Andrzej had quit his job at the village and was to teach in Jaroslav. He and his wife were to live at his parents' house. Andrzej had made all these plans without Frania's knowledge.

She kissed her father first, lightly on his cheek, although she wanted to hit him instead. On the second day of the reception, she had heard him advise Andrzej to be the king of his castle. That day, she vowed to herself to help Andrzej be a good husband and father.

"I love you, Mama," she said, putting her arms about the older woman.

"I'll have you over for a dinner soon," she told her sister, Marysia, while hugging her.

"Don't cry, Aniela. We'll visit each other often. I promise."

Then she went down on her knees to embrace Jozia. "Be a good little girl to Mama for me." She held the child close to her chest. Jozia was Frania's second favorite sister and a perfect image of herself.

"Goodbye, sweet angel," she said to Helcia, the toddler of the family, who was napping. She threw a quick kiss down to the crib and ran out of the house.

Andrzej was waiting with his parents inside their fancy carriage. When Frania came out, he stepped down to help her up to her seat beside him. He clicked his tongue and pulled sharply on the reins. The pair of healthy horses stepped forward and started to pull her away from the only home she knew. Tears filled her eyes when her family followed her out of the house to see her off. She waved to Marysia, and then to Mama. Both women were crying. The sight of her mother's reddened nose and puffy eyes stayed with Frania until a different feeling began to overwhelm her. Villagers had come out to say their farewell to the newlyweds. After all, Andrzej had taught their children well, and Frania was liked by everyone.

"Dowidzenia," she and Andrzej shouted to each face looking up at them. "Until we see you again." Pride and joy suddenly expanded Frania's chest as she thought of her fine husband and her future in the city. Ah, every girl and mother she knew must envy her good fortune.

Julek! She saw him standing in the front yard of his thatched-roof home. His parents and his younger sisters, Veronka and Basia, waved at the carriage as it passed by, but he didn't. Frania's heart gave a painful tug at the sight of his sober face. But the change of view that came next made her forget her old dancing partner. Now the horses turned along the curve in the road, and her village faded away from sight.

A fear of the unknown, of tomorrow, crept into her heart. Was she good enough for Andrzej? Maybe not today, but she would improve by learning to speak better. She would read books on how to be a lady. But what if she failed him? Oh, no. She had to stop worrying about that. She moved closer to Andrzej and put her head on his shoulder. His closeness reassured her that all would be fine.

But what about her in-laws? Would she get along with them? No, she wouldn't think about that today.

It was noon when Andrzej brought Frania home to a two-story brick house in a nice suburb. The grocery store occupied the first floor, and flower and vegetable gardens filled the front yard. Upstairs served as the living quarters. The newlyweds were given an apartment in the east wing. It was small, but nicely furnished. There were snowy-white curtains in the large windows and potted plants on the sill. In the combination kitchen-living room stood a brick stove covered with yellow tiles. A safe distance from the stove there was a table with four chairs. A sofa leaned against one wall and above it hung a picture of Karpaty, the Polish mountains. Electric lamps stood on both sides of the sofa. Electricity amazed Frania with its brightness.

A tub with running water in the bathroom and a sink with running water in the kitchen were luxuries Frania had never enjoyed in her village.

"I love this bed," she said. "It's big. The spread is beautiful, made out of pure green velvet. It must have cost a lot of money."

Andrzej smiled because he was glad to see her excited about her new home.

"And these huge pillows at its head. They're so fluffy and soft. Are they stuffed with goose down?"

"Yes, I guess they are."

"Who embroidered the cases?"

"Mother did."

Frania turned away and looked out the window. "Mother," she repeated.

"What's the matter, beloved?"

"Nothing. It's just that I already miss my family."

He took her in his arms then and made her smile.

The day before Christmas, it snowed all day. By Christmas Eve, millions of snowflakes had fallen upon the city and covered it with a crispy white blanket.

Andrzej's mother invited Frania and her son to a traditional supper called Wieczerza Wigilijna. As was the custom, the meal started the minute the first star appeared in the sky. The table was covered with white linen under which a layer of hay had been placed. The hay on the table and under the tree was to remind people that Jesus was born in a stable. The oplatek—a thin wafer symbolizing peace and good will on earth toward all men—lay in the center of the table. It was to be broken and shared among the family members before supper. Good wishes were exchanged with hugs and kisses.

Andrzej's father passed the wafer around. He looked very handsome in his beige suit and tie. His white hair was neatly brushed and shone in the electric light that still impressed Frania.

"All the best to you, our pretty daughter-in-law," he said to her. "Accept this wafer from your old father-in-law."

"Thank you, Father." She now stood up to let him hug her. "And all the best to you, also."

"Dear, dear, Frania," he said and sighed, placing a kiss on her cheek.

Did he know how she felt about her new life? Did he suspect? His son did not. He was too busy molding her into a perfect lady. Tears came into her eyes. She sat down quickly and lowered her eyelids to hide them. She wore a white woolen dress with a red belt and red trimming around the neck. Her hair was piled on top of her head to make her look sophisticated. *Sophistication: the process of becoming cultured.* It was one of the words she had learned last week. She had begun to resent what she was doing. She was changing, that was certain, but did she like what she was becoming? She had the feeling she was losing herself in trying to be something she wasn't.

"Tell us, Frania, how does your family observe Christmas Eve?" asked Andrzej's mother, spooning mushroom soup out of her fine china bowl.

Frania had difficulty swallowing a large piece of mushroom, then she wiped her mouth with her napkin again—she used it much too often, she was sure—and said, "At this moment, they're also eating—dining, I mean."

"What kind of dishes does your mother prepare?"

"More or less the same as you've made: a soup, various hot cereals with butter and honey, compotes, pierogies stuffed with cheese, potato—"

"I've not made pierogies," the woman said, her lower lip protruding above her upper. "Don't like them. Don't your people believe in serving fish like the one I had stuffed and baked?"

"We have pickled herring at the beginning of the meal," muttered Frania in a low voice. She didn't like the direction this conversation was taking and looked at Andrzej, willing him to come to her rescue.

"Frania's mother is an excellent homemaker," Andrzej said. "We all tasted her cooking and baking at our wedding reception."

"Yes, her pastry was sweet and moist enough, but some was too cheesy or too eggy."

Frania's eyes moistened again. No matter what she said or did, she could never please her mother-in-law.

"Peasants—" began the older woman.

"Villagers, you mean, dear," corrected her husband.

"All right then, villagers. They don't have electricity, and they light their trees with candles."

"That's true," said Frania, glancing at the tiny tree on the small table in the picture window. "My father cuts a big tree out in our own woods. It's so tall it reaches the ceiling as it stands on the floor."

"Good for you," said the woman. "But tell me, deary, doesn't your family believe that your domestic animals speak at midnight, and that's why you share oplatek with them? Isn't that ridiculous?"

"We don't really think our cows and horses speak on Christmas night. We give them oplatek because they're part of our family, and we love them."

"That's a heart-warming custom," Andrzej's father rushed to say. "After all, who deserves oplatek more than the animals that were present in the shelter where Jesus was born in Bethlehem."

Frania smiled at the older man. She was grateful for his tact and kindness. She had never heard him say anything against the lower classes.

"My great ancestors and Andrzej's grandparents had none of the barbarian customs," the woman said, her long nose stuck up in the air.

Frania blushed and blinked her eyes. She wanted Andrzej to say something good about her people, but he was too busy eating.

"As you already know, they were a blue-blooded people and very rich. They had peasants working in their fields and as house servants."

"Dear, I don't think it's necessary tonight for you to be talking about your relatives, which, by the way, are poor today," said her husband.

Andrzej finally spoke up. "Father's right, Mother. It's Christmas. Let's not argue, but enjoy each other's company."

A group of carolers, bundled up against the cold, came to sing outside the windows, and that put an end to the conversation.

At ten, the young couple returned to their apartment.

"It's chilly here," said Frania, cuddling herself for warmth in the middle of the living area.

"The fire is dying out," he said. "I'll put more logs in the stove."

She walked over to the easy chair and picked up an afghan that was draped over the back. She had made the small blanket herself out of lavender and white yarn and kept it handy just in case she or her husband needed it.

"What's the matter, Frania?" Andrzej asked after he had stuffed the stove with firewood.

"Nothing," she said and shook her head. Tears were welling in her eyes again, although she tried to keep them back.

"Is it my mother?"

She nodded.

He rushed to embrace her. "What is it that bothers you most about her?"

"Why does she always have to put down my family, Andrzej?"

"Is that what you think she's doing?"

"Yes."

"You're wrong, Frania. She can't help being proud of her relatives. After all, they were not just plain people from any village."

"Oh, Andrzej, you just don't understand," she cried out and moved away from him.

Silence frosted the air between them.

After awhile, he sat on the sofa and patted it with his hand. "Come on, darling, sit by me."

She did what he told her, as she had ever since their honeymoon ended and the lessons started. First, she had to learn how to behave at public gatherings and home parties. She now knew that a lady held her pinky up when drinking her tea. A lady didn't laugh too loud, but smiled often and tried to be a good listener when in the company of a gentleman. Oh, yes, she learned very quickly how to be a good hostess to Andrzej's friends. She was a good student, and he was an excellent teacher. Her good looks charmed her guests. Yet she wasn't happy. Maybe she could get used to it all?

"What are you thinking about?" she heard Andrzej's voice in her ear. She realized she was in his arms again and smiled.

"Thinking?" she repeated. "I was just remembering things."

"What things?" he said, his lips on her cheek.

"Nothing important, Andrzej."

"Let's go to bed, my wife."

"No. Not yet, please. Let's talk."

He sealed her mouth with his and kissed her.

She readily responded, hoping he would caress her slowly the way he had on their wedding night, but he soon pulled her down to the floor and took her in a hurry. After it was all over, she was disappointed. Had he forgotten already how to make love to her so she could be satisfied, too? Was he selfish enough to believe a lady shouldn't desire sex? If she could only tell him how she felt. No, no. She couldn't discuss such things with her husband. All her life, she was forbidden to talk about the subject. Her church warned her that merely thinking or talking about lovemaking was a sin to be confessed to the priest, and such confessions were embarrassing.

For the first time since their wedding, Frania went to sleep without responding to Andrzej's good night kiss.

Chapter Three

FRANIA BEGAN TO EXPERIENCE LIFE AS IF SHE WERE A ROSEBUSH THAT grew more thorns than flowers. Just like a plant that had to withstand all sorts of bad weather, she went through various painful experiences. Every season had its effect. Spring commanded the bush to unfold, grow, and bloom. And so the springtime of Frania's youth grew into maturity, and she saw the birth of her first child. Then fall and winter stripped the rosebush of its leaves and put it naked into a dormant state for winter. And so an avalanche of tragic events stripped Frania and her dear ones of all human dignity and forced them to exist in poverty of the lowest kind.

Ten months after her wedding, Frania gave birth to a son, Henio. The baby was born at home with the help of a midwife. Frania got out of bed several days later.

On September 1, 1939, when Henio was eight months old, Hitler invaded Poland with his powerful army. Hell opened up, swallowing the Poles in a sea of horror and brutality. Ugly monsters on the loose, performing their bloody tasks, moved across the land amid the destructive sounds of artillery and bombs. People were burned by blazing fires in the cities, thrown up in the air by exploding shells, cut into pieces, killed by guns, run over by tanks.

To avoid death, city dwellers evacuated with their belongings. They crowded the roads and villages, moving from west to east. Unknowingly, they were headed into the arms of a different enemy: Russia. The Red Army wasn't coming to help fight Hitler, as the Poles had anticipated, but to help occupy the battered nation.

Most villagers felt safe in their settlements, and they stayed home to finish gathering the year's harvest. Their crops sustained their livelihood and fed their people. But they listened to the distant booming of war while fear grew large in their hearts.

When Andrzej was called to join other young men fighting the invaders, Frania cried hard and long as she said goodbye. After he had gone, she felt completely lost and out of place with his parents. During the first days of the bombardment of Jaroslav, she decided to go back to her family. She tried to persuade her in-laws to go with her, but they wouldn't budge.

Frania's family was happy to see her back. Even her father smiled at Henio and tickled his chin.

One sunny day, she was out threshing wheat with the older members of her family. With the help of a rented machine and good neighbors, the work went smoothly. By nine in the morning, several bushels of grain were waiting to be bagged, and a hill of straw rose skyward.

Usually, at such gatherings, the workers enjoyed themselves talking and singing, but not today. Only the machine's motor roared as it threshed. Now and then a pitchfork rang out when it hit a hard object.

Suddenly, Frania dropped her pitchfork to the ground and stood looking up at the sky. Her companions stopped because she did. And then they all heard what Frania had heard: the familiar but terrifying sound of distant planes.

"One, two, three, four, five, six…" counted Marysia.

Her father shook his fist at the sky. "The Nazis bombers will keep bombing Jaroslav until they level it to the ground."

Right away, Frania thought of her in-laws in the city. Were they still alive? "Vultures," she shouted, and she also shook her fists at the planes passing above her head. "Killers! Murderers!"

"Oh, God Almighty," Frania's mother moaned. "Why do You let the Germans start their wars?"

"Look, look what's happening!" said a voice.

"Oh, yes! Two of the bombers are heading this way!"

With horror in her heart, Frania watched as the two planes came low to the ground. One of them circled the neighboring village, then dropped two bombs. Mushrooms of smoke and spears of fire flared up-ward. The other bomber scanned the wooded banks of the river. It flew so low that it almost touched the treetops. The pilot machine-gunned the terrain. Bullets strewed the ground and fell all too close to the pasture where Aniela and Jozia watched over the grazing cattle.

"My girls!" screamed Frania's mother. "They will be killed!" Without any hesitation she ran forward and headed toward the pasture, her husband close behind.

Frania couldn't believe her eyes. Tata was risking his life in order to save his daughters? Was it possible he loved his children so much?

"Tata, Mama!" cried out Marysia. "Don't go into an open space."

But they didn't listen.

Frania's first thought was to go after them, but then her baby came to her mind. She rushed into the house and picked up Henio from his cradle, the same cradle she and her sisters had used in their infancy.

"My poor baby," she whispered, cuddling Henio to her bosom. "You have no idea what terrible times you've been born into."

When she heard her parents returning from the pasture with the girls and the cattle, she sighed with relief, but she stayed indoors with her son for the rest of the day.

After that day, Frania and her family hid in the nearby forest for several days. But soon the battle over Poland ended with the Germans and Russians sharing the occupation. The two enemies were brutal and heartless in their treatment of the defeated nation. In Frania's village, news came of many Poles who were shot, beaten, starved or tortured to death.

First, the tanks of the helmeted and high-booted Nazis invaded Frania's village. Then the Russians came to stay for good. The soldiers kept watchful eyes on the villagers and often entered their homes without warning, under any pretense.

The fall of 1939 brought sadness to Poland, although the season was beautiful. The flaming leaves matched the blood of those killed in the war. Poland's soil reddened with the blood of the fallen. Whenever the sun wearied of seeing the Poles endure their misery, it hid behind clouds that rained in torrents on the cities and villages. The rain tried in vain to wash away all the ugliness.

Days grew gray and cold, and the land was like a worn-out bear, groaning and stretching before going to sleep for the winter.

Frania was helping her sisters dig potatoes out of the ground one late afternoon.

"Hey, Marysia and Aniela, slow down."

"There's work to be done, and we're doing it," sang out Marysia, her potatoes flying faster into a large bucket. For the first time in her life, she was beating her oldest sister in her work, and she appeared to be enjoying the moment.

With a wave of her hand, Frania let Marysia's remark go by. Let them kill themselves if they wanted. She straightened up and looked out over the others working the field without seeing them. Not far away, in the already harvested field, a fire blazed, and in it potatoes were being baked. She could smell the pleasing aroma. Wind blew the fire, making the flames sway in her direction. She felt suddenly cold, left her hoe on the ground and walked over to warm up.

"Andrzej," she whispered to the flames, feeling delicious warmth on her face and arms. "When are you coming back to me and our son?"

Wooo, wooo, said the wind, clawing at her scarf.

"Julek and many others have returned home. Why not you?" she said to the wind.

That night she couldn't sleep no matter how hard she tried. Lately, she worried about lots of things, but mostly about Andrzej. Had he survived the war and the occupation? If he was alive, where was he? Was he suffering cold or hunger or abuse from the enemy?

Everyone else around her was in dreamland, and she was envious. She was in and out of bed and pacing the floor most of the time. Now and then, she added a log to the fire in the stove. When she heard rain pat-a-patting against the pane, she rushed to look out the window at the dark and cold out there. Was Andrzej warm and dry, as she was? She missed being in his arms so much, she ached.

Around midnight, Henio woke, hungry. She changed him and sat down on the bench before the fireplace to feed him. While he suckled greedily at her breast, she thought about all the disbanded Polish soldiers still hiding in forests all over the country. Many of them shuffled to her parents' house at night, asking for food. Frania and her mother made cheese and baked bread every day, so that no hungry soldier walked away unfed from their doorstep.

Too often, she saw Germans on horses, forcing her countrymen to walk with their cattle on the highway that ran east from her village. The Nazis shouted at the Poles and whipped their backs to make them move faster.

Tap, tap, tap. She heard a sound behind the door and listened more carefully. *Tap, tap, tap.*

"It must be another starving soldier come looking for food," she whispered to the baby, who was already sound asleep in her arms.

Tap, tap, tap, tap, tap. The tapping was louder this time.

She called out in a low voice, "Coming. Wait just a minute, whoever you are." Then she got up and carried her son to his crib, putting him down and covering him with a quilt. As she straightened up slowly, she felt as if a burden rested on her shoulders. She sighed deeply, moved to the door and opened it.

"Who is it?" she said, straining her eyes to see more clearly in the faint light coming from the fireplace. "Come on in, soldier," she said. "Sit down by the fire and warm up. I'll make you something to eat."

"Frania," a familiar voice said.

"Is…is that you, Andrzej?"

"Yes, it's your Andrzej."

She screamed with joy and ran into his outspread arms the way she had the day he came to court her. He was dirty and smelled bad. He needed a shave, but she didn't care, only kissed his lips over and over, while she clung to him.

Her cries woke the whole family. Everyone was happy to see Andrzej. They embraced and kissed him, and welcomed him home. That night he was bathed, fed and put to bed as if he were a baby. He didn't open his eyes until noon the next day, and then, after more pampering, he told Frania and her family all about what he had been through the past several weeks.

"Shortly before Poland was crushed by our enemies, I was captured by the Nazis," he said, sitting on the bench by the stove, warming himself at a crackling fire.

"Did you have to stay outdoors in a fenced-in place, the way our soldiers did near Jaroslav?" Frania said.

Andrzej nodded.

Frania's arm tightened hard around his waist.

"You poor man," said Aniela.

"Yes, we were poor, poor beings—all of us prisoners. We lived under the naked sky and starved."

"Oh, no," moaned Frania, moving closer yet to his side.

"You see, the Germans didn't bother to feed us like humans. When they felt like it, they threw raw cabbage, potatoes, or badly rotting pears and apples at us. Each time they did that, they shouted, 'Eat! Eat, you Polish swine!'

"Twice they brought in bleeding cows' heads. Laughing hard, they yelled, 'Here you are, dogs. Bite off the meat and chew it like animals.'"

"Dear God," said Frania's mother. "I can't believe the Almighty lets the Nazis be so cruel."

"God has nothing to do with the world's evil," said Andrzej.

"Devils take over people's actions during wars," said Frania, the tears dropping down her cheeks.

Andrzej nodded, cleared his throat and swallowed hard. Then he said, "Every day the townspeople visited our camp. They brought bread, cheese, and fruit with them. Our guards let them throw goodies over the fence, but too often they shot or beat a prisoner to death when he bent to pick up some of the food."

"We've heard of such things happening," said Marysia.

Frania put her head on his shoulder. "The important thing is that they didn't kill you."

"God took care of me," he said and patted her hair. But he sat still, staring into the firelight that spilled out the open door of the stove.

"Tell us when and how you escaped from them, Andrzej," said Aniela.

"All right, but first let me catch my breath." He managed to smile now, for he was looking down at the cradle by his feet, where Henio napped peacefully, as if not a thing was wrong with the world.

"Please do tell us," said Frania.

Andrzej took a handkerchief from his pocket and wiped a tear from his eye. "Last Monday was wet and very cold, as I remember. Early that morning our watchdogs ordered us to line up before the gate, and we did just that. An hour later, they told us to march out of the camp. We were made to walk for miles and miles in the cold rain, wet and shivering. The Germans on their horses wore raincoats and galoshes. We didn't even have hats."

"I hate those Germans," said Frania, shaking her fist at the fire.

"I detest them with all my being for their cruelty," said Andrzej. He shifted on the bench to get more comfortable, then continued. "Many of us were wounded, many were ill, and all were weak from starvation. Those who fell behind were whipped. Those who fell to the ground and couldn't get up were shot or trampled by a horse, their corpses left by the roadside or even on the road."

"How awful!

"And where were the Nazis walking you to?"

"We had no idea. Perhaps to another camp. Anyway, that afternoon I ached all over, yet I kept on plodding, plodding, plodding. In spite of the cold, perspiration trickled down my face and back. I tried hard to stay on my feet. Something told me that, if I went down to the ground this time, I might not get up ever again. Dear God, I didn't want to die, for I longed to see my son and my wife, all of you…and my parents—do any of you know where they are now? Are they all right?"

"After the Germans took over Jaroslaw, we couldn't go to check on them," said Frania. Down deep in her heart, she felt guilty for failing to bring them to her village when she escaped with her son.

"I'm sure they'll be all right," said Frania's mother. "And we're happy to have you back. But please—keep on with your story."

"Thank you," he said, glancing at his mother-in-law. "As I dragged my feet forward, I looked about and shuddered because I saw nothing but mud, mud, mud. It lay slimy and thick on the fields and roads. It was such a pitiful and depressing sight. Suddenly, my knees gave in under me and—and I collapsed."

"No, you didn't. God, you didn't," sobbed Frania.

He patted her head and said, "I did fall and face first, straight into a puddle."

"And what happened next?" Frania's father wanted to know.

"Nothing, for awhile. You see, my face was submerged in the mud, and I kept it that way even after one of the Nazis kicked me. Thinking I was dead, he left me lying there on the road."

"Thank God for that!" said Frania. "And what did you do then?"

"Very carefully, I lifted my head and turned it to one side so I could breathe. I lay there until my companions and the Germans were out of sight. When finally I sat up, I smiled and wiped mud from my face with my sleeve. I knew I was free."

"God was good to you," said Frania's mother.

"How did you manage to keep away from the Germans?" asked Marysia.

"I walked only at night or very early in the morning and kept away from villages and cities."

"And where did you sleep?"

"In woods on dry days and under bridges when it rained."

"But what did you live on?"

"On vegetables and wild fruit I found in fields and by roadsides."

"I love you, Andrzej," said Frania. She looked adoringly at his profile. "You're our national hero, as far as I'm concerned."

"I love you also, Frania," he said and turned to her so he could give her a kiss on her forehead. She wished it were her lips. "I'm not a hero, just a survivor."

In order to absorb all that had been said, the family stopped talking. And then a new fear overwhelmed them. The Nazis were murderers and brutes, but they had left Eastern Poland. And they had left it to Russia. There were rumors that the Russians were secretly planning something bad for the Poles. The question was what?

Chapter Four

A HARSH WINTER BROUGHT SNOW, SLEET, WIND, AND A SKY LOW AND gray. But Christmas in Poland arrived as usual, as if nothing had changed. Trees glistened in the windows, and carols were sung in low voices, but there was no real joy in the frosty air. The people were in mourning, not only for the many fathers, brothers, and cousins lost in the war, but also for their country's loss of precious freedom. The survivors of the first battles over Poland worried about what tomorrow might bring.

January of 1940 was a tedious month, the night of the tenth extremely cold. Winds shook the skeletons of trees in the back yards and threw snow at the houses. Frost painted fantastic designs on the windowpanes.

Frania was dreaming about being lost in a strange, wild forest that night. She was all alone and climbing up a wooded hill, when a pounding on the door woke her. She couldn't move at first. Henio's shrieking brought her back to her senses. She slid down her bed, scooped him up in her arms, then climbed back under the covers and put her nipple in his mouth.

The pounding came again. "Open up!" a voice shouted in Russian.

Frania heard everyone stirring in their beds nearby, the whole family gathered in one large room because it was the only one they could heat.

"Open up in the name of Russia," came the command. "If you don't, we'll break in."

Frania's father was out of bed and stumbling about in the darkness.

"Don't let them in," hissed Frania's mother from under her covers. "They must be bandits. The noise they're making will waken our neighbors, and they'll come to save us."

Frania's father rubbed a hole in the frost on the window. "I see two uniformed Russians and one civilian," he said.

"Open up in the name of Russia! We are asking you for the last time."

"Don't open the door, Tata," said Frania. Now she saw Andrzej shivering by her side, and wondered at his lack of bravery.

"I have to," her father said. "If they break the door down, they will kill us all." He opened the door.

They came in, bringing cold from outside. Their figures were silhouettes in the semi-darkness.

"Light!" barked the same voice they'd heard all along.

Frania's father groped in the night shadows and struck a match. He lit a lamp on the table.

The first thing Frania saw was two Russian soldiers, their guns pointing straight at her and her family. A Ukrainian from the other end of the village stood well behind. Frania recognized him as the one who kept stealing firewood from her parents' woods. Whenever he was caught and had to pay a fine, he threatened to get even with her father. The expression on his face now told her the time of revenge was here, and he was happy with it.

"Is everyone home?" asked one of the Russians. He then motioned to the Ukrainian to translate his words into Polish.

The Ukrainian repeated the question in accented Polish.

"The whole family is here," said Frania's father, standing still in his nightclothes by the table.

"I'll call names, and you answer, one at a time."

Having performed this task, the Russian ordered his companions to search the house for weapons. The two men turned things upside down, but found only two butcher knives in the pantry. They brought the knives out and placed them on the floor behind their leader.

"We have orders from Moscow to evacuate you," the leader said.

"Evacuate?" said Frania. "Where to?"

"To Lwow." He moved his gun to point straight at her. Henio was still nursing at her breast. She lifted a corner of the quilt to cover his face. Why didn't Andrzej move in front of her to protect her and the baby?

"Why out there?" asked her mother.

"We have orders from a higher authority," the man said.

"You mean you're deporting us," said Andrzej in a small voice. "Have a heart and leave us here."

"Get out of bed and get ready for the road, all of you," the Russian said. He swung about so his gun now pointed at Andrzej.

"Please, don't force us out. Can't you see we have little children here?" said Frania's mother.

"Shut up, woman!" the Russian shouted and stepped toward her, his gun much too close to her face.

The children began to cry, Henio bawling the loudest.

Now the other soldier, whose gun was pointed at Frania's father, spoke for the first time. "I advise you to get ready for the trip and to pack things you will need for the road."

Frania managed to quiet Henio down by shoving her nipple back into his mouth.

"No! No! We are staying in our beds!" her mother screamed. "Shoot us all here and now. It would be better for us to die quickly in our home than die slowly of cold and starvation in your country."

Frania closed her eyes tight, expecting to be shot, but nothing happened. When she opened them, the other soldier had moved his gun closer to her father. "Get ready," he said, his voice low.

"We are not budging," said Frania's father.

"Do you want us to carry you out in your nightclothes?"

Silence.

Frania's father raised his hand the way a pupil does in school when he wants to speak. "We will get ready."

Thus, at gunpoint and under threat of being exposed to the raw cold, the family pulled on their warm clothing. Frania's father and Andrzej hastened to fill two trunks with towels, bedding, fine linens, some kitchen things, and extra clothing.

The sky was beginning to lighten by the time Frania and her family left their beloved homestead. Escorted by armed Russians, they were seated in sleighs pulled by horses. As they neared the curve in the road, Frania glanced up and saw the chimney on her parent's house. She watched it slowly disappear from view, afraid she might never see it again in her life, afraid she was leaving her birthplace and Poland forever.

They were brought in front of the school. Soon they found out that two-thirds of the villagers were in the same situation. Among them were Julek and his family. A long row of sleds carried the other Polish people. Heads of solemn-faced men, puffy-eyed women, and their bewildered children stuck out above the quilts and blankets. It had stopped snowing before daybreak, and now the sun climbed up the sky, looking like a giant egg yolk. In the daylight, Frania could see sleighs lined up on the road leading to the nearest railway station. When the first horseman gave the sign, the lead sleigh moved forward. The rest soon followed.

The ride to the station seemed to last forever. They came to a halt in front of the freight wagons that stood on the tracks like tall coffins lined up on a cemetery lot.

The soldiers barked out orders, using their guns to prod the people forward. "Get down and climb into the wagons. Hurry and get in quickly."

Frania and the others obeyed without saying a word.

The boxcars, still smelling of the cattle they had once transported, were now furnished with lower and upper plank berths divided by a narrow space in the middle where an iron stove stood. The shape of the stove reminded Frania of her grandfather's old pipe. She stayed close behind her father as he moved the children into one of the upper berths. She found a spot where she could lean into a corner and cuddle her baby. A small window let in a streak of sunlight and some fresh air. Andrzej settled by her side but didn't put his arms about her, and she was disappointed. She wanted him to be strong, to hold her safe, but he looked pale and distant.

The cars were soon packed full from corner to corner, and then they waited for the train to move. Anything, Frania thought, would be better than the stillness of these wagons. It felt like the stillness of the grave.

After a while, Mama spread bedcovers over the hard planks, and everyone tried to sleep, but the space was too small for the whole family. No matter how they sat or lay, someone was squashed. Frania tried to lie still, her arms pulled in close to her sides. Henio lay heavy against her stomach, and her nipples ached from his nervous sucking. He cried often from being bundled up all the time; every time he cried, she fed him. She would have cried, too, had she any tears left in her. She avoided looking at his sweet little face and tried not to think of what might happen to her son the next day or the day after that. Thinking led to worrying, and worrying could drive her to madness. She pulled a temporary screen around her heart to protect it from breaking.

The first day and night passed, but the train did not move. Soon, people were licking frost from the nails and iron parts in the walls to ease the awful want for water. Frania felt lucky to be near her small window, breathing in the cold but fresh air. It was like her own private window to the world outside. But when she peeked out, she saw Russian soldiers, carrying guns, pacing past her boxcar.

Frania ached all over the second night in the wagon. No one had eaten for two days, yet all she felt was thirst. The awful thirst dried out her throat, the insides of her mouth, and her lips. Often she put her face to the small hole and breathed in clean air seeping through it. Its delicious coolness went into her nostrils and down her throat the way cold water does. But no matter what she did, she couldn't get rid of the terrible thirst.

Much later, when people were dozing from exhaustion, someone opened the door and pushed in five buckets of snow.

Snow!

Frania was among the first to reach the buckets. She scooped up the precious white stuff. It was ice-cold but melting fast in her hands and her mouth, and she kept swallowing, swallowing. When she had enough, she returned to her place in the upper berth and was soon fast asleep.

At midnight, a sudden jerk of the train woke her.

"Sweet Jesus and Mother Mary!" voices cried out in the dark. "The train is moving. We are leaving Poland!" Panic spread anew throughout the car. Men were pounding the walls now with their fists, yelling, "Let us out!" They cursed Russia and spit into the air. Women sobbed and children screamed. One young man stood kicking the door and shouting until he fell down, exhausted.

Amidst all the clamor, a strong beautiful voice started to sing. "Jeszcze polska nie zginela, poki my zyjemy (Poland is not lost as long as we are alive)."

Frania glanced in the direction of the voice and saw it belonged to a bearded, middle-aged man in the opposite berth. In no time, other passengers began to sing. Their singing was loud enough to muffle the awful sound that the wheels underneath were making as the train roared down the tracks.

Soon Frania was singing too. She sang as if her life and happiness depended on the loudness of her voice, and the strength of it. Maybe, just maybe, the Almighty, hearing the pleading words of young and old, would soften the Russians' hearts, soften them enough to stop the train from rolling toward the east.

Alas, no such miracle happened. In the dark night, like a bandit, the locomotive sped forward, carrying the Poles away from their birth land.

Chapter Five

A VAST REGION OF THE SOVIET UNION, AN AREA OF ABOUT 5,000,000 square miles, is called Siberia. It covers the northern third of Asia and stretches eastward from the Ural Mountains to the Pacific Ocean. From north to south there are three different vegetation zones. The land running along the Arctic Ocean is covered with cold and treeless tundra. Most of Siberia, though, is overtaken by the taiga. The taiga is made up of immense evergreen forests of spruce, larch, and fir. The steppes—grassy plains—lie mainly in the southwest.

Among other big cities in Siberia are Krasnoyarsk, Novosibirsk, Komsomolsk, Vladivostok, Omsk, and Tomsk. The Lena, Venisei, Ob, and Irtish are important rivers here. For six to nine months of each year, these rivers are frozen.

Siberia had long been a place where political prisoners, religious offenders, and criminals were sent in exile. Because of the harsh climate and lack of sufficient transportation, living conditions there were difficult.

Somewhere in the district of Omsk and in the depth of taiga, several barracks awaited their next occupants. These old shelters were furnished only with prycze (plank bunks) and iron, pipe-like stoves. For years, these barracks tried, without success, to make a home for men and women exiled into this wilderness. If only the dirty walls could talk, they could tell horrid stories of the misery of those humans who suffered and died there of cold and hunger.

One late afternoon in early March, 1940, Frania and her traveling companions were brought to one such place. These people were exhausted from the long trip, having traveled by sleighs, trains, trucks, and then sleighs again. Some of them were ill. On the train in Frania's wagon alone, two of the passengers had died. One elderly woman was taken out sick from her bed. One young man went under the train to relieve himself the first time the Poles were let out to stretch their weary bones in Russia. When the train started to move again without warning, he was run over by its wheels.

Frania and her family were given a space in one of the barracks: a two-level berth by the door, the bottom one for sleeping and the upper, much smaller, to store the few belongings they had brought with them from Poland. She was lucky to have some extra clothing, fine linens, and all of her bedding. These pillows, quilts, and blankets kept her and her dear ones from freezing while riding in sleighs. Now, they would keep them warm at night.

The first thing she did that evening in the shelter, warmed up now by wood burning in the stove, was to unbundle Henio. He stretched, kicked, waved his little arms all about and gurgled happily. She smiled at him through her tears. Then she changed him into nightclothes for the first time since the night they were deported. She fed him with her breast and put him down to sleep.

Hot soup and bread were brought in, and she ate with relish.

Ah, it was good to lie down on blankets without feeling bumps in a road. And she had enough room to move about, all she wanted now. Smiling, she brought her arms above her head, straightened her spine and legs, and yawned. Then she turned on one side, her knees and elbows bent. This luxury she enjoyed before falling into a deep sleep.

But she was still riding in her sleigh in her dreams. Snow fell on her blanketed head. White flakes came down in the form of a lacy net.

"How dare you humans enter my kingdom," she heard mean voices saying in the treetops of the taiga.

"We've not come here willingly," she said to the voices, pulling a blanket over Henio's forehead.

"That doesn't matter. You will pay dearly for disturbing us."

"Please, don't punish us for something that isn't our fault," she sobbed out.

"You will die, die, die. All of you."

"Oh, no. No! Please don't kill my son."

Next she found herself lying in a bed that was drowning in fog. She was tired, so tired, and falling into a deep slumber. Yet there was something trying to interfere with her rest. Who or what was it? Something was prickling her skin as if with tiny needles. Voices were buzzing about her ears the way an insect does about a bush.

"Go away," she mumbled, tossing and turning on her bunk. "Scat, you pesky creatures, and let me be."

Before she opened her eyes, she realized she was in the barrack and scratching herself something awful.

"Bedbugs! Bedbugs! Bedbugs!" voices in the bunks cried out. "They are coming out of the walls and dropping down from the ceiling."

It was frighteningly cold in the forest, but it wasn't snowing. Temperatures plummeted to about thirty below zero, but Frania sweated under her clothing because she labored so hard. She teamed up with Marysia to load logs onto one of the carts.

"People, move faster! Work harder!" one of the Russian overseers, named Ivan, shouted, warming himself by one of the fires. He was tall and stocky.

"Psiakrew (a dog's blood)," Frania cursed under her breath.

"Hush up, my sister," said Marysia, getting ahold of the next log and lifting one end of it. "You don't want him to hear you."

"I hate him," Frania whispered, bending to pick up the other end. "He and all the other Communist watchdogs are here to see that we Poles work to the last drop of energy before we drop dead."

"Come on, Frania, let's lift together. One, two, three."

"All right, then, let's get the dumb thing into the cart."

Ten minutes later, the cart was loaded. Frania wiped fresh sweat from her forehead and said, "It makes me mad to see these creeps stand around in their thick coats, boots, and furry hats while we, in our thin clothes, do all the hard work."

"You're much too slow!" another overseer shouted, standing next to Frania's father and Andrzej, who were cutting down a tree with an old, two-handled saw. They grunted as they pulled and pushed, trying to make the rusty teeth sink deeper into the bark.

When Frania glanced at Andrzej, she noticed how much he had changed since the war. Now he looked at least ten years older. Lately, he shuffled as he walked and hardly ever smiled. She could understand that. But why had he stopped communicating with her and her family? He kept falling into periods of silent gloom. His only enjoyment seemed to be holding Henio and rocking him on the bunk after work.

For some reason—maybe because he didn't want a child born in Russia or maybe because of the lack of privacy—he never tried to make love to her and did only what he was forced to. Even in Poland, after his escape from the Nazis, he hardly ever kissed her and simply sat around, unwilling to help her family with the farming. He wasn't much help to her during the journey to Siberia, either. And now she had to yell at him every morning to make him get up and go to work. What was it that was slowly dragging his spirit down to the ground? She supposed it was partly the loss freedom—his and Poland's—and now the deportation. But thousands of other Polish deportees in Russia were just as bad off, she knew. Something else chewed at him. All his life, he had been told that God made him to use his mind, not his hands, and he firmly believed it. Frania decided he was ashamed to be forced into hard labor along with her father and all the others who had been farmers in Poland, but now cut trees in the taiga.

"Will he ever learn?" she muttered to herself.

"Zakurek (time for a cigarette)!" Ivan called out, and Frania's thoughts scattered all over the snow.

She ran to the nearest campfire that spat sparks into the air. Freshly cut branches smoked and hissed in spite of the wind blowing at them. Now she shivered. She stamped her feet and slapped her arms against her chest for warmth. She noticed Julek standing nearby. He stood tall and straight as always, though he was much thinner. She had seen him in the company of girls now and then, but never twice with the same one, and he was not married yet. Did he ever still think of her? Now she saw him looking at her, and she lowered her eyes. Did he hate her for marrying Andrzej? No, he wasn't capable of hate. He had probably forgotten all about ever liking her.

The hours passed slowly, as usual, and the day dragged its feet across the snow like a man wearing chains on his ankles. The Poles cutting trees in the forest could hardly wait for the sun to cross over to the low western horizon and, when it finally did, they were permitted to go back to their barracks.

Right away, they poured into the cafeteria for supper. There were always long lines before the kitchen windows, and they had to wait for their thin soup and bread, but this meal was the only cheery moment in their dreary exile. Single workers ate in the cafeteria. Those who had non-working relatives shared their food with them in the barracks.

One evening, a meeting was to be held in the cafeteria. All the working Poles were told they had better be there.

Wronsky was a big NKWD man and the top watchdog over the deportees. When he walked in that night, fearful eyes turned toward his uniformed bulk. What was he up to this time? The Poles knew he had a wife and a small daughter living somewhere else, and they guessed that was where he spent his time when away from the barracks. They also knew he wasn't as cruel as he pretended to be. When he was around, soups were thicker, the bread lighter, and his assistants a bit easier going. Wronsky acted like a lamb one day and a bear the next, but he hadn't hurt anyone yet. He often confused the exiles, though. After awhile, they were certain of one only thing: he was great on promises he couldn't possibly keep.

"Good evening, Comrades," he began, standing on a raised platform and looking down at the exiles sitting on benches. "I've called you here tonight because I want to talk to you as a...a friend."

A scornful murmur washed across the room. "Friend? Hah!" someone said.

Wronsky searched the faces in the front benches. He cleared his throat and continued. "As I've said before, you people need to work harder. I hear from a higher authority in the nearby city of Tara that you're not putting out enough lumber."

"Give us more bread, Commander Wronsky, and then ask us to produce more in the forest," called out Julek from the depth of the room.

"Feed us better, and we will work harder," said someone else.

Wronsky raised his hand and smiled, but only with his teeth. "Show me what you can do, and I promise to add meat to your diet, and milk for your children."

"We were supposed to get boots last week to keep our feet from freezing."

"And warm hats."

"Where are they, Commander Wronsky?"

"They are on the way," said the Russian. "Don't you worry. You will get all you need with time. As you know, our beloved Daddy Stalin is merciful. He wants you to be happy."

"If you want us to be happy, send us back to Poland."

"We can't do that," said Wronsky, "but we have great plans for you here."

"Plans? Oh, no!"

"In the summer, we will move you to Bialy Jar."

"What is Bialy Jar?"

"It's a nearby settlement."

"Oh, are we to live in barracks like the ones we have now?"

"No. We will build you houses modeled on villages in Poland."

"But we don't want to stay in Russia forever. We want to go back home!"

"Yes, yes. We all want to go back."

Wronsky's smiling face turned grim. "You ungrateful Poles!" he shouted. "We have saved you from your capitalists and want to make citizens out of you. And what do you do? You yell and complain all the time!"

"You've done us wrong by exiling us. Your government took away our farms!"

"Shut up! Shut up, all of you! I've had enough. The first one who says a word is going to jail."

Silence.

Spring came to the forest. As soon as the snow melted, all the fresh greenery sprang up and began to reproduce. Wildlife was awakened to multiply as nature intended it to. Birds laid eggs in their nests, feeling themselves at home, but what did they know of the misery of humans living in barracks that looked shabbier than ever against the beauty of Mother Nature?

While leaves unfolded on trees and bushes, and wildflowers bloomed in the clearing of the taiga, people in the shelters were dying. One by one, the elderly and the infants weakened. Those exiles unable to acclimatize to life in Siberia without medical care and proper nourishment eventually grew ill and passed away.

One early spring morning, Frania was ready for work, yet she stayed in for awhile. Holding Henio close to her, she hugged and kissed him on his cheeks. He was warm and soft, but ten pounds lighter than he had been in Poland. His eyes looked glassy, his skin yellowish.

"Take good care of your only nephew," she said to Jozia, who was seven now. Then she handed her son to the girl.

"I will, Frania. I will," Jozia said, her large sad eyes on her big sister. Jozia was small and thin and bent under the weight of Henio.

Frania patted Henio's head and sighed deeply. Tears came to her eyes. "Holy Mary," she moaned, "the poor darling looks like a wax statue."

"Yes, he does, but he's the only baby here still alive."

"Yes, he's alive," repeated Frania, "but will he survive his first summer in Siberia?"

"He will. I know he will," said Jozia.

Frania said nothing now. She just stood there staring at her son and feeling guilty. Had she tried hard enough, she would have managed somehow to be excused from the labor in the woods because of Henio. But she knew that, if she stayed in the barrack day and night, she would go insane in no time. And then she would not be any good to anyone.

"Warm up some soup on the stove and give him that for lunch. Whenever he cries too much, let him suck on a lump of sugar wrapped in a rag."

"Sugar," said Jozia. "You were lucky to get some of it the other evening in the store."

Frania nodded. "But it would have been better if they brought milk for our little ones, instead," she said, and went outside.

A week later, Frania awoke in the morning and discovered Henio had stopped breathing. "Oh, no! God, no," she cried out. She stared at his little corpse with its eyes closed as if in sleep. She touched him over and over again and shook him by his shoulders, hoping to waken him. She refused to believe her son was gone. Why was his face so cold and his tiny arms stiff? Sweet, innocent child, what have you done to deserve death before you had a chance to live?

"Frania." She heard Andrzej's voice and felt his hand on her shoulder.

"Wha—?" she said surprised at the nearness of her husband. "Andrzej," she sobbed out then, "our baby, he…he's…"

"He's dead?" said Andrzej.

She nodded.

Andrzej's head went down and stayed down for a long time. Frania broke into convulsive crying. She was expecting his arms to surround her, but they didn't. After awhile, she stopped crying and looked at Andrzej. She saw him staring at the body, a strange expression on his face.

"Andrzej. Andrzej?"

He didn't respond.

She reached out and touched his arm, but he winced and pulled away.

"We have to bury him."

"What? We can't put Henio into the ground," he said.

"We have to," she said, then repeated, "We have to."

"No, no, no!" he cried, covering his face with his hands. "No, no."

She pried his hands from his face and, holding them in hers, whispered hoarsely, "Andrzej, you have to make a coffin."

Again, he pulled away from her touch. He held his hands out in front of him, studying them, and said, "I…I can't."

"Why not?" she suddenly yelled at him. "Why?"

Still staring at his palms, he said in a low voice, "Because I c-can't."

"What?"

"I don't know how to."

For a moment she looked hard at him, and then she said through her teeth, "Why do I have to do everything in this family?"

"Ask your father," he said and lowered his head back down to his chest.

In late afternoon, the family carried the little wooden box to the freshly-made cemetery in the taiga, about a half-mile from the barracks. As they were lowering it into the grave dug out beside many others, Andrzej suddenly broke into pitiful sobs.

Frania stepped closer, wanting to embrace him, but he elbowed her away, and then fell down on his knees. "Why did you have to die, my son?" he said, beating the ground with his forehead. "They killed you. They did. The Russians murdered you."

Frania's arms went limp by her sides. She stood there, silently crying, not even knowing that she was crying. She looked down at the coffin, and then at Andrzej, so completely bent under this new tragedy. What was happening to her family? Had she lost her baby and her husband, too? Had he slipped so far away from her that he would never find his way back? Was she now all alone in this Hellish world?

A strong arm suddenly went about her shoulders. It was her father, offering his comfort to her.

"Oh, Tata, Tata," she moaned leaning against him. "If only I had stayed with Henio in the barrack, he would still be alive."

"No, Frania, your son would have died the same as all the other babies, and you know it."

"Maybe you're right. It wouldn't have made any difference if I worked or not."

"Just think, my daughter. Henio now is happy with God in Heaven."

"That's right. He's happy," she said, managing to lift the corners of her lips upward.

The Siberian summer, in contrast to the long, severe winter, was hot and short. Warm weather brought in mosquitos, flies, and all sorts of reptiles to plague the exiles.

Bialy Jar, of which the exiles had heard already from Wronsky, was a large village located on the Irtish River, on the opposite shore from Tara. It was made up of a school, a combination cafeteria and store, and small houses built half in and half out of the ground to keep them warm in winter and cool in summer. Its dwellers lumbered collectively for their meager livelihood. Each family owned a cow and a small lot to grow vegetables on when weather permitted.

In June, Wronsky chose two dozen of the working exiles and took them to Bialy Jar to help him realize his plan to erect Polish Village on the edge of the taiga, neighboring with the settlement. This was the only promise the Russian kept. Thus, under his supervision, the Poles cut trees. They soon made two rows of wooden, two-room houses and covered them with thatched roofs. These shelters were made in a hurry and by unwilling Poles, who refused to believe, even for a moment, that they would have to stay in Siberia for much longer, much less occupy these houses for the rest of their lives.

Before the first snow fell that year, the exiles were indeed transported to the new location.

Frania and her family found the new life somewhat different, but essentially the same. Food was still far from being sufficient and work was exhausting. They continued to cut trees in the forest, and now they sailed logs down the river to Tara. The Russians were, as always, watchful and suspicious of every move the Poles made. Only the land, especially in warm season, was strikingly beautiful. Another good thing about the new shelters was that they were free of bugs.

Going south from Polish Village, the Irtish glistened in the sun. In summer, boats of all kinds glided along the surface of its wide waters. A barge laden with passengers went back and forth between Bialy Jar and Tara.

The second winter in Siberia was even harder for Frania to bear. She was not only dispirited, but also lacked the physical strength needed to keep up with her six-day-a-week labor in the taiga. There was work awaiting her each day in the shelter—cleaning, washing, and repairing clothes. Besides doing her chores, she helped her mother when Marysia was ailing. Frania's family occupied the other room in the same house as she and Andrzej. In the evenings and mornings, she heard them moving about, talking, shouting, and sometimes fighting with each other.

"Why don't you do something, Andrzej?" she said to him one evening. She was mending his shirt by the fire that burned in the brick oven.

Andrzej didn't stir. He sat, silent, in a room filled with shadows and streaks of firelight.

"Don't just sit there with your head in your hands and your elbows on the table. I can't stand seeing you this way," Frania said.

"What do you want from me?" He spoke to the kerosene lamp, not to her.

"Read a book or write something," she said, twisting the edge of his shirt on her lap.

"What's the use," he said, his eyes half-closed.

She suddenly threw the shirt to the floor and jumped to her feet. "Snap out of this gloomy mood!" she screamed, standing now behind him. "You aren't a man anymore, Andrzej."

"I work in the taiga like everyone else," he said.

She leaned over and said into his ear, "Yes, you work because they are forcing you to work." Now she grabbed both of his shoulders and shook them with all her might. "You don't want to be put in jail. But maybe you would be better off in the cell. Have you ever thought of that? You wouldn't have to do a thing in there but sit and think."

He didn't respond. Instead, he hid his face in his hands.

She let go of him, walked to the other side of the table and sat across from him on the stool. "Look at me, Andrzej," she whispered.

He sat, unmoving.

She reached out and pried his hands away from his face. "Open your eyes and look at me."

But his eyes stayed shut against her.

"Andrzej," she said, and lifted his chin upward. "Please don't shut me out."

He glanced up at her and muttered, "Leave me alone," then closed his eyes again.

"No, I won't leave you alone until I tell you what's on my mind this time."

"I...I don't want to hear."

"I'm young, and I need to be loved. Why don't you take care of yourself and pay some attention to me? Shave that ugly beard and comb your hair. I wash your clothes and do all the work in the house; the least you could do is retain your dignity as a human being by keeping yourself looking decent."

"Leave me alone."

"Sweet Jesus," she said, letting go of his face and getting up. "Talking to you is like talking to the floor or that lamp." She heard the slight trace of self-pity in her voice. Quickly, she returned to her mending by the fire.

When was this horrid life in Siberia going to end, one way or another? Right now, logs were burning in the brick oven and she was warm, but in an hour she would have to crawl beneath cold covers in her bed. Tomorrow, she would be shivering in the taiga. Tomorrow and the day after that. She labored every day to the point of exhaustion and ached all over every night from the strain. Right now, she was hungry. She was always hungry. She couldn't remember the last time her stomach felt full. If it wasn't for her family living in the other half of the house, she would be the loneliest person in the world. Andrzej was getting worse every day, and she couldn't help him. Why couldn't he be like Julek or her father, who had made Frania's bunks, a wooden table and stools, and shelves to keep the pots and pans they brought from Poland.

As Frania and Andrzej sat at their separate spots, absorbed in their own thoughts, a strong wind rose from above the Irtish and soon came down to claw at Polish Village. In its fury it shook the houses and threw snow at the thin glass windows.

"You are poor excuses for homes," Frania seemed to hear the wind howl outside her door. "Polish Village in Russia. Ha, ha, ha. You houses are as out of place here as your dwellers are. Your walls are too thin, and their clothes are too thin. You will never keep warm when my cold breath blows on you."

Chapter Six

ANOTHER WINTER PLODDED AWAY.
Frania awoke one morning with a dismal feeling that her life wasn't worth living any longer. She put on her dress, clean but with too many small patches and stitches showing. Then she washed her hands and face in the bowl filled with water near the stove. Looking into the tiny mirror on the wall next to the window, she combed out her short light brown hair and tied a threadbare scarf around her neck. Her face was pale and thin, but her eyes seemed larger than ever and maybe even bluer than yesterday. She made up her bed. Andrzej's bed beside hers was empty. He had broken his arm and injured his back while working; a falling tree cracked his bones in three places. They had taken him to a hospital in Tara.

She closed her eyes tight against the sunlight pouring in through the unshaded window, and she wished she could just stop breathing. How much easier that would be. Her ears strained toward the adjoining shelter where her first family must still be asleep, for no sound came through the wall. "Mama," Frania whispered, her hand on the doorknob. Maybe she should wait to say goodbye to them? Just for a moment she let go of the knob, only to grip it again.

Quickly, she stepped out into the young day. The air was still cool and scented with moist wilderness. Birds chattered in the treetops. Her head lowered to her chest, Frania began walking along a dirt road flanked by two rows of small houses, hastily built above ground for Polish exiles. Across Bialy Jar where the natives lived, their houses were half built into the ground to keep them cool in hot weather and warm in the freezing cold.

The Poles and the Russians were still asleep or perhaps just stirring in their beds; there wasn't anyone outside yet, and Frania was glad. She came close to the Irtish River and saw it through the foliage of bushes. The river shimmered and glistened in the sun, which had managed to rise above it by now. She saw Julek emerging from behind the curve of the path, carrying two pails of water.

"Frania!" he called, and she could tell he was happy to see her. "What are you doing here so early in the morning?" He quickened his steps to meet her halfway.

"I...I'm taking a walk." She came close to him and asked, "But why are you up so early, Julek?"

"Couldn't sleep. Mother needed water for breakfast," he said, searching her face. "How are you, Frania?" He lowered the pails to the ground and pushed his hair back from his forehead.

She shrugged and stared across the Irtish at Tara, the city located on the opposite shore. "Andrzej's still in the hospital," she said.

His eyes also on the river, Julek said, "That was an awful accident. I saw how the tree hit your husband and barely missed your father."

"Thank God, Tata is all right. What would Mama do without him, and what would I do? He fixes everything for them and for me. Andrzej never has been good with his hands." She paused, looking down at her feet. "Born to teach, I suppose."

"That was a bad accident," he repeated.

"Yes, it was," she said.

An uncomfortable silence fell between them, but it lasted only a few seconds.

"Frania, let's go for a picnic," Julek cried out.

With wide eyes, Frania turned to look at him. Had he gone mad? Whoever heard of a picnic in Siberia? "I don't know," she said in a small voice.

"We can go deep into the forest and spend all day there, just you and me," he sang out. "It would be nice to talk about old times. Do you ever think of those Saturday nights in Poland, when you used to sneak out your bedroom window to go dancing with me?"

"Oh, yes," she said and smiled sadly, still stunned by the idea of going into the taiga all alone, just the two of them. "But how can we go? It wouldn't be proper. I should visit Andrzej today, and we aren't allowed to leave Polish Village."

"What do you care what's proper and what's not? And haven't you heard that Wronsky gave us permission to go mushroom picking?"

She shook her head. "Why this sudden change of heart?"

"You know there's not enough bread, and soups are thinner in the cafeteria lately."

"We are practically starving," she said. "Twice this week they ran out of bread before I reached the bakery window. I wonder why?"

"Don't you know? Wronsky has been waiting for a fresh supply of food to come by boat from Omsk, and so far it hasn't come."

"And if the boat doesn't come soon—" she rushed to say.

"We'll starve."

"So what?" Frania blurted out her true feeling. "We have to die sooner or later."

"Frania!"

"We would be better off in our graves."

"Don't talk like that," he pleaded in a soft voice, touching her cheek. "It's not like you to be so gloomy."

"Oh, I don't mean to," she said, and managed a crooked smile.

He stepped closer and whispered in her ear. "Please come for a picnic with me. Please."

Her heart quickened at his nearness, but she took two steps away from him. "All right," she said, knowing he wouldn't give up. "Let's go, then. But aren't you going to take the water to your mother first?"

He picked up the pails. "I'll be back. Wait for me here."

"I will wait," she said, and waved him away. She watched water spill on the dusty road behind him. Finally, he was gone from her sight.

Julek hadn't changed, except he was thinner. But he was still handsome, strong, and thoughtful. She could easily fall in love with him again. Dear heavens! What was she thinking about? She couldn't love any man but her husband. It would be a mortal sin.

Frania stepped closer to the river and stood on its shore looking down. Ripples in the water seemed to invite her to jump in so they could rock her to sleep, eternal sleep. Yet something kept her standing. She turned and looked at the taiga right behind her. She closed her eyes and felt the urge to run, just run away. What would happen if she threw herself blindly into the thickness of the forest? Soon enough she would smash her head against the bark of a tree. Here was the solution to her misery. She opened her eyes and stared at the forest with its magnificent pines, birches, and hardy larches all crowding each other, all trying to reach higher and higher toward the life-giving sun.

A bird screamed, and she turned back toward the river. Perhaps it would be easier, after all, to jump into the deep waters, where she would drown easily, for she couldn't swim at all.

"Oohoo, Frania!" a voice called behind her.

"He's back already?" she whispered. "Now what am I to do? I've wasted my time and the chance to do what I came to do."

He strolled close to her, a bundle slung across his shoulder, and smiled the way he had in Poland, ages ago.

"Julek, you look happy," she said, and swallowed hard. She ran her hands over her eyes and mouth, wanting to wipe away any traces of her morbid thoughts. "You've changed your clothes. Where did you get such a nice outfit?"

Grinning, he smoothed out his yellow sport shirt open at the throat, then touched his brown trousers. "I brought this from Poland and saved it to wear on a special occasion like today."

"What occasion is this?"

"Being with you," he said.

"Oh," she said, but didn't smile.

"Don't worry, dear Frania. In the taiga I will behave like your brother or good friend, nothing else."

She sighed with relief. Without another word, they began walking along the path that ran by the wooded shore of the Irtish. Soon the taiga grew thicker, full of dark moist shadows and golden streaks of light. Mosquitoes swarmed around their heads. They swatted at the insects and ran to get far, far away, not only from them but from Polish Village and their miserable existence there.

Time passed, and Frania and Julek kept walking. Holding hands now, they followed a path that wound through the trees and thick undergrowth. It ran parallel to the river, across moist ground lined with grasses, pine needles, and ferns. Without resting, they plodded on and on, two tiny specks at the bottom of the immense taiga filled with bears, wolves, and foxes. No wild animals chased them. No Russian labor overseers forced them to keep moving. Not even Wronsky, with his watchful black eyes, caused them to trudge onward until they were exhausted and sweat ran down their spines.

Frania stopped on the path. "Let's rest here." She was out of breath and pale.

"A meadow! The perfect place for our picnic," Julek said, trying to catch his breath. He looked with longing at the luxurious shade under a huge larch right in the middle of the heart-shaped clearing.

As soon as they reached the shade, they kicked off their shoes and sprawled on the cool grass. Frania stared up at the dark green fringe of the taiga overhead. "I wish I were a bird," she said. "I could fly home to Poland."

Julek sat up. "Look, Frania, look at this place. Isn't this a beautiful sight? Sit up and look."

She rose, but not willingly, and then she was glad she had. The glade reminded her of an enchanted castle she had once read about as a little girl. But this castle in the taiga—on a rise of land, breezy, with fewer insects than in the thick forest—was made by nature herself. Here, fallen trees thrown across the carpet of grass served as benches. In the middle of the clearing the larch under which they rested laid its blue pattern like lace on the velvet grass. Bunches of yellow, pink, and purple wildflowers embroidered their secret room. Tall trees walled them in, but a window opened to overlook the vibrant, milky river.

Frania turned to look at Julek. "Why would God make such a beautiful world, then fill it with flesh-eating animals and stinging insects and poisonous plants? Why did God make evil men like Hitler and Stalin to rule their countries and start wars?"

"I don't know why things are the way they are, but I believe in the goodness of God."

"Are you saying that God is just?" She leaned close to see his face. "Yes."

"Well, then, tell me what I have done to be deported from my homeland, to have my first and only baby dead?"

"Oh, my dear Frania, only God has the answers to your questions."

"Look at me, Julek." She pointed at her chest. "I don't even have a real husband. Andrzej has changed so since the war." She hugged her knees and began to rock back and forth.

Julek placed his hand on her shoulder to still her rocking. "Please, Frania, forget about this life in Russia. Remember our walks and talks in Poland, when your father thought you were at the river with your sisters? You even let me kiss you now and then. Until *he* came to teach in our village."

"We had good times, didn't we?" she said, and managed a small smile. "You were a good dancer."

"So were you." He leaned forward to look into her face. "The prettiest one, too." Then he quickly straightened up and looked away.

"But now all of Poland seems like a dream."

"Our kisses are real to me still," Julek said. He leaned close to her again, and his hand almost touched her knee. "Why did you have to marry Andrzej? Did you love him so much?"

"Love?" she repeated, and stopped her rocking to turn and look at him. "I don't know. He was so different from you and the other boys in the village..."

"And represented a higher class," he said derisively, but she pretended not to hear.

A cool breeze blew in from the Irtish River. "I'm tired," Frania said. She lay back, her hands pillowing her head, and soon fell asleep.

She awoke to the aroma of boiling soup. A wood fire burned beneath a pot balanced on fieldstones. She sat up and saw Julek stirring the soup with a long wooden spoon.

"Lunch will be ready soon," he called out.

She rose and walked over to the fire. "Where did you get all the food?" She peered into the pot and licked her lips.

He straightened up by her side and smiled. "Let me think. I brought potatoes, onions, and carrots from home."

"Carrots and potatoes!"

"Mother exchanged her silky shawl with her Russian friend for goodies this week. She gave me some today for our picnic."

"It smells delicious." Frania's mouth watered, and she swallowed.

"It would taste even better with mushrooms," Julek said. "I saw some in the forest, near the edge of the clearing. Why don't you go pick some?"

"Mushrooms," she murmured. She untied the scarf from around her neck and walked away.

Her scarf was almost full when she heard Julek call, "Soup is ready!"

"Why didn't you wait for the mushrooms?" she called out, but he didn't answer. She bent down to pick one more, then stopped, frozen by the sight of poisonous mushrooms nesting side by side with the edible ones. She quickly looked in her bundle. Had she picked any bad ones by mistake? But no, her scarf held only good ones.

Still, she lingered by the mushrooms. A handful of the deadly ones mixed with the good ones would kill her. If Julek ate some, too, she wouldn't have to die alone. They would both be free.

"Frania! Soup," Julek called.

"Coming," she cried out. Quickly, she stooped and pulled up several bad mushrooms and threw them in with the good ones. Later on, she would break them in pieces, mix and boil them in the pot for a dessert. Her jaw set tight, she strolled over to Julek as if nothing unusual had happened.

He had brought bowls and spoons in his pack, and the bowls were filled with steaming supper. They settled down together in the shade of the larch. Julek ate like a hungry man, but Frania had to force herself to swallow each spoonful. She hadn't eaten since last night, but now— maybe for the first time in Siberia—she wasn't hungry. The broth was too hot, and the solid pieces grew large in her throat. Her trembling hands kept spilling soup all over her lap. She willed Julek to eat faster so the meal would be over quickly, but it seemed to go on forever.

As soon as his bowl was empty, she knocked hers off her lap. "Dear heavens," she moaned. "Look what I've done."

"And what are you going to eat now?" he said, staring at pieces of vegetables scattered all over the grass. "You need strength to walk back."

"I'll make it," she said. "I'll fill up on those," and she pointed to the bundle of mushrooms at her feet. "I'll break them into pieces and boil them. You can have some, too." She tried to smile, but couldn't, and her voice cracked.

Julek picked up the bowls and spoons. "All right, then. Do your cooking. I'll go down to the river to wash these, but I'll leave the pot with you."

Frania nodded. She watched him go. No good future awaited him in Russia. He was an exile. He would never marry a pretty girl and have children, not in these hard times. Nothing good would come his way. Yet he tried to feed her and cheer her up. Why couldn't Andrzej be more like Julek?

Frania had the mushrooms boiling by the time Julek appeared before her, the clean dishes dripping with water.

"All done washing?" she said, just to say something, and stood to look in the pot. "Hand me the bowls," she said, her voice hoarse. "I'll serve my dish now. We can pretend we're having a dessert."

They sat down under the tree, in the same spot as before. "You should be eating all this by yourself," Julek said, looking into his bowl, which would have to be washed again.

"Nonsense. There's enough for both of us."

"Why aren't you eating? Aren't you hungry?" he said, still looking into his bowl.

"N...no...yes. I'm waiting for you to start."

"What's wrong, Frania?"

"Wrong? What do you mean?"

"You look so pale."

"Oh, I've a terrible headache," she said, staring ahead but seeing nothing now: no heart-shaped glade, no lacy shadows, no wildflowers.

"It's cooler by the river," Julek said. "Would you like me to get you a cool drink?"

She shook her head. "I miss Poland," she said. "I miss our birth land."

Julek picked up his spoon. "I miss our farm, too, our fields and meadows. But I believe we'll go back someday."

"How can you say that? We'll never go back." She stared at the spoon in Julek's hand.

"Frania, why are you so gloomy? You didn't used to be—"

"Let's eat our mushrooms."

"Let's."

She glanced at him sideways and saw him bringing the spoon close to his opened mouth. Her arm leaped out and knocked it from his hand. "Don't," she cried out. "Don't eat this!"

He stared at her, his eyes wide.

Her head lowered, she muttered, "I...I just remember seeing bad mushrooms growing near the good ones. And maybe I picked some by mistake."

Julek removed the bowls from their laps and emptied them on the ground. For a long time he didn't speak, and then he said, "Frania, it's a good thing you stopped me in time."

"I'm sorry, so sorry." She started to cry.

"Hush, my beloved," he said, putting his arm about her shoulders. "The important thing is no one got hurt, right?"

She couldn't answer him. Something big and painful broke inside of her and poured rivers of tears from her eyes. She felt his face in her hair, and she leaned against him, crying and crying and letting him rock her. How long, she had no idea, but when she stopped, she realized he was holding her tight. She felt better now. She wiped her eyes with her hands and half smiled at him.

"Do you like me still, just a little bit, Frania?" he whispered.

She nodded and cuddled closer to him. "I do like you a lot," she blurted out, then looked at the Irtish, flirting shamelessly with the sky.

"You do, I knew it." He turned her face to his. "There's still hope for us, Frania."

"It's too late for us, Julek." She tried to turn away, but couldn't. Her eyes followed the curve of his lips.

"Frania, let me love you, just for today," he pleaded.

"Oh God, we can't—" she said, but his lips stopped her words.

Then they were locked in each other's arms, whispering sweet words, right there on the carpet of grass. Frania imagined she was back in Poland, making love to Julek on the shores of Lubaczowka, the river that ran south from her parents' land.

Suddenly, a low, throaty growl came from the woods. They heard branches breaking.

"Bear," gasped Frania, pushing Julek away.

He jumped to his feet and grabbed a big stick lying nearby. "Run, Frania, run!"

"I can't move," she said.

Julek leaned forward, knees wide apart, facing the woods and shielding Frania from whatever was lurking there. "For God's sake, save yourself," he said.

She stood up then, but said, "No, I won't go without you." And she prayed to God for the animal to go away. She didn't want Julek to die. She didn't want to die, either. She wanted to live for Julek, for her mother, for the rest of her family. "Let's run, Julek," she said, and grabbed him by the hand.

And so they ran on and on, for what seemed like an eternity, until they could run no longer. When they stopped, they looked back and smiled, for there was no creature running after them.

Chapter Seven

IN JUNE OF 1941, THE SAME SUMMER FRANIA WENT PICNICKING WITH Julek, Hitler invaded Russia; the codename was Operation Barbarosa. The invasion wasn't publicly announced in the Soviet Union until July 3. That day, Stalin spoke in a radio broadcast, describing Nazi war aims as the enslavement of the Russian people. He summoned the nation to a ruthless and merciless struggle against the Germans.

Hitler deployed about 3,000,000 soldiers and the best weaponry, including about 15,000 tanks, in his attack on Russia. He also sent bombers. By the end of the first month of fighting, nearly 175,000 square miles of Russia had fallen into Nazi hands. When the Germans drew near Moscow, Stalin turned to the West for help. On July 12 and August 16, he signed agreements with Britain to fight Hitler. Stalin also signed an agreement with the Polish government in London to grant amnesty to any Poles who had been deported to Russia and gave permission for a Polish Army to be organized in Russia, using deportees.

News of the war slipped through to the exiles from mouth to mouth. But the announcement of their freedom came as a complete surprise to Polish Village.

"I have something to tell you, Comrades," said Wronsky one evening to the Poles sitting on the benches before him.

"Comrades? He called us Comrades?" whispered voices in the cafeteria. "What's going on?"

Wronsky smiled, searching the faces before him in a fatherly way, as if he were about to forgive them for something they might have done. "I have news for you."

"News?" fearful voices repeated. Their faces showed they expected all news to be bad.

"It's good," said Wronsky.

"Tell us then, please!"

"As I've already told you many times, our Daddy Stalin loves you, the Poles, as much as he does his own people."

"Oh, no. Not again," moaned Frania, glancing at Andrzej sitting beside her. But, as usual, he didn't respond.

Wronsky cleared his throat. "Our merciful leader has granted you all amnesty."

"Amnesty? I didn't know we were criminals to be granted amnesty," came a voice from the crowd.

"Maybe you didn't understand me. You're being freed."

"You're right, Commander Wronsky. We don't understand."

"You're free...free...free."

"To do what?"

"You can move from place to place. You don't have to send your children to our school anymore, and you don't have to work if you don't wish to."

"Can we walk out of Polish Village any time we want?"

"Yes, but why would you want to do that?"

The exiles stirred in their seats, humming and buzzing like bees in a beehive when something excites them. They turned to their neighbors, hugging and kissing one another. Some broke out crying, while others laughed aloud. Some women fell to their knees and, raising their eyes heavenward, thanked God for the miracle they were certain He had performed for them.

But the mere joy of it exhausted them too soon. One by one, these men and women returned to their seats and slumped down on their benches, suspended in bewilderment and a happiness they weren't prepared to experience.

"Any questions?" Wronsky asked them.

"I have one," said Andrzej quickly, and that surprised Frania.

"Yes?"

"You have said that we can leave Polish Village, right?"

"Right."

"But will you give us permission to do so?"

"Of course. But, I repeat, why would you want to leave?"

"We want to go back to Poland," several voices said at once.

Wronsky raised his hand in the air, and the voices hushed. "Poland doesn't exist any longer."

"It does in our hearts!" said Andrzej.

Frania turned to look at her man again, and the old admiration for his wisdom stirred in her.

Wronsky threw his head back and laughed long and loud. "In your hearts!" He wiped his eyes. "That's the only place your country exists, indeed. Now, be smart and stay with us."

"No, we want to go!" cried out Julek next. "You deported us to Siberia, and you should transport us back."

"Don't be naive, Comrade. You are here to stay for good."

"But it's too cold at Bialy Jar. Can you at least relocate us to a warmer climate?" said Frania.

Wronsky shook his head vigorously. "We cannot do that."

"That figures. What good is this amnesty to us?" someone called out.

"Since you are free persons now, we will treat you equally with our people."

"Equally? There's no equality in Russia, and you know it, Commander Wronsky."

"Be quiet, if you know what's good for you!" Wronsky shouted.

"You can't keep us here by force anymore."

"No, but lack of transportation and money will."

"We can always walk, if we have to," said Frania's mother.

"Walk? Don't be foolish. Do you know how many miles it is from here to Poland? Of course, you don't. Let me see—1,837 miles from Omsk to Moscow alone." Wronsky made no mention of the war going on in Eastern Europe.

"With God's help, we'll find a way to return home."

"There you go, depending on your God, as usual." Wronsky waved his hand at the Poles as if he were chasing a fly away from his face. "Can you see the air you and I breathe? No. And you never will. It's the same with your birth land. It will remain invisible to you for the rest of your lives." Wronsky said the last sentence slowly, weighing each word carefully. Then he walked away, carrying his body tall and straight like a hero who has just won a battle with his enemy.

"What do you think of this amnesty, Andrzej?" Tata asked the next day when Frania and her husband went visiting her parents. They all sat around the table, the young couple and the grownups, drinking their "coffee." Mama had invented the drink: boiled water darkened with dried-out bread burned and pounded to a powder.

"What do I think?" said Andrzej thoughtfully, looking into his half-emptied cup. "Whether farce or gossip, we should try to take advantage of this favorable situation and leave Polish Village."

"Yes, let's walk out before Wronsky changes his mind about letting us go," said Mama, her voice eager.

"Whoa…slow down, woman," said Tata. "First, we have to find out where we're to go and how we're to get there."

"It's easy to answer the first question," said Andrzej. "We have to get to the nearest railway station."

"But that's about 300 miles from here," said Tata. "It would take weeks to walk there."

"We can go faster if we make a wooden barge and sail down the Irtish."

"But that has to be done before winter," said Frania.

"That's right, and before ice covers the river," said Andrzej.

"All right, let's say we have already arrived at the station," said Frania. "Where are we going from there and how?"

"We'll get on a train and travel through Central Russia to a city, such as Buzuluk."

"Why Buzuluk?"

"Because it's one of the points where Polish military units are springing up under the leadership of Anders."

"You're going to join our soldiers, aren't you, Andrzej?" said Frania.

"I would like to, and maybe your father can, too, if he's not too old."

"Old? I'm strong as a horse, in spite of hard work and hunger."

"But…but what will happen to us?" asked Mama.

"You'll stay as close to us and our Army as possible. I'm certain many other civilians just like you will also be staying near our soldiers. And we'll do all we can to care for you, somehow."

"Besides, Central Russia is much closer to Poland than Siberia," said Tata.

"That means we'll all be nearer Poland when the war ends," Andrzej rushed to say.

"Wait a minute," said Frania. "I just thought of something. Aren't you, as a soldier, signing up to help Stalin win the war?"

"Don't think that way, Frania. Just imagine—the Polish Army born in Russia will be fighting to defeat the Nazis first. And then—"

"Oh, I know. Then you turn on Russia and regain Poland's freedom."

"Exactly."

"Let's go, then," sang out Marysia.

"We can't just go," said Tata. "We have to gather food, we'll need money for train tickets, and so on."

"Food and money…hmmm," said Frania. "How are we to acquire that?"

Her mother walked over to the coffee pot and looked into it. "God gave us brains so we could figure things out for ourselves."

Chilly days sneaked into Bialy Jar and Polish Village. Each day the winds from the Irtish blew stronger and colder, doing their best to lower the temperatures. Winter was nearing, and it exhaled breezes that could freeze the river suddenly. If that happened before another freighter came with food from Omsk, a tragedy would strike both Russians and Poles.

Fear of possible starvation gripped at the Poles' hearts. Most of them kept on working for food alone. It was no wonder the exiles, in their spare time, came out on the shore just to stare at the sleepy Irtish as it rippled in the grayness of the season. Prayers quivered on their lips, and their hearts desperately clutched the hope that the ship would arrive before ice halted all river transportation.

Days were passing by, and still there was nothing to see but the same miserable barge crossing the Irtish every day, carrying passengers. At that time, the exiles unwillingly shuffled their feet from work back to their houses, where their hungry children waited to be fed. Mothers avoided glancing at their little ones, trying not to think of how it would be to watch their children slowly waste away. Husbands and wives couldn't look at each other throughout those days without wondering which of them would die first.

"Are you awake?" said Frania to Andrzej one morning. She raised her head to look at him lying beside her, but dropped back instantly.

"Yes, I am," he said staring up at the ceiling.

"Do you think we should go to work today?" She also looked up, lying on her back.

"What's the use of going? They haven't given us anything to eat for the last three days."

"Rubles. At least, they are paying us with money lately."

"What good is money when you can't buy bread?"

"Have you forgotten, dear? We need rubles for train tickets."

"You're still thinking of that trip to Central Russia?"

"Yes, I am."

"Forget it, Frania."

"Don't say that, Andrzej," she said in a thin voice.

"What else do you want me to say?"

"Talk like a person who doesn't easily give up on an idea that could improve the future for all of us."

"Frania, we can't even hope to leave Polish Village while facing starvation."

"Hope? Not only do I hope and pray, but I know we'll be going someday, somehow."

"Frania, look what happened to our plan to sail down the river. First, your father came down with a strange flu, and then Aniela couldn't stop coughing for weeks. And now—"

"Things will change soon, dear," said Frania.

"Like what, for instance?"

"Like that boat we're waiting for; it could come any day now."

"And what are we to live on while we wait?"

"I'll try to barter some of my Sunday clothing with the Russians for potatoes or whatever I can get. And, starting today, we can stay in bed as much as we can to preserve our energy."

"Let's go back to sleep, then."

While Frania and Andrzej were dozing, the sun climbed in the clear sky. In the brilliance of its light, the river glistened, winking hopefully at Bialy Jar. That morning, the temperature rose considerably, and there was no wind.

Then something woke Frania. "I hear voices outside. What's going on?" she said, and sat straight up in bed. That woke Andrzej and, with renewed energy, they both dressed and rushed outside. They saw many Russians and Poles heading toward the Irtish, men and women who had abandoned their work and children who had turned around while walking to school.

"It came!" Voices rose from the streaming crowd. "Indeed, it came!"

"What came?" asked Frania.

"A boat. A boat came."

Frania thought that it was the freighter with food, but it wasn't. Her eyes widened when she saw small children stepping down to the shore.

"Who are they, and where did they come from?"

"They're orphans brought here from Kiev because of the war," a middle-aged Russian man told Frania.

"There must be hundreds of them," said Frania to Andrzej, holding his hand.

"At least two hundred," he said. "And so young. Many of them are just toddlers and the older ones, no more than six or seven."

"Look at the poor things. Their heads are shaved. Why?"

"Because of lice, I suppose," was the reply.

At that moment, a young blond matron with a child in her arms passed by Frania. The woman glanced at Frania and smiled. Frania smiled back, and the child smiled, too.

"Did you see that, Andrzej?"

He nodded. "So what?"

"I have a feeling that this orphanage will bring luck to me, to us."

He let go of her hand. "Don't have too high hopes," he said.

She grabbed his hand back and held it tight. "Andrzej, please hope with me for good days to come."

Frania was right in thinking that the arrival of the orphans was a good omen. Two days later, the supply of food came to Bialy Jar. Now everyone, Russians and Poles alike, breathed easier.

Cold air slipped into her shelter, but Frania had a good fire going to keep it warm as she busied herself with laundering. By noon, she had the second load of wash boiling in the banged-up kettle on top of the stove. Boiling, she had learned from her mother, prevented grayness on white clothes and killed germs on colored articles.

She heard a knock on the door and rushed to answer it.

"Marysia and Aniela! Come in."

"We brought you another four pails of water from the river," said Marysia, stepping inside.

"Put them by the stove," said Frania, watching out for spills.

"Yes, Frania. We have done what we promised," said Aniela, lowering her pails to the floor. "Hope that's enough for your rinse."

"It has to be," said Frania. "And I thank you, my sisters, for your help."

"You're very welcome," said the girls, both at the same time.

Frania thought her sisters looked as if they would like to stay awhile. "Would you like some tea?" she asked.

"Tea?"

"You have tea?"

She nodded, grinning. "Real tea."

"Good, very good. I've not tasted the delicious stuff since we left Poland," sang out Aniela.

"Where did you get it, Frania?" asked Marysia.

"From my new Russian friend," she said, filling a small pot with water. She moved over to the stove and placed it by the steaming kettle.

"I know," said Aniela. "The woman who gave you that smile the other day?" She settled herself at the table.

"The same one. Yesterday, I gave her my blue silken blouse, and she handed me two loaves of bread and the tea."

"Is that all?" said Marysia, and she sat down on one of the stools across the table from Aniela.

"No. She also hired Mama and me to do the laundry in the orphanage."

"Terrific! When do you start?"

"Tomorrow. Be sure to tell Mama."

"She doesn't know about her job yet?"

"I only found out the good news an hour ago."

"What are you getting for the work?"

"Three meals a day for the whole family."

"Good. We'll be eating again, regularly."

"Yes, hopefully, you and I won't go hungry from now on. At the orphanage they serve thick soups, fried fish balls, and good bread, too."

"Yummm," said Aniela, licking her lips and rolling her eyes.

One evening, three weeks later, Frania and Andrzej had many more visitors.

"I have called you all here," said Andrzej, his eyes traveling from face to face about the table, "so we can talk about the trip we're to undertake this winter." He stood before them the way he had when talking to his students in Poland.

"What do you think we should do first, dear?" Frania asked eagerly. She was happy to see Andrzej taking an interest in something.

"We all know where we're going, don't we?" he said, squinting at the faces.

"Nieznajdowka, the nearby railway station," said Marysia.

"Right." Andrzej smiled, nodding not only with his head, but also using his hand. "And then?" he looked at Frania's mother next.

"Omsk, and…and Buzuluk," she said.

"Very good."

"Now we know for sure where we're going, let's talk about how to get to the station," said Julek, his voice laced with impatience.

When she heard Julek speak, Frania felt her heart miss a beat.

"We'll walk," said Tata.

"Walk?" whined Aniela.

"Walk," repeated Andrzej, his shadow swaying to the left as if to blend with other shadows on the wall opposite the fire.

"Walk?" The women's voices swelled with sudden fear.

Andrzej straightened up and stood tall above his sitting guests. "Do any of you have a different idea how to travel?"

Silence fell heavily on people's heads and on the single lamp glowing in the center of the table.

"So now we can get ready for the road!" Marysia's voice rang out like a bell in the room.

"How do we start?" asked Andrzej, taking on the pose of a leader again. He pulled a pad and pencil from his pants' pocket.

"First, we men make sleighs to carry our small children and belongings," said Tata.

Andrzej, nodding, wrote in his pad. "But we're still lumbering in the taiga. How will we find time to do this?"

"Quit working," said Frania.

"What?"

"Stay in and make sleighs," she said. For weeks, she had been dreaming every night about leaving Polish Village; when awake, she tried to figure out how to make the dream a reality. And here it was, her chance. She had tried to talk about it with Andrzej, but only recently was he willing to listen.

"But if the men don't work, can we survive on what our women are bringing in?" said Julek, glancing at Veronka, then at Basia. His sisters had started working in the laundry last week. Frania and her mother had managed to pull them in.

"Aren't we bringing you enough food?" asked Veronka, her dark eyes on her brother. She was a tall girl, taller even than Julek.

"Lately, we have more than enough bread in our house," said Basia, her blue eyes flashing with pride.

"Attention!" cried Andrzej. He raised his hand and, when all eyes went up to his face, he said, scribbling in his notebook, "Food. That's Number Two on our list. Now, how to go about acquiring enough to carry us through to Buzuluk?"

"Save as much bread as we can," said Marysia, excited.

"We'll do that," said Mama. "Make sure to dry out slices well before storing them away, so they don't mold."

"Yes, Mama," said Marysia.

"We need more than just bread," said Julek, glancing at Frania.

When her eyes met his for just a second, she felt warm all over. She glanced up at Andrzej. Did he know about her spending a day with Julek in the forest? Probably not, for he had never said a word about it.

"I want to speak," said Aniela in a voice fit for a student.

"Please do," said Andrzej in a voice fit for a teacher.

"We still have some of the nice things we brought from home. How about exchanging those with the Russians for food for the trip?"

"A fine thought," said Mama. "I have a lacy shawl, and we have Sunday dresses too thin to wear in Russia."

"And we have Mother's clothes and Father's, lying in the trunk," said Julek. His parents had died two months earlier of an unknown illness.

"No, no! We can't touch their things," cried out Basia.

"Calm down, my baby sister," said Veronka in her deep, throaty voice. "Do you think our parents—God rest their souls—would not want to help us any way they could?"

"I—I don't know," whispered the girl, tears in her eyes.

Julek, sitting next to Basia, put his arm about her and said, "If they were alive, they would do all they could to take us back to Poland. Right?"

"Right," the girl said and nodded.

Frania fought back sad memories of Henio stirred up by Basia's tears. "Andrzej and I have a beautiful bedspread," she said to help push away her painful thoughts.

"That should supply us with potatoes and onions. It's lucky for us the Russians can grow so much on their small lots, or they would have no food to barter," said Andrzej.

"Do you remember that blue gown you bought me for our first dancing party in Jaroslav, Andrzej? I still have it."

"You're not thinking of parting with it, are you, Frania?"

She nodded. "What good is putting on silk and lace when I have no parties to go to?"

"That makes sense," he said and sighed deeply.

"For that gown I should get at least two or three buckets of their delicious sauerkraut mixed with pickled green tomato or carrots."

"Mmmm," Aniela said, patting her stomach. "That's good stuff."

"I want your attention again," called out Andrzej. He waited a bit until everyone was quiet, and then spoke while writing in his journal. "Clothing. That's Number Three. We have to make sure we're all bundled up against freezing temperatures while walking."

"Wish we could buy boots, fur coats, hats, and gloves," sighed Frania, "but there's not much money and nothing like that to buy at Bialy Jar."

"There's no use wishing," said Mama.

"What can we do, then?"

"We have to use what we have. Let's go through our wardrobe, find every rip and hole, and stitch and patch them all."

"Aniela and I can start work on this right away," said Marysia.

"There's one more thing we can't overlook," said Frania.

"What's that?" asked Andrzej.

"Our bedding. We have to fix our quilts, blankets, and pillows."

"Bedding. That's Number Four. And Number Five will be getting our passports and written permission from Wronsky."

Chapter Eight

ON A COLD AND QUIET MORNING IN FEBRUARY 1942, SOMETHING unusual was happening at Polish Village, while Wronsky was still sound asleep in the darkness. Nine pairs of feet crunched along the snow-packed road. Four sleighs, weighted down with belongings and food, swooshed forward, pulled and pushed by humans. In one of them sat Jozia and Helcia.

Frania heard her blood going *pound, pound, pound* in her ears as her heart pumped blood in and out. She pushed the sleigh while Andrzej pulled it. Since he had taken on the role of leader, their sleigh was first in line.

Wronsky. As usual, he couldn't be trusted. Although he had given Frania and her companions the papers they needed to travel within the Russia borders, he could easily stop them from going at the last moment. Frania thought of the day she and Andrzej went to visit the Commander for the last time, and she shuddered.

Wronsky had readily handed Andrzej the passports, but took his time signing the permission slip. "So you're going?" he said, his pen poised over the slip on the desk.

"Indeed, we are," said Andrzej, and he winked at Frania, who stood beside him.

"You have no idea what dangers you may encounter while walking to the station."

"On the contrary, Commander Wronsky, we are fully aware of every difficulty, and we're prepared to handle everything that might come our way."

"Then go and die, you insane people," Wronsky said, furiously placing his signature on the slip. He thrust it across the desk toward Andrzej.

"Thank you, Commander Wronsky." Only now did Frania speak, for she had noticed Andrzej's hand trembling slightly as it received the paper. She couldn't help but watch lately for any sign of his depression coming back.

Wronsky shook his head and waved Frania and Andrzej away. He was still shaking his head as they walked out of his office.

Now, in the semi-darkness on the snow-encrusted road, she muttered to herself. "Insane people, eh? A big surprise is waiting for you today, Commander Wronsky, you big Communist." She smiled. "Someday, I will write you a note from Poland." At that, she heard an answering whisper—*danger, danger, danger*—from treetops bending to the ground under excessive snow. Her hands gripped hard at the sleigh. Then she sighed, and something in the forest sighed, too.

A light smudge cracked the darkness on the eastern horizon, and she grinned. Soon apricot-tinted beams came streaking across the earth. Next, the sun popped up. Frania's smile was as dazzling as the new day.

Everyone else on the road smiled along with her. At that moment the walkers knew they were a safe distance from Bialy Jar and Wronsky. They were indeed free of him and free to move from place to place. Their first taste of freedom was a glorious one, like a giant bird soaring into the sky. If only they could climb on its golden wings, they would fly through the air, fly straight back home to Poland. Freedom brought a joyful light to their eyes, and this light gleamed bright the way snowflakes sparkled in the sun, the way their sweat as they walked froze on their eyebrows and glistened in ice droplets.

Hope—a purple jewel in the spiritual crown of many others—appeared before the Poles on the road. It stirred their imagination. In it they saw themselves already living happily in their village near Jaroslav. The joy of freedom and hope glowed in their hearts and created happiness. Happiness—mistress of feelings, desired by all living things—beamed on the walkers' faces and drifted from their open mouths as their breath steamed in the cold air.

Squinting her eyes against the sun, Frania labored hard at the sleigh. She was going uphill and feeling it. Up, up, up, her steps crunched, devouring her energy much too fast. She was sweating profusely now. When would this ascent end? Never, it seemed. She wondered what was up ahead, beyond this endless hump in the earth. Maybe a village, where one could get a kipiatok (boiled water) to warm up one's stomach. Up, up, up, she kept moving. But why so slow? She exhaled with every push to ease the pain in her chest.

"I will make it," she said to the biggest lump in the sleigh loaded with belongings. "We'll all make it up this horrid hill, and then back to Poland."

Finally, the obstruction in the road was behind them, and she blinked at the white sameness of the view that spread sadly before her.

"Do...do you th...think we could stop to rest now, Andrzej?" she stammered.

As soon as she said these words, he halted on he road. The other travelers also came to a stop.

Frania climbed up on her sleigh to rest and was glad to see Marysia come up to keep her company. Andrzej had stayed down to talk with the other men, and she didn't want to be alone, even for a moment. For a while, the two sisters sat in silence, trying to catch their breath.

A cloud drifted close to the sun and soon covered its face. Shadows fell on the forest and on Frania's head. She stared at the track running in the direction of Bialy Jar, Polish Village, and then to the barracks. Suddenly, warm wetness came to her eyes.

"Poor Henio," she whispered into her own breath.

Marysia heard the sorrowful words. Following Frania's gaze, she said, "Don't feel bad about your little son. You know he's happy with God in Heaven."

"God. Heaven. Just words, for all we know. The fact is that my only child's body lies back there in the hard, frozen ground."

"Frania," said Marysia, "don't talk that way."

Frania glanced up and saw the sun peeking from under a cloud. Something inside her stirred. "I'm sorry for having upset you, Marysia. Maybe I should try harder to believe that Henio is safe and warm up there."

"But he is, Frania. You know he is."

Frania said nothing, but looked away at the wooded landscape. Beyond it, the lonely trail stretched out into an unknown tomorrow. She felt small and helpless against the immensity of Siberia. "Marysia, you're right about Henio. He must be better off dead. At least, he's free of pain and fear. Who knows what awaits us all at the end of this trip?"

"Poland," said Marysia. "Poland is awaiting us."

"But the other day you said the lines in your palm told you that you were never again going to see our village."

"I...I was just talking," Marysia said, taking off her glove.

"And what do you see in your hand today?"

"Nothing. Nothing much."

"Put your glove back on, or you'll freeze your fingers, dear sister."

The sisters stopped talking when they overheard the men discussing things concerning the trip.

"Three hundred miles is a long distance," Andrzej was saying, looking at the map, which he held up to Julek's face. "See those dots scattered all along our road?"

"Yes, I do."

"What are they?" asked Tata, leaning over Andrzej's shoulder to see the map.

"Villages. Where we can sleep at night."

"That is, if we find good people to let us in," said Julek. His voice rang out like a song to Frania.

"We will; I'm sure of that," said Tata. He stared at the horizon as if already seeing houses up ahead. "I know the Russian people are basically good. Frania and her sisters made friends with many of them."

"Too bad their government isn't good, like the people," said Julek, pulling at his sleeve to cover up bare skin between it and his glove.

"Too bad," repeated Andrzej. He carefully folded the map into a neat square and slipped it back into his coat pocket.

"Andrzej, how many miles did you say we have to make a day in order to get to the station within three weeks?" asked the older man.

"Let's see. We take three hundred miles and divide it into twenty-one days and...and..."

"We come up with fourteen," Julek rushed to say.

"Fourteen miles a day," said Tata, his fingers picking ice droplets from his eyebrows.

"Better start walking again, then," said Julek.

Andrzej nodded. He turned around to face the women and children on the sleighs and raised his hand in the air. "Rest time is over, my dear ones!"

With a painful sigh, Frania slid down to the ground, but not before Marysia had. Marysia moved faster now and with much less effort than Frania. As a teenager, Frania had been able to outrun and outwork everyone in her family and in her neighborhood, but that had changed now. It wasn't due to age, for she was only twenty-one. And it wasn't the war or deportation—everyone she knew was affected by those tragedies. Mostly it was because she worried too much. She had worried first about her husband when he was away at war, and then about Henio's health. His death settled heavily on her shoulders and pulled her down. In addition to that, she never stopped fearing for Andrzej's mental health.

She shuffled along, crunching through the snow, and the sound seemed like her feet complaining, cramped as they were inside her crooked shoes and wrapped in rags. Her legs ached, and so did her head. What had happened to her spirit? It came down from the heights to the level of her eyes, forcing her to face reality. Here she was, with this small group of beings, pushing her belongings on a sleigh and dragging her feet along the road that led to an uncertain destination. Were her dear ones and she ever to reach Nieznajdowka, Omsk, Buzuluk, and Poland? These places were so far, far away, they might as well be at the other end of the world.

It was noon that day before the travelers stopped a second time. They ate frozen pieces of bread and washed them down by swallowing snow. Before sunset, the weary group stopped at a small village made of charming wooden houses. They all found places to stay overnight.

It was Friday in the second week of their walk to Nieznajdowka, and it started the same as all the other days. At seven, the Poles began plodding along the snowy road. As usual, the seconds turned tediously into minutes, and then into hours. The hours folded painfully into a day.

In spite of their spiritual and physical exhaustion, the travelers labored like a team of mules at a milling wheel. Their worst enemy was the dreary monotony: performing the same motions over and over, looking out upon the same landscape. They spent most of their time daydreaming of when they would arrive at their birth land.

Frania, laboring at the sleigh, observed Andrzej carefully; she watched for signs of his old gloom coming back. And, too soon, she noticed how his shoulders rounded up, how his head sunk in between them the way a turtle backs into its shell when something frightens it. Andrzej shuffled his feet like an old man and fell into a silence that was hardest to bear, especially in the evenings. Poor Andrzej. Poor Jozia and Helcia, who looked at the world now with the eyes of grownups. The cord of their joyful childhood had been unexpectedly severed by war and deportation.

Would Andrzej give up his leadership? She knew he would, and the day he passed it to Julek she saw tears in his eyes. But Frania was used to seeing him sob like a child. Too many times, she had seen this. And now Julek's sleigh was first in line, and Frania's was last.

Her disappointment in her man was great and would probably have overwhelmed her but for one thing: now she could watch Julek up ahead, pulling his sleigh while his two sisters pushed it. The sight of her beloved brought warmth to her heart in the freezing weather and made her pushing easier, somehow. During the trip, she and Julek acted like strangers to each other, but Frania knew that, secretly, the special feelings they carried were a precious gift in these hard times.

On this Friday, Frania ached and sweated more than ever. When would this strength- and time-consuming march come to an end? Maybe never. Maybe the last happenings were not real. Maybe she was having a nightmare from which she would never awaken. In it, she and her walking companions were trapped forever. They were all dead and in Hell already. Oh, no, God, no!

A strange sound came to her ears and broke through her troubled thinking, bringing her attention back to the road and forcing her to listen. She saw Julek stop suddenly down the hill. The sleighs behind him halted, too, and Andrzej brought their sleigh to an abrupt halt.

"What's the matter?" someone asked.

A guttural, echoing sound was their answer.

Julek motioned the others to come close to him and, when all except for Helcia and Jozia had moved near, he pointed down the road and said, "Do you see those dark spots in the snow?"

"Where? Where?"

"Look to your right by the roadside."

"I see nothing," said Tata.

"You must have good eyes, Julek," said Mama.

"I see them!" called out Veronka. "One, two, three, four, five, six, seven—"

Suddenly, Frania shuddered, for now a story came to her mind of a lonely traveler who was attacked by animals and eaten by them. She had read about him in a book in Jaroslav.

"Mama!" cried out Aniela. "I'm scared."

Mama went to Aniela and placed her arm about the girl's shoulders. "Calm down, dear. Panicking won't do us any good."

"What are we going to do?" said Basia in a trembling voice.

"Yes, what can we do?" asked Marysia.

They were all looking at Julek. He searched their faces, one by one, as if trying to read their minds. "I see two things we can do," he said.

"What?"

"We can turn around and go back to the last village where we slept last night, or we can try to pass by the wolves."

"No!" cried the women. "We have to go back."

"Hush, everyone!" shouted Tata. "Listen to me."

"Yes?"

"We can't turn back. That wouldn't work."

"Why not?"

"Do you think the wolves won't follow us? We can't outrun them, and you know it."

Silence.

"That's a fact."

"Why not just keep on walking and try to pass them?" said Mama.

"Too dangerous for the children and our women."

"Then?"

"We will scare the wolves away," said Julek resolutely. "If that doesn't work, we men will have to fight them with sticks."

"That's insane," moaned Andrzej, who was shaking all over.

"Better than waiting for them to attack us, standing on the road."

"No, no. If we have to die, we'll die all together," said Mama.

"Yes, we'll die together," repeated Frania, who couldn't imagine life without Julek.

"Women, you mind the children and the sleighs, and let us do what we have to," said Tata.

"But—but—"

"Silence!" He roared the way he used to, long ago in Poland.

The women bent their heads downward in acquiescence.

Five minutes later, Julek, Andrzej, and Tata began walking down the road toward the dark specks in the snow, their hands gripped tight around the sticks they carried.

The women at the sleighs fell to their knees and prayed to God for help.

"Our Father, Who art in Heaven," Frania started to say, but stopped, for in her imagination she already saw Julek being pounced upon by two giant animals, their sharp teeth and claws tearing his clothes and skin. She saw blood all over his dear face.

The guttural sound rose to a shrill howl, and Frania leaped to her feet and started to run toward the men. "Get away, wolves, get away!" she shrieked, waving her arms above her head.

"Get away! Get away, you monsters!" the other women cried out hoarsely at the top of their lungs. They began running fast behind Frania.

Helena and Jozia in the sleigh were yelling, too, in their thin voices. When the men heard them, they also started shouting and waving their sticks. "Get away! Get away, if you know what's good for you!"

"Scat! Scat, if you don't want to be beaten to a pulp!" Julek screamed.

At that moment, a strong wind picked up. It rushed across the snow and blew handfuls of it into the humans' faces. It also took hold of treetops and shook them in anger. *Hissssss, hisssss,* it seemed to be saying. The trees were asking a question: *Wha'sssss going on?*

"Away! Away, you run! Away, you mean creatures!" People on the road screamed and ran, screamed and ran. Seven dark figures in their raggedy clothes drew closer and closer to the dark spots on the white surface.

Then the unexpected happened. One of the wolves rose to his feet, lifted his muzzle and howled, stirring his companions to action. He was a big animal, leader of the pack.

Without slowing his stride, Tata shouted back toward the women. "Go to the sleighs and protect the children!"

"Yes, please go!" shouted Julek, but he kept running forward.

The women paid no attention. They ran forward even faster, shrieking obscenities at the wild beasts.

Now a dozen wolves sprang up from the snow and turned toward the creatures who were running and screaming at them. A few of the animals lifted their sinister muzzles and howled again, but the others were already turning away.

The humans running down the road toward the wolves no longer felt any fear. They were hunters, merciless and mean. They were going to kill…kill…kill…

And then it happened. The wolves were leaping, leaping, leaping with a dreadful grace. But, oh, thank you, God, they were leaping away into the depths of the forest.

After awhile, the Poles returned to their labor on the road. All seemed fine now. But was it? Most of them believed that the mere sight of wolves was a bad omen. At noon, the sky turned black. It started to snow, at first lightly, but then harder and harder. The gentle breeze that sighed in the trees earlier in the morning had changed into a roaring wind that clawed the snow and bushes.

Trying to oppose the blizzard's evil force, the taiga replied insolently to the winds and to the sky that kept dropping more and more snow, as if determined to bury the earth in the white stuff. The storm stood its ground, and broken branches fell down like bats.

Wooooooooo, wooooooooo. Something horrid howled in the wind.

Hisssssss—shshsh, hissssss—shshsh. The vegetation bent low and swayed dangerously in all directions.

At the tail end of the caravan, Frania struggled to move ahead. Like all the others, she floundered and panted but moved ahead, knowing all their lives depended on finding the nearest village. How far away was it? No one knew. But their survival today lay in their strength and willingness to go on. The road was quickly filling with snow and reaching a level with the rest of the land. The trail was marked by telegraph poles and wires, but the visibility was so bad they could stray off the path. If this happened, the travelers would get stuck in the deep snow and freeze to death. Wronsky had predicted such an end for them. But this group of Poles would not be overpowered by men or nature, for they were too stubborn to give in. They would make it to a settlement today, even if only to prove Wronsky wrong.

Hours passed, but there was no sign of the snow letting up. That mean wind threw snow into Frania's face, knocking the breath out of her and weakening her. Every time she received such a blow, she held tighter to her sleigh and pushed with all her strength. Too often she stumbled over her own feet and went down. Fortunately, she managed to scramble up each time. She felt numb from exhaustion. Had it not been for her love for Julek and her family, she would have stopped fighting long ago. It would be so easy to sit down and let the snow cover her head, her nose, her mouth.

For a moment, the storm lifted. Frania took two deep breaths and relaxed a little. Again the wind pounced upon her, but she braced herself against it.

Her sleigh came to a stop. Andrzej had fallen again. Lately, he was more hindrance than help. She slid down and leaned against the sleigh, waiting for him to get up. Seconds were turning into minutes, but there was no movement on the other side of the sleigh.

Had he fainted? Was this the end for him and for her? If that was to be, let it, she finally decided, smiling faintly and resting her head on her arms.

Wooooooooo, wooooooooo. She heard the wind, but wasn't frightened anymore.

Hisssssss—shshsh, hisssssss—shshsh. The vegetation still fought loudly with the storm for its existence, but not Frania. She was giving in to a cruel fate. Sleep…sleep…delicious sleep…so welcome. She closed her eyes.

"…aniaaaaaaa," something called out to her. She opened her eyes and stared into the moving lace of snowflakes, but saw nothing. There it was again…that voice…

"…drzejejejej."

Who or what was calling her and Andrzej? Was it the ghost of her grandfather, inviting them to cross the threshold to another world?

"Fra—niaaaa…"

Or was it her father calling? Or Julek? The thought of her dear ones made her get up and move to Andrzej's side. He lay like a big, dark lump, face down in the snow. She went to her knees, lifted his head, turned it to one side. She gently slapped his cheek to revive him.

"Frania, Frania!"

"Here we are, Tata!" she cried out, helping Andrzej to rise.

Night was settling upon the land early, and finally the winds died out, although snow continued to fall. The travelers rested on the road more than they plodded. They were like flies drowning in a bowl of milk: still moving, but ever more slowly. Without even knowing it, these Poles were becoming resigned to their fate. If freezing in the snow was to be their end, let it be, let it be.

Then, through the semidarkness, they saw something. What were those golden pinpoints up ahead of them? Was it a village or the glowing eyes of wolves? God Almighty, not that again! But no—it was a small settlement. Glory be to sweet Jesus and Holy Mary.

Never before in her marching days had Frania been more grateful to anyone than she was to the Russian family who shared their small home with Andrzej and her that night. It was a wooden, two-room house covered with a slanting, thatched roof. The rooms were furnished simply, but cozy and, above all, warm. Warmth! Ah, this was luxury she didn't often have in Siberia. This home was lit not only by the light coming from the kerosene lamp on the table and the fire burning in the fireplace, but it was also bright with the smiles of its dwellers, a young couple and their beautiful two-year-old daughter, Ninushka. The child giggled and chattered constantly under the adoring glances of her parents.

Henio would be about Ninushka's age by now.

Frania was too exhausted to make soup that evening. Fortunately, the merciful hostess gave her guests a small loaf of bread, some cheese, and tea.

The minute her head hit the pillow, Frania fell asleep.

Chapter Nine

OMSK, A DISTRICT CITY IN SIBERIA LOCATED 1800 MILES EAST OF Moscow, was an important commercial center of the steppe belt on the Trans-Siberian railway, with steamer trade down the Irtish. Omsk had a regional museum, the Siberian Agricultural Academy, the Medical and Veterinary Institute, and Central Pushkin Library. Dostoevski, the Russian novelist, had been confined in the old fortress at Omsk for four years, and he described his imprisonment in *The House of the Dead*.

A week had crawled past since the awful storm. This day, Frania was inside the waiting room of the railway station in Omsk with her mother, Jozia, and Helcia. In the overcrowded hall, they sat by their bundles near the door, and every time it opened and closed a cold stream of air hit their backs. They huddled together for warmth.

"Can't believe we have finally made it to this big city," Frania said, turning to look at her mother.

"Yes, it was easy to get on the train at Nieznajdowka," sighed Mama, "but here, who knows when we will get our tickets."

"I had no idea the trains would be so crowded," said Frania. She scanned the passengers who packed the waiting room.

"These are bad times, even for Russians," said Mama.

"People are being evacuated, and soldiers are going to the front lines."

Mama nodded and sighed again. "I wonder if Aniela, Veronka, and Marysia will be able to buy our tickets today?"

"Isn't it time to for us replace them in the line?"

"We have ten more minutes. Someone needs to check on the men at the food window and see if they need help."

"You want me to go?"

"Not yet."

For a moment, both women fell into the flow of grim thoughts as if they'd been dropped into a swift ocean current. They still had a long journey ahead of them to Buzuluk. Three more such train changes and traveling for days and nights in freight wagons awaited them. Why should they go to Central Russia to look for the Polish Army supposedly being organized there? What if there were no such army? What if all the talk about it was nothing but a lie, fabricated by cruel Communists who wanted to draw the Poles out and onto the dangerous roads, so they might freeze or starve to death?

"I'm hungry." A child's voice scratched at Frania's ear.

Frania looked in its direction and saw Helcia pulling at Mother's sleeve for attention. Her mind lifted out of the current of dark thoughts and back to the present, which seemed bleak enough. "Stop your whining," she said to her baby sister.

"My tummy is empty, too," said Jozia, as she leaned against Frania. The girl was a perfect replica of Frania, but in a smaller frame.

Frania patted Jozia's head and said in a soft voice, "We'll eat today. Soon, I hope."

As if in response to her last words, Jozia called out in a happy voice, "They're coming!" The child jumped to her feet and began waving her arms in the air.

Frania looked toward the cafeteria door and smiled, for she saw her father, Andrzej, and Julek elbowing their way toward her. And they were carrying bread and a pail of steaming soup! Pure happiness filled her heart. Pure joy overwhelmed the little girls, too.

Mama swallowed hard and said, "We will have to eat fast."

"I know," said Frania. "We have to stand in the ticket line so the girls can eat, too."

Four days passed.

"Can you tell me what time our train arrives, Comrade?" Frania asked one of the officials as she paid for their tickets.

He looked at her, his eyes cold and dark. "When it comes, it comes, and it's up to you to get on it."

She opened her mouth to say something else, but he waved her away with his hand, long-fingered like a woman's.

On Friday, she and her dear ones waited outside for the train to come. They had been waiting since dawn, and a crowd of people, all sexes and sizes, waited with them. Everyone, including Frania, stood patient and calm by their bundles, but inside they were bracing themselves for the coming fight to find room in one of the railcars. Above their heads a cloud, pregnant with snow, waited to empty itself.

Finally, the locomotive came into their view, pulling several boxcars behind. The crowd stirred the way a lion does before pouncing upon its chosen victim. The sky began to snow. Exhaling dark twists of smoke, the engine pulled into the station and stopped. Even before the doors slid open, the crowd pressed together and became a huge pulsating mass moving toward the wagons. Amid cursing, screaming, and name-calling, hundreds of arms lifted in the air, holding up children and bundles to keep them safe from the crushing mob.

Too soon, wagons filled up from corner to corner, yet the crowd still flowed toward the portals. Those who had managed to get in were blocking the way with their bodies. People fought brutally, not only with words, but with their teeth, claws, elbows, fists, and feet. It ended only when the doors closed. Those unfortunate ones left on the outside breathed hard with envy and shook their fists at triumphant faces peering out through tiny windows.

Frania was extremely happy to be among the lucky passengers, and so were her traveling companions, all of them. Thank God! She and Andrzej settled on an upper berth on the right side. He collapsed beside her. Lately, any physical exertion tired him more than the others. Frania squeezed in between him and Marysia, breathing hard, glad for a chance to rest. She could still hear terrible cursing and shouting outside. Her body burned where she had been elbowed or kicked. Dear Lord, she was lucky not to have her ribs broken.

How could they call themselves human, these madly shoving people, many of them someone's parents, sisters, and brothers? How could they change so suddenly into a savage crowd ready to trample over anyone just to get on the train? But Frania knew she was guilty of the same cruelty. She remembered using her feet and elbows in order to get closer to the door. What did she feel then? Nothing but fury and the need to overpower anyone who stood in her way.

She looked around for her mother and saw her sitting on the same berth. Helcia and Jozia leaned against her. Good for them. The girls needed time to recover from the frightening experience of boarding the train. Julek sat on the opposite berth, leaning against the wall, and his sisters sat next to him, their bundles pushed all the way behind them.

"My beloved," Frania whispered to herself.

"What did you say, Frania?" asked Andrzej.

"Nothing," she answered. A strong desire to be in Julek's arms overwhelmed her other feelings.

When she saw the fire going in the iron stove, she smiled. The stove stood in the passage between left and right side double-decker berths. Through holes in the stove door, golden-red flames shot out. This warm, bright sight made Frania think of her life in Poland.

In wintertime, the biggest room in her parents' home was heated by burning wood in the built-in brick oven/stove. Evenings, the whole family sat in front of the fireplace and did things together. While they listened to someone tell stories or sing songs, they plucked goose feathers for pillows or quilt stuffing or spun thread out of flax or hemp. Flax made good weaving material for towels and sheets. Out of hemp, they made ropes and bags needed to transport grain to the nearest market. Frania loved to embroider flowers on her white blouses. She also helped Mama hand-stitch new dresses out of colorful materials they brought home from Jaroslav.

Jaroslav. That's where she had left her in-laws in the fall, just before the deportation. Did Andrzej ever think about his parents? He had never talked about them during their exile. Frania wondered if they both survived the bombing and the German occupation. And her parents' homestead—were the buildings still standing? If they were, the livestock would be sheltering in the barn still. Who was taking care of these precious animals? She remembered how her favorite pet, a dog named Aza, had howled so the evening before the Russians came to deport them all to Siberia.

Andrzej's snoring punched her down from the heights of daydreaming like a fist. Oh, dear Heaven, what had happened to the man she had adored and loved, first as a teacher in her village, and then as her husband? He had been altered completely by the changes brought down on him through mean fate. Back then, he was handsome, young, and dressed neatly. Now, only two years later, he looked like a fifty-year-old bum. It wasn't the way he looked that bothered her so much, but his helplessness under pressure and his unwillingness to survive made her angry.

For the rest of the day, the train stood motionless on the cold tracks. Night came and the passengers, lying close to each other like sardines in a can, fell asleep. At midnight, a sudden jerk as their car bumped into one next to it woke everyone. Small children screamed. Some men cursed, and most of the people were wide-eyed, their eyes trying to pierce the darkness.

Someone shrieked by the stove. Frania sat up and tried to see what was happening. By the light of the fire, she could see a woman near the stove moaning and holding up her arms. Evidently, she was warming some food when the abrupt movement of the train caused her to fall, and she burned herself against the hot stove.

Stoo-koo, poo-koo, the wheels of the train repeated underneath her, and Frania listened for hours to the constant rattling. Tonight, she couldn't get to sleep no matter how hard she tried. It wasn't because she worried about an uncertain future, and it wasn't because of the fact that the closer they drew to Buzuluk, the harder it became to change trains and buy food at the stations. It was because Julek and her father were missing.

Journey across Russia just now was difficult. So many Russians rode the freight trains and, after the amnesty, hundreds of Frania's people streamed out of their places of imprisonment, traveling toward Central Russia, where they hoped to find the Polish Army. There was no water to wash up in the boxcars and never enough soup and bread available. It didn't matter if they were buying or exchanging clothing and linens with the Russians; there just wasn't enough food to go around.

Frania and her group had run out of dried-out bread, so they lived on potatoes and onions baked in the hot coals. Tata and Julek kept getting off the train at each stop to search for food. Sometimes, they would buy half a pail of soup; they seldom found bread. Andrzej went with them only once. Such trips away from the wagons were risky. Passengers never knew when their train might depart. Leaving even for a few minutes meant possibly being left behind, separated forever from your dear ones. Every time Tata and Julek got off the train to look for food, Frania and her mother worried they might not get back in time. Frania's heart would pound, skipping beats, as she waited and prayed for them.

Frania kept having the same bad dream every night. In it, she saw the two men running, running toward their train, which was speeding away. She also saw herself, her arms outstretched, standing on the platform of the last car and watching them run in vain to catch up with her. When the distance between them grew too far, she screamed, "Faster! Please run faster!" Then she would wake up covered in a cold sweat. Awake, she felt blessed to hear the sound of her father's snoring. She could recognize his snoring anywhere. At home, it was a constant irritation, but here it sounded like music to her ears. She knew that Julek slept on the opposite berth and would sigh with relief and smile. After that, she usually fell back into a restful sleep.

She couldn't image life without Tata or Julek. Her father was the main provider of food for the family. Julek was the main reason she fought to exist in these bad times. Was it a sin to love him? Even if it were, she didn't care anymore. She didn't feel wicked. Did Andrzej suspect anything? She didn't know. Maybe he knew how she felt and laughed secretly at her hopeless situation. She was married, and divorce was condemned by her society and her religion. Adulteress: that's what they would call her, and the name was unbearable to her.

And then one day her nightmare came true. The two men left to search for food, and the train departed before they returned.

Thinking these thoughts tonight, Frania finally closed her eyes, hoping to fall asleep and wake to find only her nightmare was real. Her own voice woke her suddenly. Someone swore at her for disturbing his sleep, and then silence fell upon the wagon. She strained her ears to hear

Tata's snoring, but only heard one of her sisters mumbling. Her heart sank. Julek and Tata, the two men she loved and needed most, had been left behind only yesterday, and she wasn't to see them ever again.

Ne—ver, ne—ver, clattered the awful wheels.

"Never, ever," she mumbled, staring up into the darkness and feeling the rocking of the train. If only the rocking would put her to sleep. Oh, sweet Jesus. Time crawled like a turtle. Maybe it had stopped moving for good, like a fly caught in a spider web. She checked her pulse and felt it thumping under her finger. She was still alive in a world where things moved and changed with the certainty of a clock ticking.

She felt a slight change in the train's movement. Was it slowing down? Yes, it was, dear God. Up ahead the locomotive sounded out its hoarse, dark signal. Then the wagons did their usual bumping into each other, which never failed to wake the passengers.

The train stopped in a small town just before the crack of dawn. Before Frania could say a word to Andrzej, she heard voices outside the door. Her ears perked up, but she couldn't pick up clear words yet. Who was making such a commotion outside?

She sat up. The door slid open, and up came Julek's dark head like a seal surfacing through a hole in the ice. Next, she saw the gray head of her father. Frania smiled and hurried to welcome her father by hugging him.

"How did you and Julek manage to catch up with us?" she asked.

He didn't answer until he had embraced all members of his family and his wife had asked him the same question.

"You see," he started to talk, and then cleared his throat, "we were lucky to jump one of the passenger trains yesterday afternoon."

"You rode in one of them?" exclaimed Marysia.

He shook his head. "We rode it lying low on the roof of one of the wagons."

"Oh," said the girl.

"Oh," repeated voices from the surrounding berths.

Chapter Ten

COULD THERE BE A POLISH ARMY IN THE U.S.S.R., THE ENEMY AND occupier of Poland? Yes, indeed, such an army was born in 1941 and created out of Polish deportees. When Hitler attacked Russia, the fate of Polish exiles changed. When the Nazis came too close to Moscow, Stalin realized that he desperately needed help and looked to the West to come to his rescue. A treaty between Russia and Great Britain was signed in the summer of the same year. The two countries allied to fight Hitler. Soon after that, the Polish government—residing in London with General Sikorski as its head—also signed an agreement with Russia.

One of the points of the agreement contained these words:

A Polish Army will be organized, as soon as possible, in Russia, and it will be part of the military power of Poland...The Polish Army will fight for the Russian Army and other friendly nations against the German Army...After the war, the Polish Army will return to Poland...These Polish units will be sent to the front lines when they are ready to fight...Polish soldiers in Russia will obey Polish laws and regulations...Weapons, equipment, uniforms, automobiles, and so on will come partly: a) From the Government of Russia; b) From the Polish Government in London.

General Anders, a great Polish statesman, had been nominated as commander of the prospective army. After his release from a Moscow jail, he appealed to all the Poles in Russia to join him. In response to his call, thousands of his countrymen left their detention camps and prisons and streamed toward Central Russia. These people, like Frania and her group, walked hundreds of miles and rode freight trains. Men, boys, and single women signed up for the Polish Army. Mothers with small children and men unfit for active duty came also, just to be close to their soldiers. The Polish Army then was placed in Buzuluk, Tatishchev, and Tockoje. Homeless civilians made rings around each camp and had to be taken care of by the army.

But the army itself was forced to develop in deplorable conditions. The soldiers weren't getting a sufficient supply of food. There was a time when 80,000 men lived on the rations for 44,000, which they also shared with the civilians encircling their quarters. Some of the soldiers received Russian uniforms, but the rest wore their own ragged clothes. Later on, a few others received English uniforms. The shelters weren't what they were supposed to be. The military unit in Tockoje, for instance, spent one wintertime in small tents put up in the snowy woods.

What saved the Polish Army and thousands of civilians was massive evacuation, first to Uzbekistan, Kirgistan, or southern Kazakhstan, and later to Iran in the spring and summer of 1942.

This pitiful army born on the Volga Steppes between Kuybeshev and Chkalov developed later into a powerful military force in Iraq. This was the Polish Secondary Corps, which fought beside the British Army and won battles with the Nazis. One of the battles they fought was over Monte Cassino in Italy.

About 114,000 of the deportees not only crossed the Caspian Sea, then, but also stepped into a normal life on friendly lands. But that was a small number of lucky Poles compared to the one and a half million who were exiled into the wilds of Russia at the beginning of the war. What happened to those left behind? Many of them starved to death or died of illness, cold, or hard labor. Those who survived suffered a hellish existence in the U.S.S.R. Very few returned home to Poland after the war ended.

Frania and her dear ones made superhuman efforts in order to arrive at Buzuluk located in the Chkalov Region, about 110 miles from Kyubushev. Kyubushev was chosen as the alternative administrative center of the U.S.S.R. when Moscow was threatened by the Germans. This event added even more chaos to the already existing confusion in Russia, making it increasingly difficult for the Poles to travel.

In Buzuluk, a city of small wooden houses and narrow streets, Frania came in contact with Polish soldiers for the first time.

After stepping down from the train that Sunday, she and the others sat on top of their bundles and waited under the naked sky. For what? They didn't know. Snow fell silently upon their heads and shoulders. Mercifully enough, winds were absent, and it wasn't as cold as in Siberia.

Frania's eyes kept searching the crowd milling about the station. Most were Russians, both adults and children. Some were soldiers, but they all wore Russian uniforms. She saw none of her countrymen who looked like members of the Polish Army. So had the Russians lied to her and all the exiles? Hit with this sudden realization, she closed her eyes in pain and rocked herself.

"People, you have to move away from here!" she heard a male voice shouting in Russian. She opened her eyes.

"But—but we have no place to go," she said, blinking tearfully at the big soldier looming over her.

"Move!" he repeated, his right hand touching the rifle swung over his shoulder.

Julek slid off his bundle and walked over beside the soldier. "Comrade," he said, "we came here from Siberia."

"So what?"

"We came to sign up for the Polish Army being organized here. Can you tell us where it is located?"

"Polish Army, huh. Never heard of it," said the Russian.

"But we were told—" cried out Mama, still sitting on her bundle, Jozia and Helcia at her side.

"Move!" roared the soldier. "You're blocking the way to the station. Go, you ragged Poles!"

Their heads down, dragging their belongings behind them, the poor exiles shuffled their numb feet along the snowy street of Buzuluk, a drab-looking settlement. Dispirited and worn out, they moved at the speed of a turtle. Was this the end of their journey? The end of them all? They had no place to go. They could try to go back to their birth land, but they knew the fierce war there stood dangerously in their way.

While passing a barracks-like building, they heard men singing and halted on the spot, as if struck suddenly with some heavy object. They stood listening, and their eyes widened.

"…God, who throughout ages surrounded Poland with the splendor of power and glory…" The melody and words were dear to them. Every Pole knew this song in Poland.

They listened intently, soaking up every word and note of the music, and their hearts, battered so by the cold waves of exile, began to warm. Smiles came to their otherwise grim faces, and joy reflected in their eyes the way tiny stars shine in the darkness of night.

When the door opened, out came soldiers in a strange mixture of uniforms, mostly English. Some still wore their own ragged clothing. The ones with uniforms on had white eagle pins fastened to their hats. A Polish eagle with a crown on its head!

"We have found our Army!" shrieked Mama. She got down on her knees and held her hands up to pray. "Oh God, God, I can't believe my eyes. Thank you. Thank you for making this miracle happen for us."

One of the soldiers stopped by her and said, "Please, dear lady, get up." He offered his hand to her.

"Thank you," she said and rose to her feet

Two more soldiers stopped to talk to the newcomers.

"Where did you come from, my good people?" asked the first soldier, who was an officer.

"All the way from Siberia," said Frania.

Marysia took two steps toward the youngest soldier and asked, "May I touch your eagle?"

The soldier took off his hat and handed it to Marysia. She smiled, her two fingers placed carefully on the crowned head of the bird. "Our precious eagle. Our Polish, Polish eagle." Then she kissed the symbol.

Other voices called out. "May I touch it, too? And I?"

The officer also took his hat off and handed it to Frania. She enjoyed the touch as much as her sisters and mother did.

Finally, the hats were returned to their owners.

Tata was first to speak. "We need help badly," he said.

"We are here to join the Army," said Julek.

"I know," said the officer again, but he didn't smile. "I wish we could accept you, but unfortunately we cannot."

"Why not?"

"Stalin has forced us to cut the flow of men who would enlarge our military units."

"Why?"

"We don't question his reasons. The only one who talks to the Red leader is our General Anders, and even he can only do as much as he is allowed to."

"Look at our children, dear countrymen," said Mama, pointing to Jozia and Helcia still sitting on one of the bundles. "Look and see that they are cold and thin. They need food and warm shelter."

The soldiers looked at the little girls and said nothing.

"Are you going to let them die on the street?"

The officer shook his head and said, "No. We will do something for you and them."

"What?"

"We will put you in one of the wagons reserved for civilians. We have thousands of them surrounding each camp."

"Thousands?" said Andrzej. "Why do you want to put us on a train?'

"Have you not heard of the upcoming evacuation?"

"No."

"Stalin has agreed to evacuate soldiers and their families south."

"Why south?"

"It's warmer there. Besides, we are to cross the Caspian Sea and step down on the shores of Iran."

"Iran? Stalin is helping us to get out of Russia? It's like another miracle..." said Tata.

"It's not a miracle performed by God, my dear man," said the officer. "This evacuation came from the hard work of General Anders."

"God bless the General," said Mama.

"Iran!" called out Frania, all excited. "We all want to go there."

A day later, she and her companions were on their way to Uzbekistan. This trip was barely more comfortable than the previous one. The four wagons filled with Poles were no cleaner or less crowded, but now, at least, hot soups and bread awaited them at each station, and coal for heating was regularly provided. In addition to these goodies, the passengers were also sent to public baths in larger cities. Bathing had become a luxury for them.

Frania spent hours looking out the window and daydreaming about the better future she and her dear ones were to have outside Russia.

"Andrzej, how much do you know about that country called Iran?" she asked one day.

He glanced at her with that special light he always had in his eyes whenever someone wanted him to share the knowledge he had acquired through his schooling. "As you know, I've never been there," he said, combing his fingers through his tousled hair. "I can tell you, though, what I have learned in classrooms and from books."

"Tell me," she said.

"Iran is a kingdom located in Southwest Asia. It's bounded on the north by the U.S.S.R. and the Caspian Sea."

"What kind of a land is it?" Frania interrupted impatiently. "Is it covered with forests or fields?"

"Iran is a great tableland raised 4,000 to 8,000 feet above sea level. Across the country, from the Elburz Mountains to the Gulf of Oman, there is a desert."

"Desert? My God. Nothing grows in a desert."

"There are fertile plains in Iran."

"That's good. What do Iranians grow that's fit to eat?"

"Wheat, barley, rice, sugar beets, corn."

"You can make delicious meals out of those," said Frania, licking her lips.

"Iranians also fish for trout, carp, sturgeon, salmon, and herring from the Persian Gulf and the Caspian Sea."

Frania smiled and rubbed her stomach like a child, which made Andrzej smile also.

"Are Iranians friendly people?"

"I think so. They are chiefly modern Persians, descendants of the ancient Medes and Persians. What's interesting is that, before 1935, Iran was known as Persia. Riza Shah Pahlevi officially changed it to Iran."

"Oh," said Frania. After a pause, she asked, "What kind of trees grow in Iran?"

"Let's see. There are konars, cypresses, dwarf oaks, walnut, mulberry…"

"And what kind of animals live there?"

"Rabbits, foxes, wolves, hyenas, jackals, leopards, deer, tigers, and so on."

"Iran is not a Communist country, is it?"

"No, it is not."

"Good," sighed Frania with relief.

Some people say that Fate is blind and strikes only humans who accidentally bump into it. Frania believed the opposite. Fate could see altogether too well. It was made of both goodness and evil, and it was fickle. It picked some who were to enjoy their good fortune and struck others like a snake, inflicting pain and suffering on them.

For the two past years, Fate had kept lashing her and her people with whips of tragedy, one after another. Right now, it was dozing, allowing the exiles in the wagons to breathe calm breezes. But how long would it sleep? How long?

One day, Fate opened its spying eyes and looked hard at the Poles arriving at Tashkient, which was situated in an oasis near the Chirchik River. In this big city, Fate struck the wagons a renewed blow. Suddenly, the Poles lost the caring hand hovering over them. Hunger and lack of water came back to plague the exiles traveling across this warm land. Because of dirt and heat, the wagons were perfect places for lice and germs to multiply.

Soon, a horrifying word began to pass among the passengers: typhus. With fear gripping her heart, Frania mouthed silent prayers for Julek's health as she observed him sitting at the other end of the berth. She also kept careful watch over Andrzej and all the members of her family for signs of illness.

"Mama, I'm thirsty. Please bring me a glass of that nice cold water from our well," she heard Marysia mumble in the middle of the night, and she knew then that typhus had invaded their wagon.

Three days later, Aniela opened her eyes in the morning, complaining, "Why is it so stuffy in the house? Someone open a window. I want to smell the flowers growing in our garden."

That same afternoon, Veronka woke up from a short nap and began talking to her dead parents.

Frania and her mother did all they could for the sick girls. They always managed to save some water for drinking and for sponge baths. Whenever there was food in the wagon, Frania tried hard to encourage her sisters to swallow something nourishing, but was not always successful. One time, Tata and Julek brought several cups of dried-out prunes. That day, Frania had to part with her favorite bedspread, one made of pure blue velvet, a wedding gift to her and Andrzej from his parents. The exchange was made during the last train stop on the streets of an Uzbek small town.

Ty-phus, ty-phus, ty-phus, the wheels of the train seemed to chant. They clattered constantly, and Frania couldn't shut out the sound. Ty-phus, ty-phus, ty-phus, she heard while tending to Marysia and Aniela. Ty-phus, ty-phus, ty-phus, she heard when she awakened suddenly at night, lying in darkness. Ty-phus, ty-phus, ty-phus. The constant repetition was driving her insane. Oh, God, please keep me healthy for Julek and my dear ones, she prayed. We need each other to survive.

Lately, there were moments—yes, too many moments—when she wanted to get off the train and walk away from it all. She wanted to get away from Andrzej, her parents and sisters, and even Julek. Seeing him suffer because of his sister, Veronka, made her heart bleed. Maybe she would have actually left, if it were not for the evacuation that was to come someday soon. Frania believed that only evacuation from Russia could save her sisters' lives, and she also believed the evacuation would end all their suffering. That is, if it came before...before...

Frania hated Fate for dumping these horrors on their heads. She saw more and more of her people getting sick and dying on the train. Their corpses, staring-eyed, were dragged off the platforms. Some of the sick were sent to hospitals in towns they passed. Frania knew her sisters could die due to unsanitary conditions and lack of medical care. She tried to persuade her mother to let Aniela and Marysia go to a hospital, but Mama wouldn't hear of separating the family.

"I know that once I let my sick daughters go, I will never see them again," Mama kept saying every time the subject came up.

"But what if they die?" Frania replied.

"I pray to God they won't."

Die-die, die-die, the wheels underneath Frania repeated. She listened to the gloomy sound and shuddered, but down deep in her heart she agreed with Mama. It was best to keep Aniela and Marysia with the family.

Each time an orderly with a nurse came to visit the wagon, Mama made Marysia and Aniela sit up straight and act as if they were the healthiest persons in the world.

One day, Frania noticed that Marysia was unusually restless.

"I think that Marysia's feeling worse than ever before, Mama," she said.

Worse, worse, worse, said the copycat wheels, rolling on and on in spite of the fact that three more corpses had been taken off of the train early that morning.

"She feels so hot," said Mother, her hand on the girl's forehead. "Is there any water left in the pail over there by the wall?"

"Not a drop. But the towel I've been wiping Aniela's face with is still wet."

Mother was sponging Marysia's face when Marysia suddenly opened her eyes wide. "Mama? Mama, where are you?"

"I'm right here, sitting next to you, dear."

Marysia pushed her mother's hand away and sat up. "Where did you go, Mama?" she cried out, her head moving side to side.

"Can't you see me?" asked Mama, her voice trembling.

"Mama? Mama?"

"What's the matter with you, Marysia?"

"Mama, Marysia is talking out of her head," said Frania, watching from her spot by the window.

"Is she dying?" asked Jozia.

"No, no. She's not," said Frania.

"Listen to me, Mama, I have something to say to you," Marysia said, still sitting up. But she was talking to the air.

"I'm listening."

"You were wrong about not letting us go to the hospital."

"Dear, you don't know what you're saying," said Mama tearfully, again placing her hand on Marysia's forehead.

And again Marysia pushed the hand away and said, "Because of that, Aniela here…" Marysia pointed down at the stove, "…will die."

"Marysia!"

"Veronka will die, and I will die, too."

"Please, dearest, don't—"

"And…and I'm dying now," Marysia said, and then threw herself backward on the berth as if someone had pushed her. "I'm dead already."

"Dead and talking," said Jozia, giggling into her fist.

"Jozia, you should be crying, not laughing," mumbled Marysia and closed her eyes. These were the last words she said in the wagon.

"Are you all right, Marysia?" Mama cried out, shaking the girl's shoulder.

Marysia opened her eyes, but only to stare up at the ceiling with dark, empty eyes.

Mama went to her knees. She took off the holy beads she wore about her neck and started the Rosary. The whole family joined her in praying for Marysia's life.

Shadows of the approaching evening were filling up the corners of the wagon by the time the train stopped again. Several minutes later, Marysia, Aniela, and Veronka were on their way to a hospital.

Kagan, a city located near Bukhara in Uzbekistan, was drowning in darkness dotted by streetlights and bits of brightness spilling out of the windows of small houses. The world didn't seem real to Frania as she rode in an Uzbek arba (cart drawn by horses). Was it possible she was still inside the wagon and only dreaming of escorting her sisters to the hospital? She sat by Marysia in the front seat, next to the driver, whose dark eyes would not stay still. The two scraggly horses looked like ghosts.

In a daze, Frania tightened her supportive arm about her sister's waist and patted the girl's cheek with her free hand. "Are you feeling a little better?"

Marysia leaned harder against Frania's shoulder, but said nothing.

Marysia's cheek felt clammy under her touch, and Frania's own voice rang out too loud in the air to be just imaginary.

"Isn't she going to speak?" asked Aniela from the back seat, where she was being supported by her father. Next to him, Veronka leaned on Julek, and she was snoring softly now.

"I hope so," said Frania, twisting her head to one side so she could look back at Aniela. "She has to come to before Tata and I say goodbye to you all."

Aniela sighed deeply and said in a weak voice, "What if she dies? What am I going to do then?"

"Marysia will live, I know," said Frania in a firm voice.

"I'm scared, Frania," said Aniela.

"Do you want us to take you back to the train?"

Aniela shook her head.

"Are you sure?"

"I'm sick and tired of lying on boards and riding in stuffy trains and...and I want to lie on a bed and feel sheets about me."

Frania turned around and stared straight ahead. "I can't blame you for feeling that way."

"And...and I don't really care whether I live or die," said Aniela.

"Aniela!" Tata scolded. "Don't talk that way. Remember, your mother, sisters, and I all want to see you healthy again."

Aniela sniffled. "I want to see you, too, but—"

"I don't want to hear buts from you, girl." He pushed Aniela gently away to see her face better. "You get well in that hospital. Do you hear?"

"I...I will try," said Aniela, cuddling closer to him.

"Promise?"

"Promise?" said Frania from her front seat.

"Yes, I promise."

Frania stared ahead. She looked hard at the lights and beyond them, as if to crack the night's darkness and see their future hiding in it.

"Father, tell me again how you're coming back for us," said Aniela.

"They told me at the station that we Poles are to get off the train in Bukhara. From that city, Julek and I will hop another train, and we will be here in no time to get you girls out of the hospital."

"Good."

Kagan, Bukhara, Uzbekistan: weird names, strange places, not friendly. Was Bukhara really to be the exiles' temporary destination? A stop before the oncoming evacuation to Iran? Frania had her doubts. From past experience, she had learned that Russian officials lied easily, without so much as the blink of an eye. How could she and her parents leave Marysia and Aniela in the hands of those who couldn't be trusted?

The night grew darker, the lights weaker and smaller until, finally, the cart reached the iron gate of the hospital, a several story brick building with narrow, curtainless windows.

In the waiting room, which was furnished with low benches that leaned against whitewashed walls, those who had to stay and others who had to leave said goodbye to one another. Frania cried hard, embracing each girl. Again, she begged Marysia to say a word, but to no avail. Just before leaving, she glanced at her father and, to her utter surprise, she saw tears running down his cheeks. For the first time in her life, she witnessed this man, who had bullied his family for years, display deep emotions. Right then, she forgave him completely for the ugly scene he had made at the Wroble's dance party.

Back on the train that night, she couldn't sleep. Although she had more space to lie down, an empty place in her heart burned painfully because of her sisters and Veronka. The biggest hole was because of Marysia, whose sad image in the hospital stayed with Frania vividly, causing her to cry quietly into her tattered pillow.

She heard her mother sniffling, too, and mumbling, "My girls...I won't see them ever again..."

E-ver, e-ver, e-ver, the wheels droned.

Shut up! Frania's voice shrieked inside her head. She placed her hands over her ears, but could not drown out the awful sounds.

"My poor, poor Marysia and Aniela...they will die..."

Die-die, die-die, clattered the train.

"Holy Mother, full of grace…" She recited the prayer she had known since childhood. Her sisters' lives were now in the hands of strangers. All she could do was ask God to save them.

Somewhere in the middle of the rosary, she finally drifted into a restless sleep.

Chapter Eleven

THE NEXT DAY, THE TRAIN ARRIVED AT BUKHARA, THE CAPITAL OF Bukhara province. This city had been an ancient meeting place for caravans traveling from the East and the West. Bukhara still was an important trading center in Central Asia.

The four wagons began slowing down on the far outskirts of Bukhara, and the passengers waited anxiously for them to halt. They were all ready to step down into the warm and sunny day they hoped would bring changes for the better. Here they were to wait for their evacuation.

Finally, the train came to a bumpy stop on the sidetracks. Inside, people crowded the exits, eagerly pressing against one another, waiting to spill out like a swarm of bees about to abandon its hive.

But why weren't the doors opening as usual? Why? Why?

"Let us out!" cried a voice in Frania's wagon. It was accompanied by a fist pounding against a hard surface.

"Open up, please, please," the other voices pleaded. "We are suffocating here."

"God help us," sobbed Mama. Because there was no space below, she and her small daughters still sat up on the berth.

"Water. We need water," another voice cried out by the door.

"Food. Give us something to eat."

"Open up! We need fresh air."

Pound, kick, pound, kick!

In addition to these cries, curses and swearing began to flow from some mouths. A man cursed Russia and Stalin. His voice was deep and strong, and it could be heard outside very clearly.

"Open up, Comrades, or we will break down the doors!"

Suddenly, a gunshot boomed in the air on the other side of the doors—then one, two, three more of them.

"Oh, sweet Jesus, the Russians are going to kill us," someone moaned behind Frania.

A dreadful silence fell upon everyone in the wagons.

"People! People, I have something to say to you," a male voice in Russian shouted from the outside. "Are you listening?"

"Yes, we are listening."

"You have to stay in for a while."

"Why? Aren't we supposed to get off the train here?"

"Please, let us out."

Pound, pound, pound.

Another shot sounded, silencing the people one more time.

"Don't ask questions! We are doing what we were told."

What the Poles on the train didn't know was that, somewhere in the city, their fate was being weighed by a few Russian officials. These men, after only a short discussion, decided to send the exiles back into the wilderness of Russia.

A-way, a-way, a-way, repeated the wheels, and Frania knew what they meant. She was moving away from her sisters in the hospital, perhaps never to lay eyes on them again.

Where were she and all the others going? She had no idea. She was sure the Russians were trying to murder her and her people by starving them. No food was delivered to the train, and the only stops were made in deserted areas with no human settlements nearby where the passengers could go begging or exchange items for nourishment.

Someone who has never experienced starvation can't possibly to imagine what it is to be dying of it. For weeks, the poor victim suffers terribly while desiring food, thinking of it constantly, searching for it. "I want something to eat, eat, eat," every cell in such a body screams silently, and the screaming never ceases. At nights, such a person dreams only of how he or she has eaten in the past and awakens hungrier than ever before.

The need for nourishment overwhelmed Frania too soon. How long since she had had a piece of bread or a spoonful of soup? Four, five, six days? Weeks, months, or years ago? Now she was like an animal looking for any tiny morsel and thinking of no one else but herself and her pain. Hunger was a rat with sharp teeth, gnawing constantly at her insides.

Once, she found some old breadcrumbs at the bottom of a sack, and she licked them off when everyone was asleep. She was like a cat, cleaning its bowl after a meal.

Mornings, late afternoons, all were the same; they brought no relief. When looking out her tiny window and seeing a village passing by, Frania drooled just thinking of the meals its dwellers were eating. She often pictured families sitting around their tables, consuming steaming dishes in front of warm fireplaces. Ah, what she wouldn't have done for a good lunch!

"Why don't you go out there and look for something to eat?" Frania read this plea in her little sisters' eyes one day, while the train rested silently somewhere in the depths of the steppe. The girls kept glancing at Tata, too, and much too often. Once in a while, Mama looked at her husband, but in her eyes there was an understanding.

An hour passed, or was it eternity? Somewhere in the wagon someone moaned, asking for water. A child whimpered and stopped, and through the open window a cool breeze rushed in. Frania inhaled it.

"Oh, Lord in Heaven, I can't just sit here anymore," Tata suddenly cried out. His voice rose from the very bottom of his soul. "What a horrid world we're living in. How can anyone let children starve?"

Their eyes wide with interest, Jozia and Helcia looked at him.

"There's nothing you or I can do to change this," said Mama, reaching out for her man's hand. Her eyes were unusually large and dark, not only from her own suffering, but for her family's, also.

"Oh, yes, yes! There's something I can do," he said. "I don't know why I've not thought of it before."

His little girls' eyes shone with hope now.

"What? What are you thinking of?" asked his wife.

"I will go outside."

"For what?"

"To look for food."

"But...but there's nothing out there but that awful hill," she said, pointing out the window.

"That's it. I'm going to walk to it. Maybe I will find people living on the other side."

"Dear husband, that hill is too far away from here for you to make it to the other side."

He waved her words away. "We all have to die sooner or later. At least, I won't go without a fight."

Mama's eyes filled with tears. "Our children and I need you more today than ever before. And the ones in the hospital..."

"I'll be careful and rest on the way. Besides, I will take other men with me, so don't worry."

She nodded.

"Now, my woman, look in our bundles for something I can exchange for bread."

Jozia and Helcia smiled as they watched their father prepare for the trip. In their minds, they could already see him coming back with an armful of goodies they could put into their mouths.

It hadn't occurred to Frania that Andrzej would even hesitate to participate in the on-coming walk. She picked out one of her nightgowns from her trunk and a silken shawl too light to have worn while in exile.

"Here, take these with you, Andrzej," she said, handing him the two items.

"I...I can't go," he said, looking down.

Her mouth opened wide and stayed open for too long. "Why can't you?" she asked.

"Because I'm too weak," he moaned, and then raised his eyes to her face.

In them she saw pleading for her to understand, but she shook her head vigorously and shouted, "Pull yourself together, my husband, and try to be a man like my father and...and Julek."

"Sorry," he whispered, cuddling up to the bundle behind him.

When she saw Julek stepping down off the platform, she said quickly, "I'll go in your place." She slid down the berth and got out. Secretly, she was glad Andrzej was staying behind, for she saw a chance to be alone with her beloved.

The grasses, thick and tall, hissed as the walkers plunged through them. The sky above was grayish-white and covered here and there with jagged clouds that looked like wolves' teeth. When the sun peeked out from behind, it was too warm for human comfort. The dry wind was sharp and swatted at their sweating faces, and the hill—the hump in the earth—loomed darkly ahead at a mocking distance.

"God give us enough strength to make it," the ones who moved toward it prayed, and the ones in the wagons prayed too.

Frania and Julek lagged behind on purpose.

"Andrzej looks bad," Julek said.

"Yes, he does. The trouble is that he's not a fighter at all." Frania sighed and glanced sideways at her companion. His face was pale and thin, but his eyes were shining with love for her.

"It's because our life in exile is harsh," said Julek, quickening his steps.

She stayed a little behind, but then caught up with him. "It's true. Our life is hard, especially now, but we all suffer. He's not the only one."

Julek nodded silently and stared ahead at the hill, which didn't seem to be getting any nearer.

Frania reached out for his hand, and he wrapped his fingers around hers.

"Wish you were my wife instead of his," he said.

My wife, something in the grasses repeated.

"I love you," Frania said.

"Frania, Frania, my beloved." He squeezed her hand harder yet. "I love you more than life itself." He stopped on the spot and made her stop, too.

Next, they were in each other's arms and kissing passionately, although their companions were still dangerously near.

"I want you now and here," he whispered into her ear. "Please don't say no." He kissed her.

"I...I want you in the same way." She opened her mouth wider to let his tongue explore it even deeper.

Their bodies pressed hard against each other, and they fell to their knees. Down they lay in the grasses, two starved souls aching to express true feelings so long suppressed.

He kissed her neck and slipped his hand into her blouse, touching her breast.

"Yes, yes, sweetness, make me happy even for a moment," she whispered.

A bird screamed high in the air and brought her abruptly to her senses. "Julek, please, we can't go through with this."

"I can't stop now," he said and planted another hot kiss on her lips.

She pushed against him with all her strength. "You have to, before it's too late. Let go of me right now!"

And he did.

They got up slowly, with great effort. After smoothing out their clothing and hair, they resumed their walk, but now they walked in awkward silence.

"Are you mad at me?" Julek finally said, not looking at Frania.

She shook her head. "No."

"Will you forgive me for forgetting myself?"

"It was my fault, too."

He said not another word, but moved faster, and she kept up with him. With a miraculously renewed energy, the young couple caught up with the men walking ahead of them, who evidently had no idea what had almost happened behind them in the grasses.

Indifferent to their suffering, time ticked its minutes away, neither rushing nor slowing on their account. When its ticking brought on the noontime, this great master of change continued to march forward, although the walkers were still about a mile away from their destination, too far from it for their own good.

By now the marchers had reached the point of complete exhaustion. They tripped and fell, got up and tripped again, but still kept moving forward. Step by step, they pushed themselves far past human endurance. What kept them going? It wasn't the flatland with low vegetation that did it, for it held nothing but a grave emptiness for them, an emptiness like the toothless mouth of an ancient giant exhaling despair.

It was the wildlife, signs of which they saw around, that made them keep on struggling. Something low in the grasses slithered and buzzed. Birds chirped and flew above the low bushes. If these creatures could find nourishment in this forsaken place, why not the exiles?

For another half hour, Frania and the others floundered through the vegetation, bathing in their own sweat. She feared she might collapse at any moment and not be able to get up again. Her knees wobbled, and she was shaking all over. She looked toward the hill, which seemed closer now, yet still too far, and she took two more torturous steps. Then she glanced back and saw one of the men crawling on all fours. Dear God, the man, who always sat in the center of the opposite berth with his small grandson constantly clinging to him, was about fifty.

Something stirred in Frania's heart and went out to the poor grandfather, the only relative the boy had. Compassion brought her a new flow of energy, and she turned back to help him rise to his feet.

At this moment, her father called out, "Hey, everyone, let's rest for awhile."

"Good," she said.

"Good," whispered the grandfather.

"Oh, good," cried out several voices all at once.

So they all sat down. They were not only hungry and tired, but also thirsty now. Some glanced about, hoping to hear a stream flowing nearby, but found none. A fluffy cumulus drifted close to the sun and soon covered its too warm face. A shadow, together with a gentle breeze, rushed to touch their sweaty foreheads. Ah, it was sheer luxury to feel coolness on the skin. It was almost as good as a cold sip of water going down a dry throat. They needed rest, water, some lunch to regain their strength so they could reach the other side of the hill. And then they still had to return to the train.

Too weak to talk, the walkers listened to their own heartbeats and to small sounds that the steppe made. They heard twittering, whistling, shee-sheeing and...and barking...

Barking? Yes, dogs barking. Coming from behind the hill!

Behind the barren hill, under an unfriendly sky that never provided this land with sufficient moisture, a small settlement squatted low to the ground. The flat-roofed huts were tiny, made out of mud, with narrow doors and small windows. No gardens or shrubbery grew about them. On the grassy ground behind the village, a herd of sheep grazed. Villagers and their animals showed traces of having starved for much of the year.

"Who are you? Where did you come from?" asked the natives, who had quickly surrounded the Poles when they showed up at the edge of their village.

"We came from the train that stands on the other side of your hill," said Frania. "We are awfully thirsty." She licked her parched lips.

"We have water," said one man, acting as leader of his people. He told his men to bring drinks for the visitors.

"You have walked all that way, huh?" he said, after the visitors had drunk their fill.

"We have not eaten since Monday," said Julek. "Please give us some bread."

The man shook his head and said, "We don't have enough for ourselves." He pointed to a skinny little girl hugging her mother's knees.

"There are little children riding on the train," said Frania's father in a shaking voice, "and they are starving to death. Have mercy on them."

But the leader shook his head again, and women behind him did the same, backing away.

Suddenly, Frania stepped in front of her group and said, "Isn't my shawl beautiful?" With her nightgown thrown over one shoulder, she spread the shawl across her arms for everyone to see.

A pretty girl, probably a new bride, rushed to Frania's side, pulling her husband behind by his hand.

"What do you want for this?" she said, her dark eyes shining like two pearl buttons.

"Bread, cheese, milk," said Frania, swallowing hard. Just the thought of food made her drool.

The girl motioned Frania to follow her and her man into their hut. She offered Frania two flatbreads, several strips of dried-out meat, and a chunk of cheese, which Frania accepted in exchange for the shawl.

For her nightgown she bought more cheese and a large bowl of grain from another woman.

While Frania carried out her bargaining, others did, also. The villagers were very hard to bargain with, but the Poles stood their ground firmly. They soon walked away with enough provisions to keep them alive for some time.

On Easter Sunday, the Poles were brought to snow-covered Aktyubinsk, a capital city in Kazakh Soviet Republic. Here the passengers were allowed to leave the train. Glory be to God. A city meant people, and people had food.

Although proud by nature, the exiles went on the streets to go begging. It was not an easy thing for them to do, but there was no other way for them to survive this trip toward an unknown destination.

Frania took Jozia with her. When they both came to a house with a wide door and large windows with curtains in them, she pushed her sister in front and asked her to knock. A good-looking woman came to greet them. Through the open door, a delicious aroma of boiled ham, potatoes, and fried onions drifted out. Frania inhaled the aroma and swallowed hard.

"We're very hungry," said Jozia to the lady of the house. "Would you, please, give us something to eat?" Jozia shivered in her ragged coat.

"You poor, poor child," sighed the lady. "Where did you two come from? Are you sisters? You look alike."

"From the train," said Frania, standing at the bottom of the steps.

"Where are you going?"

Frania shrugged her shoulders. "We don't know. We are Poles. Your government is taking us somewhere."

"Oh. Wait here, you two. I'll be back."

While waiting for the woman to return, Frania moved her legs and beat her arms against her chest to keep warm. Through the small opening in the door she saw a fire going full blast in the fireplace. She smiled to see such a dreamy picture.

"Here you are, little girl," the good lady was saying to Jozia, as she handed her a whole loaf of bread.

"Thank you," said Jozia, her eyes fixed on the bread. She licked her lips.

"Thank you very much," called out Frania, not quite believing what she was seeing. Bread—white bread! When had she last eaten such a goodie?

"God bless both of you." The woman smiled and backed away. Too soon, she closed the door behind her.

From other dwellers, Frania and Jozia received boiled eggs, pieces of sweet pastry, and—oh, sweet Heaven!—slices of ham.

On this day when Christians celebrated the resurrection of Jesus Christ, not only Frania and her sister collected food, but so did every Pole strong enough to go begging. Into eager hands, Aktyubinskans gave a variety of things to put into their empty stomachs, including dried fish, pierogies stuffed with cheese and potato, and many other good things. This day the Poles feasted in the wagons almost as well and joyfully as they had in their Polish homes on Easter Sunday.

Kazakh Republic lay in Western Central Asia, covering a vast area largely lined with dry plains called steppes. On the east, Kazakhstan was bounded by China; on the west, by the Caspian Sea. Sixty percent of the population were Kazakhs who, before 1927, had lived as free nomads, breeders of livestock. Now, with the help of irrigation and hydroelectric power, the Kazakhs were forced to raise grain, cotton, flax, sugar, beets, rice, and tobacco, in addition to raising their cattle. But, as Frania soon found out, the extra effort wasn't bringing these people prosperity.

Somewhere in Northern Kazakhstan, the Polish passengers were dropped off by a wagon at different collective farms called kolchoses. Frania and her companions were brought to Narod in early spring. They were given an old school, long unused, as a shelter. The next day all the grownups were taken to a brickyard to work. Here they labored all day for two bowls of oat soup and two thin slices of bread each.

Because Frania's spade was dull, she had to place her foot on its steel edge and push down with all her might in order to cut the ground with it. Next, she had to scoop up a shovelful of dirt and toss it into a cart. The air was still ice-cold, but she was sweating from exhaustion. At times, she felt she might faint, but she never did, no matter how bad her muscles ached.

In another part of the yard, where bricks were formed and laid out to dry in the sun, Julek, Andrzej, and her father worked. Julek had found shelter in an old building at the other end of Narod. Frania was keenly aware of his presence in the yard and kept glancing in his direction, as if fearing he might disappear from her sight any moment, any day. She now thought of him constantly and wanted the whole world to know how she loved and was loved by him. Why did she have to hide her true feelings, so precious to her in these harsh times? Why did she have to pretend? Was it even necessary to pretend in a place where people cared about nothing but food and warmth? It was mainly for her mother, who would be hurt had she found out that her oldest daughter desired to be with a man other than her husband.

Next to Frania's hole, her mother worked at the same chore. The older woman's breath whistled dangerously.

"Mama, why do you keep looking at the road?" Frania asked.

Mama shrugged her shoulders and threw a shovelful of dirt into her cart. Automatically, her hand went to her back, and she moaned.

"Do you believe Marysia and Aniela will come to Narod?"

"I pray to Jesus and Holy Mary that they will, someday, and soon."

"I so hope they do," said Frania. She gazed at the dirt road that ran toward the creek, crossed it, and then led all the way to the nearest railway station. Lifting her head, she saw a dark cloud hanging low above the horizon, almost touching the land. The cloud looked like the distorted face of a giant sneering at her, and she winced.

"What if—and I only mean if—they don't know our whereabouts? How do they find us after they leave the hospital?"

"Your sisters will go to the railway station in Kagan. Any clerk working there can tell them where our train went."

Frania glanced up at the cloud again and saw that the giant's chin had grown a crooked fist into which the giant snickered.

"Can't trust Russian Communists," said Frania.

"I trust God," said Mama, "and believe in Him only."

A young stout Kazakh shouted at Frania and her mother. "Hey, you two women over there. Stop dillydallying and get back to filling your carts with dirt if you want your supper."

"Dillydallying?" muttered Frania. She thrust the spade into the ground and spit on it, imagining the Kazakh's face.

Several minutes later, three females appeared on the road on the other side of the creek. They walked slowly from the direction of the station and were not recognizable from so great a distance.

"My daughters and Veronka are coming!" Frania's mother suddenly shrieked with joy. "They have found us. Thank God."

"Oh, yes, yes, there they are," cried out Frania, and she smiled.

Their excited voices brought work in the yard to a halt and angered the overseer. "People, go back to what you're supposed to be doing," he shouted. He turned to Frania and her mother. "What are you two women gaping at? You're wasting too much time for your own good."

Frania's mother pointed to the creek and cried out in a high-pitched voice, "Comrade, look! Do you see those women walking over there?"

He nodded. "So?"

"They are my daughters and their friend. They have found us."

"How do you know they're your daughters, and where are they coming from?"

"I would know them anywhere. They're coming from the hospital, where we had to leave them because they were sick with typhus."

"Typhus?" said the Kazakh, and backed away as if the older woman could inflict the illness upon him.

"Please, Comrade, let me meet them at the creek?"

"Can't you wait for them to get here?"

"No, no. Don't you see how slow they are moving? They must be still very weak. Someone has to help them cross the 'walk' on the creek so they don't fall in."

"Please, Comrade, let one of us go," said Frania, trembling.

He looked at Frania, then at her mother, who was visibly shaking, and then looked toward the approaching figures. "You stay and go back to work. I'll go and get them."

"Thank you, Comrade," said Mama, picking up her spade.

"Thank you," said Frania, and bent to her digging.

The Kakazkh strolled away. How could he be so calm? Both women tried to keep at their labor, but couldn't. While filling up their carts, they kept spilling half spades of dirt on the ground, because their eyes were constantly on the Kazakh and the three figures. Why was he walking so slowly? The women on the other side of the creek were now much closer to it than he was. What if they reached the 'walk' before he did?

But he did cross the river first and met them. Frania and her mother sighed with relief. Leaning on their spades, they watched the four people talking. What were they saying? Why were they talking for so long? All the girls had to do was identify themselves so the Kazakh could bring them to the yard. Were the figures shaking their heads, or did it just seem that way?

"Oh, no, no," whispered Frania, refusing to believe what she was seeing next. The Kazakh separated from the group and soon was crossing the 'walk' back, but he was alone. "Please, God, make him go back and get my sisters."

"Marysia! Aniela!" Mama screamed in a voice that frightened not only Frania, but all the workers in the yard. "Where are you going?" She let her spade fall to the ground and leaped forward with an energy no one imagined she still possessed. "My daughters, come back to me!" She stretched out her arms.

The figures on the other side of the creek stopped and stared.

Frania could see, now, that they couldn't be her sisters. They were much taller and wore strange clothes.

"Your family is here at Narod. Marysia! Aniela!" Mama cried out, her voice weaker now.

The three women shrugged their shoulders, and then went back to their walking as if nothing in the world was happening.

Frania watched her mother start to run, and horror gripped her heart. She wanted to go after the dear woman, but couldn't move. Her legs were as heavy as if they were made out of lead.

"Mama, please stop," she called out, but in a voice too thin to carry far.

By then Mama had reached the Kazakh, who was returning to the yard. Frania saw how her mother grabbed the man by his shoulders, how she was shaking him, and how he pushed her away so hard that she fell to the ground. And only now she started to run toward her mother, who wasn't getting up. Had she fainted?

"Mama!"

She heard footsteps behind her and knew it was her father. She slowed down to let him pass.

When Tata reached his wife, with Frania right behind, the woman was lying motionless on the dusty road. He got down on his knees and touched her head. That seemed to trigger a violent reaction in her, and she suddenly kicked out, hit the ground with her face, her body arching up and down, up and down. Her fists beat the road and her nails dug into the dirt.

Frania's eyes widened with fright. Was this person her mother who, until now, had always been the foundation stone of her family's sanity?

"My dear wife," murmured Tata, "don't go crazy on me." He grabbed Mama's shoulders firmly, held them down, and started to massage them.

Mama responded with cascades of sobbing.

"Cry, cry, all you want." His fingers worked the back of her neck. "Marysia and Aniela will show up at Narod, someday. You'll see."

"No, they won't. They're dead."

"Hush, hush up, don't talk that way. I know that both our girls are alive and well, and God will help them find us."

"There is no God," she mumbled into the dirt. Her fists began to beat the ground again, but soon stopped. "I have prayed so hard, day and night, but He doesn't answer."

"Don't talk against God," Tata said, as he massaged her spine.

"I'll say what I want!" his wife shrieked and sat up. Facing her husband, she added, "I'll say it again—there is no God up there," she pointed up to the sky, "or Hell down there. Hell exists only in Russia."

Frania's father did something unusual next, so unusual that he took Frania's breath away. He put his arms about his wife and whispered into her ear, "I love you, dear." Then he kissed her on the mouth.

And Mama, still sobbing, clung to him as if she were a little girl, cuddling up to her own father for comfort.

Frania stood above her parents, neither detracting from the scene nor adding to it. She simply observed. Though deeply involved emotionally, she was still just an observer. And she was glad to witness, one more time, her father changing for the better.

Chapter Twelve

As soon as the days grew warmer, Ivan Borushniak (Ivan B.), the biggest boss at Narod, asked all the adult Poles to work in the fields for twice-a-day meals and milk. They eagerly agreed. The fields were located within five to ten miles of the settlement.

The first season in Kazakhstan, Frania hand-sowed oats and wheat. The fields here were enjoyable to work in, though not as precious as they were in Poland. There, the freshly overturned and smoothed-out soil was soft and damp, like dark bread dough kneaded and rolled out on the board. In her parents' fields, not only wheat and oats were planted, but also rye, corn, buckwheat, potatoes, carrots, and beans. Crops grew quickly under the Polish sky, soaking up Polish sunrays, smelling like warmed-up honey and swaying in warm breezes that whispered promises of a good harvest to come. A good harvest meant a good winter ahead, with better tasting meals and more sweet pastry to munch on. In Poland, Frania loved summers especially, because she ate fresh fruit: pears, plums, apricots, cherries, and apples. When had she last sunk her teeth into something as sweet as an apple? She hadn't eaten anything so delicious since leaving home. And when last had she eaten well at all? Right now, her stomach gurgled and churned, even though only two hours had passed since breakfast, and supper was still long hours away.

She sighed deeply and straightened up. In the next row, a woman with pitch-black hair and slanting dark eyes labored. A Kazakh person. Where was Mama? Working at the other end of the same field. She wasn't attractive anymore, the way she had been in Poland. Or as energetic. Her eyes had sunk deep into her forehead, where creases were fast forming, and she was much too thin.

In other parts of the fields, Tata, Andrzej, and Julek sweated at their ploughs, which were ancient and pulled by winter-thin horses, as well as bulls, cows, and camels. The bulls and cows were hard to handle. They often refused to move. They stumbled and fell. Each time this happened, a worker went down, too. Some of the animals wouldn't rise again until one of the Kazakhs came with a lit straw torch and brought it close to the animal's side. It was a cruel way to deal with the poor creatures, but the men were desperate.

Then one day they stopped bringing bread to the field for the Poles, only very thin soups. There was a shortage of food at Narod. Too soon the exiles found out that such a shortage was an annual occurrence here, caused by poor workmanship, bad management, and high taxation.

Kazakhs at Narod had no land of their own. Thus, they had no incentive to work to their full capacity. No one cared when a large piece of land lay idle because there was no more seed left in storage. Harvesting and threshing was done carelessly and mostly by hand. Too much grain was left in the straw stacks to freeze in the winter and rot the next spring. Narod officials cared only for themselves and their families; as long as they ate, they made no special effort to correct existing situations on the collective farm. Narod, for instance, had some modern equipment for its use, but when the machinery broke there was no one to fix it, and it was left under the naked sky to rust.

No matter how good or poor the harvest at Narod, the government collected the same large quota of crops every year from its people. Therefore, Narodowians lived in poverty, and many times they were half-starved by springtime.

Frania and her people couldn't live on soup alone. They had no choice but to keep exchanging articles from their fast-diminishing belongings for food. The exchanges took place with Kazakhs from the upper crust, of course. Ivan's beautiful wife, still a teenager, loved the satin slips and silky underwear Frania brought to her. She supplied Frania with flatbread, grain, cheese, and flour. In this way, the young woman helped Frania and her dear ones to survive their first spring in northern Kazakhstan.

May came to the settlement, and it found Frania alive, healthy, and laboring, but always thinking of the three girls left in Kagan. Were they alive? Somehow, she knew they were. But she also felt in her gut that the poor things were in trouble. They had no papers to identify themselves, no money, and no other clothing than what they wore to the hospital. She dreamed at night about them wandering the streets of a strange city with no place to go, no shelter, and nothing to eat. Someone had to return to Uzbekistan and bring them back to Narod. She debated whether to go herself or to send her father.

Then she came up with an idea.

On one of their very few days free from work, she sent Jozia to Julek with a message to meet her at the other end of Narod by the crossroads, a little way from the settlement.

"I'm happy you wanted to see me," he said, when they came close to each other. He stretched out his arms to her, but she didn't rush into them. The sun was almost setting behind the fields, the crops ripening in its warmth and light.

"I came here for a reason," she said, trembling. She ached to be in his arms, but suppressed her feelings.

"Oh," he said, and dropped his arms to his sides.

"Let's take a walk in the steppe," she said, moving away.

He followed.

"Is Andrzej any better today?" He matched his long steps to her short, quick ones.

"He got sick and is still in bed. But let's not talk about him, Julek."

He nodded and glanced questioningly at her.

"I have a big favor to ask of you."

"I'll do anything for you, my beloved." His voice was choked with deep emotion. "You know that, don't you?"

She nodded and looked down at her feet. "I hate to ask." Her voice cracked. In her imagination, she already saw her sweet Julek being trampled by the crowd trying to get on the trains.

"Frania, don't hesitate to ask."

"How often do you think of Veronka?" She didn't dare look at him, so she stared at the sun, now only half visible above the horizon.

"I think of her all the time, and your sisters, too."

"You do? I...I..."

"You want me to go after the girls, don't you, Frania?"

She looked away.

"I will do it!"

"You will?" She turned to look at him.

"Of course, I will."

She wanted to throw herself at him and beg him to hold her tight, but she decided against it, for she didn't want to start something she couldn't go through with. Instead, she smiled at him and said, "Thank you, darling."

"When do you want me to go?"

"As soon as possible."

"I can go tomorrow."

"No, not tomorrow...or the day after it. You will need money for train tickets."

"I can jump trains."

She shook her head. "It's too dangerous. And you need to buy food at stations."

"I can steal sunflower seeds from trains and bread from Russians."

"Out of the question. Listen to me, Julek, for I have a good plan."

"Plan?"

"Lately, Mama and I have been talking about nothing else but your traveling to Uzbekistan."

"You have?" he said, and grinned at her.

"Mama will sell Ivan B.'s wife her blue shawl."

"Not the one she wore only on holidays to church, back home?"

"The same one...and I'll get rubles from Ivan's sister."

"What are you going to sell her?"

"The outfit I wore on my wedding day, and other things."

Julek went away, and the days passed. Frania and her mother anxiously awaited his return. They prayed and daydreamed aloud how it would be when he and the girls showed up at Narod.

"What are you going to do, Mama, when you see them standing in front of you? What?"

"I will stretch out my arms like this and embrace both of them at the same time, if I can." She hugged herself. "And I will hug and kiss them, hug and kiss their cheeks until they are all wet."

"I will welcome them with open arms, too," said Frania, thinking she would kiss Julek right on his mouth when she saw him again. She would do that in front of everyone. Someday, she even might let him make love to her somewhere in the steppe.

"I swear to God I will never raise my voice in anger to either of them, and I will always be nice to them. Always."

"And I will be the best sister in the world to them. You will see, Mama."

The whole month turned all about and hid in a deep fold of the past never to come back. Mother and daughter waited—waited and prayed.

Frania heard her mother sniffling one late afternoon, and the sound irritated her. It was still daylight, and she was going through her things in the trunk. She did this whenever she wanted time to pass more quickly. The trunk was made out of oak. Its lid was shaped like a dome cut in half, covered with pure leather and brass hardware. Back in Poland, it had shone from waxing and polishing, but now it was dull and worn like the face of an old man. Her parents had given her the trunk two years before her marriage to hold her trousseau. It went with her to Jaroslav full of handmade clothing, cheap glittering accessories, a few linens, and some kitchenware.

When the war broke out, she brought the trunk back home filled with expensive things: silky undergarments, woolen dresses, bulky sweaters. It held Henio's little suits of velvet and Andrzej's best outfits. At the bottom she put a jewelry box that played music. Andrzej had given it to her on her birthday, in Jaroslav, together with a pearl necklace. The necklace provided them both with the money they needed for train tickets to Buzuluk. The jewelry box was still there, though it was empty and cracked and had stopped playing music long ago. Wrapped in two thick towels, Frania kept an oil painting of Holy Mary, called Matka Boska Chestochowska. As legend had it, this picture saved Chestochowa (a Polish monastery) from invasion by Swedes before Poland was erased from the map for the first time by Russia, Austria, and Prussia. Frania believed she would survive as long as she had the holy image of St. Mary with her.

The sound of Mama's sniffling hit Frania's ears for the hundredth time. "Mama, stop that!" she cried out, slamming the trunk's lid. Then she ran out into the fresh air and open spaces. She kept running across Narod, the Kazakh children staring after her. One of the youngsters threw a stone that barely missed her. An old woman looked out her window and swore hard at Frania, because she was one of the Poles with whom the woman and her family had to share grain in lean times. A dog came barking, and Frania stopped to pat it. The pooch sniffed at her fingers, wagged its tail, and then followed her all the way to the edge of the village before turning back home.

She finally slowed down by the brickyard and stopped. The yard was empty of workers. The same old sight hit her like a hammer: the dusty track leading toward the creek and past it. The same old painful longing to see the dear girls, and now Julek, walking the road, tugged at her heart. It was sad to see only swirls of dust dancing in the wind.

Did all three girls die in the hospital? Or maybe they were poisoned! Had Julek perished somewhere on the way to Uzbekistan? Oh, no, no, that couldn't be. Tears filled her eyes, and she wiped them with the backs of her hands. Then she stared into the distance, blinking, blinking.

Someone appeared on the road, about as far away as the three figures had been that day when Mama clawed the ground with disappointment. Frania strained her eyes to see whether it was a man or a woman plodding down the road. She waited patiently. At that moment, the wind stopped blowing, and the grasses around her ceased to move. It was as if the steppe were holding its breath, waiting with her for something unusual to happen.

Something, indeed, happened in the semidarkness of the approaching evening.

"Julek!" Frania screamed. "Is that you coming back?"

"Yes, it's me, Frania," he called out to her, his voice heavy with a shameful sadness.

"Julek, Julek," she repeated, running toward him, but then she halted as if her feet had suddenly sunk deep into the ground. Her beloved was returning to Narod and to her, but where were Marysia, Aniela, and Veronka? Poor, poor Mama. How would she react to the bad news coming her way?

They embraced, but didn't kiss.

"Are they dead?" she asked simply, still in his arms.

He released her then and shrugged, looking down. "I don't know."

"What?"

"I couldn't find them."

"Did you not reach Kagan by train?"

"Yes, I did."

"And did you go to the hospital, Julek?"

"Several times."

"And? And?"

"I had a hard time finding anyone who would talk to me, and when I did catch an orderly clerk working in the admittance office, I asked her questions."

"And what did she tell you?"

"She took a long time checking her books, and then said our sisters' names were not written on any list of patients."

"How can that be? We left them there that night, and that is a fact. Do you suppose they all died?" she asked again, biting her lips.

"No, no. You know Communist officials; they always lie."

"Yes, I know, but did you go looking at the railway station, Julek?"

"Did you think I wouldn't?" he said, his voice spiked with hurt.

"No, Julek darling, I didn't think that at all. I know you did all you could."

"You're right. I went everywhere, asked questions everywhere. I talked to Russians, Uzbeks, our people—"

"Our people?"

"There are hundreds, thousands of them on the streets of Kagan and Bukhara."

"Did you go to Bukhara, too?"

"Of course, I did."

"What are our people doing there?"

"Have you forgotten about the evacuation and Anders' Army?"

"Oh, that. Do you think they will go to Iran? If so, we should be there with them, waiting."

"The evacuation might come eventually, and I hope it does before too many of our women and children die of hunger, dysentery, malaria, and typhus."

Frania looked at Julek carefully, and her chin trembled. "I'm lucky you're here with me, again, and that you're not sick."

"I don't feel lucky," he said, his eyes on Narod, drowning in bluish shadows.

"Are you getting ill?" she said and moved closer to feel his forehead for fever.

"No, Frania, I'm not ill." He pushed her hand away. "I feel bad because I didn't bring our sisters back to Narod with me."

"Julek, you did your best to find them. Please smile!"

"I can't," he moaned.

"Oh, come on, darling, don't be so sad," she whispered, and placed a quick kiss on his lips. "Put your arms around me and hold me tight."

He did just that, but didn't try to kiss her. Too soon he let her go.

"Tell me more about our people in Kagan and Bukhara. Is anyone helping them there?"

"There are Polish outposts set up here and there with food, and I've heard of Polish orphanages organized by our Army, but these efforts to save our civilians are like drops of rain falling into a dried-out well."

"Dear Lord in Heaven," she said, "more and more pain for us Poles, and no end to it in sight."

They went together to tell Frania's mother the unfortunate news and watched her gasp for air. When she looked as if she were about to keel over, Frania and Julek rushed from both sides to support her. But she elbowed Julek away and stared into space. Her eyes were dangerously dark.

The next morning, Mama came down with an attack of malaria and nearly died. It took her a long time to recover from her grief and her sickness. When she finally got out of bed, it was already time for harvesting.

Now, not only Kazakhs, but also the exiles ate better and gained weight in spite of the heat and hard work. Then came fall with cool breezes and dark clouds. Seasonal work at Narod was about to end as the last potatoes were dug. What were Frania and her family to do in the wintertime? How were they to earn food?

Chapter Thirteen

"I HAVE A NEW JOB FOR YOU, COMRADE," SAID IVAN B. TO FRANIA'S father one day in his office. "I can send you and your family into the steppe to tend to a hundred heifers over the winter."

"How far away from here do we have to go?"

"About two hours on horseback."

"I see. How about shelter and food?"

"Don't worry, Comrade. There's a house you can live in with a barn and stacks of hay for the heifers."

"How are we to get our supplies?"

"My men will bring them to you, twice a week."

"Good."

"Will you accept the job?"

"Of course, I will. Thank you, Comrade."

At the foot of a stark-naked hump in the earth, amid the ruins of what once had been a small village, stood one surviving structure, a barn and human shack combined. It contained an old brick stove, double bunks made out of rough planks, and a crooked table. Two low benches leaned against walls filled with holes and in desperate need of painting.

Later that week, Frania and her dear ones arrived at their new location in two horse-drawn carts. With them came Kozaczka, a Kazakh widow, and her fourteen-year-old son, Sasha.

"It looks like this winter may not be so bad after all," said Frania to her mother one day. They both were doing their laundry in the nearby creek, which was their only water supply. Jozia and Helcia were giggling behind some bushes and making mud cakes, which they were sure would turn into sweet pastry in the afternoon sunrays.

"Yes, it looks that way." Mama sighed, soaping up a tattered quilt that had gone unwashed since Bialy Jar.

"I think we did all we could to prepare the shelter for the old witch with snow and frost in her lap," said Frania, beating Andrzej's shirt against a stone. She smiled, recalling how she and her mother had smoothed out the earthen floor with a thick layer of mud mixed with cow manure. This mass, when hardened, was yellowish brown instead of a dull gray.

Mama glanced up at the sky and said, "I'm glad Kozachka is here with us. Otherwise, we wouldn't have thought of collecting manure and drying it in the sun for fuel to heat our shack on cold days."

"That's true. She told us about the fuel, but who thought of patching up the holes in the walls with mud packs, instead of just stuffing them with hay?"

"We did, didn't we?"

Frania nodded and grinned.

Winter swooped down upon the hill and their shelters the way a crow attacks a nest full of tiny birds. Snow fell often from the dark, low-hanging sky. Frost turned the surface of the creek into a sheet of ice. Vegetation on its banks stood hoary and leafless. From the depths of the land came wolves to howl outside the shelters, especially at night, disturbing both people and heifers. Life in the snowy steppe was harsh, and each day's labor devoured their time and energy. On blizzard days, the heifers stayed in. When weather permitted, first thing in the morning, Andrzej, Tata, and Sasha let the animals out for fresh air, exercise, and feeding. On his horse, Sasha circled the herd to watch out for the wolves, which were always lurking somewhere, ready to claim a heifer for their breakfast. Andrzej and Tata had to plough through the snow to the stacks of hay, which they forked out and carried to the open space, scattering feed on the snow for the cattle to eat. When the animals' meal was over, the men steered them toward the creek near a hole in the ice. Then they lifted out pails of water for the heifers to drink.

Meanwhile, Frania, Mama, and Kozachka, who had already rushed about the shelter making breakfast, doing dishes, and making up bunks, went to the barn to clean it. They shoveled the smelly waste into two wheelbarrows and wheeled it outside. The mountain of animal waste by the shelter grew higher and higher every day. But, as the women labored, the manure in the barn seemed to grow and multiply, instead of vanishing. Only when their work was done in the barn were the women free to do laundry—by hand, of course—mend worn-out clothing, and make supper.

Suppertime was the only happy period of those days in the shack. Frania's mother usually prepared it very carefully, using all her talent. From the supply brought to the shelter by Kazakhs from Narod, she made cabbage-potato soups seasoned with minced onions fried in a dot of lard. Delicious eyes of grease and brown pieces of onion floated on top of each bowl, tempting their appetites. And how they ate, slurping, clicking their tongues and swallowing aloud. Good, good meals, they enjoyed in the evening, sitting by the lit fireplace. If only they could hope to eat as well for the rest of their stay in Kazakhstan. Once, every two weeks, a loaf of fresh bread was placed on the crooked old table. The good meal-maker baked it in the oven, after she had accumulated enough grain, which she crushed and powdered between two stones.

The first snowfall this year somehow stirred strong memories in Frania of all the Christmases she had enjoyed back home. From these memories came thoughts of pierogies she had eaten in good times. These thoughts of pierogies brought on an obsession to taste the dish again. She saw pierogies in her dreams at night and daydreamed of them during the day. And when she'd had enough of this desire that wouldn't leave her alone, she decided to satisfy her palate, which screamed for such a delicacy.

Among the Kazakhs who visited the hill was a young woman of about twenty-five. She had a friendly smile and liked to talk to Frania. Her name was Irena.

"Is there any way you could bring me some flour and cheese?" Frania asked Irena one day in the middle of January.

Irena rubbed the tips of her chubby fingers against her handsome chin and said, "Maybe." Her eyes traveled to Frania's trunk, sitting underneath the shelter's only window.

"Would you do it for a yellow dress as silky and smooth as tulips' petals?"

"It's a deal," whispered Irena, and winked at Frania.

One day the following week, everyone sheltering in the shack sat down to a special meal, one that gave off the delicious aroma of boiled dough and cheese.

"Hmmmmm," Frania moaned, as she munched on one of the pierogies.

Everyone started to guzzle the food, all except Frania's mother. She sat in front of her dish and stared at it.

"Mama, this is delicious. Why aren't you eating?" asked Frania.

"I...I can't," Mama cried out, her voice suddenly choked up.

"Why? Why not?" cried out voices that came out of mouths mauling the tasty morsels.

"I can't eat such good stuff when they...they are starving in...in Uzbekistan."

"Who's starving?"

"You mean Marysia, Aniela...and Veronka?"

"That's right. They have nothing to eat, and here we are, stuffing ourselves," Mama cried out and leaped away from the table. She sat down on the floor in the darkest, coldest corner of the hut. Sobbing, she rocked herself until her husband came to comfort her. By late evening, she had finally stopped crying, but she wouldn't touch any of her supper.

After a blustery afternoon and night, morning finally arrived. Frania woke with a weird feeling that something was wrong in the shelter. It was still milky dark, but why were the heifers mooing so? And why did the air feel so heavy?

"Tata?" she called to her parents' bunk across the room. "Wake up, Tata. Mama?"

"Hmm?" her father mumbled, and turned on his other side.

"Go back to sleep, Frania," said Mama, her eyes still closed.

"I think we're snowed in," said Frania. She wasn't whispering anymore, and her words roused the others.

"What? Snowed in?" Everyone began to stir.

Kozachka slid down to the floor. Barefoot, she walked over to the window, not even shivering from the cold. "We're snowed in, that's for sure," she said, her voice surprisingly calm.

"Dear God, what's going to happen to us? What are we going to do?"

"Have to dig ourselves out," said the widow.

"Dig ourselves out? How?"

"We'll all suffocate."

"I don't want to die!" cried out Jozia.

"Mama, Mama, I'm scared," Helcia sobbed.

"Little ones, don't cry. We'll be all right," said Kozachka. "This isn't the first time I've had to dig myself out."

A heavy silence fell over the people in the shack, and now they could hear the heifers mooing in the barn.

"Tell us what to do, good widow," said Tata.

"You grownups and Sasha, get up and get dressed first. And you girls, stay up in bed and save your breath."

The first thing they did was push the door open with the weight of their bodies. A thick, white wall stared back at them.

"What next?" All eyes looked questioningly to Kozachka. They could hear the heifers complaining louder now.

"Next, we start cutting steps going upward, using our hands and the shovel that stands in the corner."

"And then...?" they asked.

"We'll climb up and out of the snow. Then we'll shovel the snow away from the doors and windows."

"Mooo..." replied the heifers.

They dug and cut—one, two, three steps—but saw no sign of breaking through. No air came in, and the atmosphere inside was lead heavy. Coughing and heaving, those who labored were collapsing, one by one. First, Frania's mother sank down to the floor. She sat leaning against the wall, gasping and pressing her hands to her chest. Next to give up was

Andrzej, and then Sasha. Frania, Tata, and Kozachka kept working on the fourth step. But the lack of air overcame the widow, and then the older man, too. One after another, they both slid down the steps like raggedy puppets and lay on the floor.

Only Frania remained. Somehow, she finished the last step and glanced up. Dear Lord, there was still that white stuff blocking the fresh air from coming in. She sat down and brought her head to her chest. She stopped moving, but still she held onto the shovel as if it were a magic thing. She heard herself whistling as she tried to breathe. There was no oxygen left for her to breathe; she knew it. She had no idea that it would be so painful to suffocate. Her chest seemed to be expanding, while her lungs were shrinking, shrinking. Something in her chest was burning like a dry fire. She closed her eyes and prayed a soundless prayer, thinking she was about to die. *God, forgive my sins.* According to her religion, she had sinned when doubting the teaching of her church, when swearing at someone, and, most of all, when getting angry with Heaven for all the hardships she had endured while in exile.

Sweet Jesus, please help me, and all of us, to enter into your Father's kingdom. She opened her eyes, raised her head and gazed, one more time, to where the snow steps ended. It was as white as a bone bleached by the sun.

"Mama!" She heard Jozia cry out and make choking sounds.

Suddenly, Frania revived. She wasn't ready to die, not yet. It wasn't written in the heavens that she was to pass away today, not this way. No! It wasn't their time to go either, she knew. She tried her arms, and they moved. Moaning, she lifted the shovel, its wooden end facing up.

Poke, poke, poke. She poked a small hole in the snow and threads of air began to slip in. Poke, poke, poke. She enlarged the opening. A stream of air poured in. She inhaled it, drank it, and swallowed it. It drifted down the steps and filled up the shelter, whose dwellers slowly came to life.

That day, the men made a path to the haystacks and carried feed to the barn. They also brought in pails of snow for the heifers to satisfy their thirst. After all the chores were done, Frania climbed up into her bunk to rest. Mama was making supper, very late in the evening.

The recent experience left Frania badly frightened and made her weak. It was so easy for death to sneak up on her and her people here in the steppe, she realized. Heavy snowfalls were dangerous, but so was fire, and what if the shack started to burn at night? No one would survive the flames. Even if they managed to escape, they would freeze in no time.

Frania couldn't stop her heart from racing, making it impossible for her to doze off. Her mind needed to escape her miserable reality, so she fled from it by sending her thoughts far away into happier times.

Spring and summer was lovely in Poland. In May, lilacs bloomed, wafting a perfumy scent into the air in her parents' gardens. Crops grew and ripened in the hot sun. Harvesting was exhausting, but joyful, when neighbors and friends came to help. They all worked, sang, and chattered together. In the evening, when she managed to sneak out of the house, she went dancing with Julek. She teased him so, but why, when she really cared about him? Was it because she had loved Andrzej, a charmer and gentleman who held her in his arms by the river in early summer and married her in the fall? And Andrzej—why had he changed so drastically?

"Supper is ready." Mama's voice cut in on Frania's deep thinking.

"Coming," she called down. Now she was relaxed and ready to eat.

Sometimes, out of boredom, Frania talked to Sasha, who had jet-black hair and dark eyes, like Julek's. Where was her beloved now? Ivan B. had sent him out on the steppe with another herd of heifers and his own group of helpers.

"Your little sisters are asleep already," Sasha said, one snowy evening after supper. He and Frania sat by the fireplace on the old beaten rug his mother had placed on the floor.

"I guess they are, aren't they?" she said.

"I like to hear them pray."

Frania shrugged her shoulders and stared into the flames that seemed to devour the dried-out manure much too fast. All the others were getting ready for bed, but not Sasha.

"Tell me in Russian, Frania, what they say in Polish," he said, glancing at her, a puppy-like adoration on his round face.

"What for?"

"I want to know what the words mean."

"Let me see," she said, hugging her knees and rocking herself slightly. "My sisters asked God to give them some bread."

"I bet you think I don't know about God."

"And what do you know, Sasha?"

"When I was a child, my grandma told me about the holy things. She said that way up there," he glanced up, "there's a place called…"

"Heaven," Frania said.

He nodded. "This Heaven is always warm and full of white bread, candies, and sweet cakes."

"Very interesting."

"A white-bearded Lord lives up there with the angels."

"That's what my church taught me to believe."

"God is good and wears expensive clothes, according to my grandma," Sasha went on.

"I see." Frania smiled at the boy.

"One day, I told my first grade teacher about what Grandma was saying to me."

"And she got very angry with you, didn't she?"

"How do you know?"

"I guessed."

"My teacher forbade me to listen to the old people's tales. She said there was no Heaven and no God, only Stalin, who took care of us, his people. I listened to her as she yelled and pounded the top of her desk, not knowing why she was making such a fuss. I was confused, and I wondered, too, why I was always cold and hungry, when I had such a great leader for a father. But she set me straight the next day."

"Next day?" Frania turned and looked at Sasha with interest.

"She took our whole class into a room where there was a stage and benches."

"And?"

"Then she told me to stand up and walk right up to the middle of the stage. And I did. She gave me and everyone a long lecture on God, Heaven, and Stalin. After she was done talking, she turned to me and said, 'Sasha, close your eyes and pray to your grandma's God.'"

"She told you to ask God for candies," Frania said knowingly.

Sasha nodded. "Yes, she did that."

"What did you do?"

"I prayed very, very hard, but nothing happened. I felt like crying, because I wanted Grandma to be right."

"Your teacher asked you then to pray to Stalin, didn't she?"

"Yes, she did that. Frania, you're not only pretty, but smart, too."

"Did you pray?"

Sasha nodded, looking down at the floor.

"What happened next?"

"This time, when I opened my eyes, dozens and dozens of sweets wrapped in red shiny paper started to fall on the stage from the ceiling."

"That figures. Your teacher tricked you."

A pause. Frania kept looking into the fire. Sasha glanced at Frania.

"And what do you believe in now, Sasha?" Frania said. She didn't turn to look at him.

"I...I am not sure," he said in a low voice, as if he were afraid the walls had ears and could hear him.

Chapter Fourteen

BEFORE SPRING CAME TO THE HILL, THE HAYSTACKS WERE GONE, AND there was no feed left for the heifers. Then the Kazakhs' authority took the cattle away from their caretakers, who returned to Narod.

Kozachka and her son went back to live with her sister. Frania and her group sheltered once again in the old school, where they slept on the floor. Luckily, they still had their quilts stuffed with goose feathers to keep them warm at night. For several weeks, the Poles couldn't find any work at the settlement, and they lived only by exchanging what was left of their belongings with the Kazakhs.

Finally, the last of the snow melted and ploughing was up for grabs. This chore was hard work even for a strong, healthy man, much less for women who were near starvation. This year, the ploughs were more rusted and dull than before, and they were pulled by gaunt bulls and old cows and camels, but no horses.

All the adults in Frania's family took to the fields. Their only choice was to plough for a bowl of oat soup daily and a glass of milk, or starve to death. This time, they worked in the field closest to Narod, so someone could walk back to the schoolhouse every evening because their food had to be shared with Jozia and Helcia. Workers in farther fields slept at night in temporary shacks.

The sky was clear and the sun warm, but ploughing was rough and guzzled Frania's strength. Her hands were soon blistered and bleeding, and the scraggly-looking bull was weak. The exhausted beast kept falling to its knees and, each time it did that, it overturned the plough, knocking Frania to her knees, too.

It was still early in the morning when the bull fell for the hundredth or thousandth time, bringing her down with him.

"Not again," said Frania, tears filling her eyes as she slowly rose from the ground.

The poor creature groaned like an old man.

She staggered over to its head and, leaning over, whispered, "Please get up."

The bull looked at her with sad, wet eyes, but didn't move.

"I wish I could let you rest," she said.

She heard someone laughing and looked to her left. It was her neighbor, ploughing in the next plot. He was a young sturdy Kazakh, a newcomer to the settlement. "Why don't you kiss him, Frania? Maybe then he would get up for you." He threw his head back and laughed some more.

She ignored him and said to the bull in a soft voice, "Up, up, up, if you don't want that Kazakh to burn your side with a lit torch again. Please get up! Do it for me."

With effort, the bull rose.

Frania went back to ploughing. It seemed she had been ploughing forever. Behind her plough, crows feasted on fat worms picked from the freshly overturned soil, and she envied the winged creatures for having so much to eat without having to work, the way she did.

"Hey, Frania, how about meeting me in the dark somewhere tonight?" the same Kazakh called out to her across the field, laughing brazenly.

She heard him loud and clear, but didn't even glance his way. The others heard him, too, she knew, including Andrzej. Why didn't he try to stop the awful man from pestering her so? Julek would have stopped him somehow, she was certain of that. But he wasn't back at Narod this year, and she missed him so much, it hurt. Why did the Kazakh abuse her so? Wasn't her life harsh enough without him adding to her suffering?

"I will get you in my bed soon," he said, and laughed again.

Tears came to her eyes. "I'd rather die than be touched by him," she whispered to the plough, which was tipping to one side. She braced herself and held to it with all her might to stop it from overturning this time. "Julek. I wish you were here." Thoughts of her beloved comforted her.

In the early summer of the second year at Narod, Andrzej came down with a strange illness. He didn't run a high fever, but complained of bad headaches, and sometimes he talked out of his head. Finally, he slipped into his own world and never rose from his bed again.

At the time, Frania had to share her meals with him, but most of the time he refused to eat. "How do you feel today?" she would ask him every morning, just before rising.

Usually, he would look up at her with glazed eyes and say nothing. Other mornings, tears escaping from under his eyelids, he would whisper, "I'm very weak."

"You have to eat more," she would say.

"I can't."

One late afternoon, she was returning to the shelter from work when she heard someone calling her name. "Coming," she answered. She carried soup in a bowl and two slices of bread.

"Frania. Frania. Frania!"

She walked across the floor to where Andrzej lay on their quilts. "I have something for us to eat," she said, placing the bowl and the bread by his head.

His body shook. "I'm not hungry."

She knelt down by his side, and only now noticed that his eyes were clear. "Andrzej, you're better."

"No," he said in a hoarse voice, and coughed.

"Did you catch cold?"

He shook his head. "Please, Frania, I want to talk," he said.

"No, not now. It's time to eat, not talk," she said, spooning soup for him. "Eat, Andrzej, eat."

He gently pushed the spoon away. "We have to talk."

Her heart skipped a beat in sudden fear. She looked at him again, but carefully. He was so thin and pale, and his cheeks were so hollow. Why hadn't she seen this before? He was almost a skeleton.

"Why don't you want to eat, Andrzej?" she said, her hand on his forehead. "You have no fever."

"It's time for me," he whispered, breathing with difficulty.

"Time?" she said.

"I'm sorry."

"Sorry for what?"

"For not being the man you deserve."

"Stop talking like that, my husband." She reached for his hand.

"I…I could have tried harder to cope with the hardships."

"You are what you are, and there's nothing you can do about it, dear," she said, squeezing his hand.

"I could have been more help to you."

"We are all human; none of us is perfect," she said with a sad smile.

He coughed again, and then took a deep breath. "Marry him, Frania," he said.

"What?"

"After I'm gone. Marry Julek, because he's the right man for you."

"Andrzej!" she said. So he knew. He knew about her affair—not fulfilled, but an affair of the heart, just the same—and he had never said anything about it. Dear God in Heaven, have mercy on her sinful soul.

Suddenly, his face contorted, and he began to gasp for breath. She grabbed his other hand and held them both in hers, knowing that he was dying.

The next fall, Frania's father was transported back to the hill, this time with only seventy-five heifers. His family went with him again, along with two of their roommates, Ala and Kazia, sisters and old maids who were teachers from Poland.

They came to the steppe with their cattle early enough to enjoy two weeks of warmth. Due to more rainfall this year, there was more grass for the heifers to graze on before the first snowfall. A good harvest had supplied Narod with more grain, potatoes, and other crops, so Frania and her dear ones were given double the food rations they had received the previous fall. Ivan B. gave Tata a horse as means of transportation. Sitting on the animal's back, the older man watched the heifers carefully, so as not to lose any to wolves.

With the cattle feeding themselves and drinking from the creek, there was less work in the barn, and the four women had more time to prepare their shelter for the coming winter. They re-sealed new holes that had appeared in the walls, painted the walls with a chalky material found in the ground nearby, and put a fresh layer of mud and manure on the floor.

"Wow! This looks beautiful," exclaimed Frania, admiring the picture of Matka Boska Chestochowska she had just hung on the wall above her bunk.

"Yes," agreed Kazia, as she mended her old, torn blouse at the table. "I like the way Holy Mary's eyes shine when the sunlight comes through the window."

"And the golden frame glows like a flame," said Frania, smiling.

"And how about that blue throw rug I put in front of the stove this morning?" said Kazia. "Doesn't it look nice?"

"The rug adds color to our gray dwelling, but I wish we had a curtain to hang in our window."

Ala, who was going through her bundle in a corner of the shelter, evidently had been listening, for she called out, "Hey, Frania and Kazia. I have something for you."

"What?"

"How about this orange beach towel?" she said, spreading the cloth for Frania and Ala to see.

"A towel?" asked Kazia.

"You think it's not good enough for this castle, my sister?"

"Don't be sarcastic," said Kazia.

"Any bright cloth will do," Frania said. She walked over to Ala and took the towel from her. "I will do the hanging, if it's all right with you two sisters."

"Nice weather we're still having," said Mama to Frania one noon, while they both laundered their clothes in the creek.

"I hate winter," pouted Frania, glancing up at the sky, where the sun grew paler each day, as it seemed to recede deep into space.

"No one likes to be cold," said Mama, and she sighed deeply. She was soaking her pile of laundry in the shallow part of the creek, between a big rock and a bush that the water licked at constantly.

Frania sat silent for a while, wringing out one of her pillowcases. She twisted and pulled, twisted and pulled, grinding her teeth as if the cloth were the neck of the old witch, Winter.

"Why do good times end so quickly?" she said, standing up. She walked over to the thickest bush and spread the case over it to dry. "Why do innocent men die or...or go away?"

"My sweet Frania," sang out Mama. With tears in her eyes, she looked at her daughter. "Don't grieve too much over Andrzej."

"I...I can't help but feel sad," she whispered, thinking first of Henio, and then of Julek. She did not think of her dead husband. Julek and his sister, Basia, hadn't come back to Narod for the spring or summer.

"Hey, you're still young and can remarry."

"Remarry? Heck, no. I will not have another husband or give birth to anyone's child in Russia."

Mama looked away and said, "Russia is a terrible place to be living in, especially during the war. We both know there's nothing more painful for a mother than to watch her children suffer. And...and to be separated from her daughters, it's just awful on a woman."

"You're thinking of Marysia and Aniela, aren't you, Mama?"

"Yes, how can I not?" A flood of tears suddenly streamed down her cheeks.

"Now, dear Mama, don't cry. For all we know, they both may already be out of Russia and living a good life in Iran." Frania embraced the older woman.

"If only I knew," Mama cried. "I would sleep better at night."

Winter fell upon the steppe quite without warning. It swooped down like a giant bird, its heavy wings stretched out from horizon to horizon. Those wings became clouds heavier yet, for they were pregnant with snow. Temperatures fell way below zero and stayed down for days. Because of the bad weather, no one came visiting the hill for weeks on end. No visitors from Narod, no food for people in the shelter.

Too soon, dreary monotony overwhelmed Frania. Day after day, she repeated the same work in the barn, or helped her women roommates with chores in the shelter. Staying in the overcrowded place was hardest, because she grew weary of her parents' sullen faces. Tata and Mama hardly spoke to anyone, and Jozia and Helcia stopped giggling behind the stove. Their eyes had begun to look old, like their mother's.

In the middle of the unfriendly season, Frania's mother came down with pneumonia. She lay in her bed, running a high fever and moaning. Now, cooking and caring for her sisters and her father fell on Frania's shoulders, in addition to her work in the barn. Somehow, she didn't mind it, because being busy to the point of near collapse kept her from thinking about herself. She and Tata did all they could to keep the sick woman warm and comfortable. But was it enough?

Monday was gray, cold, and blustery. It snowed all night and continued snowing into the late morning. More snow meant bad roads, and this meant another day without a fresh supply of provisions for the caretakers.

Just before break of dawn, Frania dreamed she was watching her mother drowning in the creek. The woman screamed as she slid out of sight down a hole in the ice. First, she went in to her waist, and then to her chin. When her head disappeared from Frania's sight and only her arms stuck up in the air, Frania tried, for the hundredth time, to reach for her mother, but she could not move. It was as if her body had turned to stone.

Finally, she mumbled, "Mama, Mama, Mama," and woke up. Thank God, it was only a nightmare. Her mother was still breathing in her bunk. Her breath was raspy and whistling, but as long as Mama was inhaling air, there was still hope for her to get well.

There was a light in the shelter, and it came from the stove. Frania listened to its merry crackling and sniffed a trace of smoke in the air. Then she got up.

"Good day, Tata," she said, standing in her nightgown above the older man, who sat crossed-legged on the rug in front of the open oven door. She spoke softly, so as not to wake the others still in their bunks, some of them snoring, some mumbling in their sleep.

"Frania," he said, glancing up at her and offering her a corner of the blanket that covered his shoulders. "Did I wake you?"

"No, I woke on my own." She tried to smile, but managed only to bring a wry expression to her face. She didn't feel like telling him about her dream.

"Sit down by me and cover yourself," he said. "You're shivering."

Frania knelt on the rug and wrapped herself with a corner of his blanket. "I'm glad you made the fire already," she whispered, feeling luxurious warmth on her face.

"I want your mother to be warm," he said.

"Do you think she's getting any better?"

He shook his head and stared into the heat that spilled out of the oven. The flames were sticking out their tongues at the two people sitting there.

The wind wailed outside, and Tata winced. "That damn blizzard," he muttered, and spat into the fire. "All we need now is to be snowed in, the way we were last year."

"God forbid that should happen again," Frania said, and pulled the blanket tighter. She could hear snoring coming from Ala's and Kazia's bunk. "I'm glad they can sleep," she said, and sighed.

"Why shouldn't they? They have no one else to worry about but themselves."

Frania's mother coughed.

"I think she's worse today than yesterday, Tata." Renewed fear for her mother's life scratched at the wall of Frania's heart. She turned to look at her father, who stared back at her. They said nothing, but knew what each other thought.

"I will go," he said, after a pause.

"Are you sure you want to, Tata?"

"I have no choice."

"But what if you get lost on the way in this blizzard?"

"I'll be careful," he said, and got up, letting his side of the blanket fall to the floor. Frania gathered it about her. From the barn came the sound of heifers mooing, but they both ignored it.

Mama coughed again.

"You get dressed for the road, Tata, and I'll warm up water for Mama's cough," said Frania, flinging the blanket to one side.

He nodded.

She rose, filled the old pot, blackened by smoke, from a pail of water, and put it on the stove to heat, while Tata bundled up for the cold weather.

"Take care of her," he said, his hand on the doorknob.

"I will," she said. "God bless you, Tata, and good luck." She came closer and kissed him a loud smack on the cheek.

"Thank you."

Mama's cough grew more insistent.

"Have to hurry," he said, but still lingered.

"What do you want us to do with the heifers?" Frania asked.

"Nothing. Just let them be."

"But they haven't eaten since yesterday morning."

"We haven't put anything in our mouths, either. If you want, fetch some snow in pails for them, to satisfy their thirst. Have Kazia and Ala help you."

She nodded.

Several minutes later, Frania was able to stop her mother's hacking by making her drink warm water. But then she wanted to stop the heifers from mooing, too. She waited for Ala and Kazia to get up, and then said, "We have to feed the poor creatures."

"But it's so bad outside, we can't let them out. Without your father watching over them, wolves may eat half of them."

"We'll keep them in and bring hay to them."

"You want us to carry hay all the way from the haystacks?"

"We have to."

"We're not going out in the storm," cried out Kazia.

"No way!" said Ala.

"All right, then. I'll go by myself."

Kazia and Ala looked at each other, and then they both looked at Frania. "We'll go with you," they said.

Outside, the three women struggled to get to the haystacks. Panting, they pushed wheelbarrows in front of them and ploughed their way forward, pausing often to rest. By now, it had stopped snowing, but still the steppe looked like the inside of a gigantic grain mill. Under the strong winds, the white stuff floated in the freezing air, and snowdrifts shifted from one place to another. From time to time, handfuls of snowflakes lashed at the women's faces, settling on their eyebrows and eyelashes, blinding their vision.

The chores exhausted Frania, but she labored long past feeling numb, and thought the whole time of her father traveling toward Narod. What if he strayed away from the track or got stuck in a snowbank and froze to death? What if wolves attacked him while riding on his horse? Maybe she should have stopped him from going. She also thought of her mother wasting away with a fever and regretted having to leave her with only Jozia and Helcia to care for her.

"Holy Father, who art in Heaven…" she prayed, but before she had finished, Mother Nature eased up on her blowing and lashing of the land. In the clear air, the haystacks seemed closer, the sky friendlier, the barn promised some warmth, and the shack offered rest after their work was done. And at the end of the day, there might be supper for everyone, if Tata returned with food and medicine for Mama.

Semi-darkness pulled down its veil over the shack window. The women inside waited for Frania's father to return from Narod. Her mother fought harder for each breath.

Frania waited quietly, her ears attuned to every small sound. When something snapped in the walls or fell to the floor, she jumped. Finally, she thought she heard a horse's footfall and then a man's steps coming closer and closer to the door.

"Tata, you came back!" Frania cried out joyfully, so happy to see him.

"Tata, Tata," her little sisters sang out, running to embrace him.

"Yes, you came back," Frania repeated.

"Didn't you think I would?" he said, but didn't wait for her to answer. He walked over to the table and placed a bundle there.

The old maids pounced upon it.

"Grain!" called out Ala, peeking into one sack. "At least a pailful!"

"And potatoes," said Kazia, opening another sack. "Onions, too!"

The little girls smiled.

But Frania came close to her father and stood face to face with him. "Did you bring any medicine?"

He shook his head.

"Did you ask Ivan B. for help for Mother?"

"Yes, I asked for a doctor and medicine, but he told me he had no such care to offer his own people during the war, much less for us foreigners."

"Dear God," moaned Frania. "What will to happen to her?"

Her father shrugged. He had done all he could.

Two days later, Mama died.

Chapter Fifteen

THE FOLLOWING SPRING SAW FRANIA AND HER FAMILY BACK AT NAROD, but the family was now reduced in size by two persons. The adult survivors went back to ploughing, while Jozia and Helcia sheltered once again in the schoolhouse.

To Frania, the hovel looked even drearier than before, and ploughing was backbreaking work this year, the pestering Kazakh even more abusive now. He did all he could to make her cry silent, dry tears.

One warm evening, she stepped out for fresh air a little after sunset and found him waiting for her in the graying outdoors.

"What? What are you doing here?" she asked, startled by the sudden sight of him. He looked taller than in the field and much stronger.

"Don't you know, my pretty blue-eyed Polish girl?" he said, and grinned like a cat waiting to pounce on a mouse.

"Leave me alone," she said hoarsely, backing away. Her eyes didn't leave him for a moment; he reminded her of a snake about to strike.

"No, I won't." He laughed his horrid laugh, and she winced at the sound. "I won't leave until I get what I came for," he said, and bounded toward her. He grabbed her hands and held them tight, much too tight.

"Please, Comrade, let go of me," she said in a thin voice. She felt his fingernails dig into her skin.

He pulled her roughly to him. "Now, give me a kiss." He wasn't smiling anymore.

"Please don't," she said, turning her face away from his lips.

He pulled her closer yet and held her so tight that it hurt. She bit her lips and stopped breathing, because his mouth was clammy and smelled like rotten eggs.

"Help!" she cried out, but only once.

"Shut up," he hissed, and clasped his hand over her mouth. With his other hand, he brought her arm backward, twisted it, and then turned her body so she faced away from him. "Now, we are walking to the back of the schoolhouse," he said, pushing her with him, "and you'd better behave, or I'll break your arm as easily as if it were a twig."

She twisted, wiggled, kicked back at him with her heels. Her free hand pulled at his hand that clamped her mouth shut, but she couldn't stop him from pushing her deeper into the back yard, where the evening's blue shadows were turning gray.

Saint Teresa, help me, she prayed silently, but nothing happened. Out of desperation, she scratched the back of his hand with her nails. He swore, his hand fell away from her mouth, and she screamed.

"Help! Help! Someone help me!" Her voice was too thin and not as loud as she wanted it to be, but still it rang out clearly in the night air.

Did no one hear her?

The Kazakh swore harder than before, licked blood from his hand, and then silenced her again. "I ought to bash your teeth in," he growled, and pulled harder on her arm.

She moaned in pain, and her head bent backward as if to meet the pain in her arm. Then she scratched him one more time and kicked with all her might, but this only made him push her faster and deeper into a dark corner of the yard. Just when she was sure her arm was about to break, for he kept pulling it upward, she heard footsteps on the ground behind her, coming closer and closer. Was someone rushing to save her? Was it Julek? No, he wasn't at Narod this year, either.

What happened next, happened quickly. Quite suddenly, the Kazakh released her, and she slumped to the ground like a puppet whose strings had been cut. She sat where she fell, staring up at not one, but two figures, towering over her. The figures rocked and swayed, cursing and breathing hard, as they wrestled with one another.

Frania closed her eyes in fright and shielded her ears with her hands against the terrifying sounds the two men made while trying to overpower each other. She stayed motionless for what seemed like years.

Then she sensed something different in the air. She uncovered her ears and heard one man trying to catch his breath. She dared to open her eyes. In the darkness, a figure darker than the evening sky stood over her. Who was it? Who had won the fight? Oh, God, don't let it be the Kazakh.

Her heart pounding, she dared to say, "Tata, is that you?"

"It's me, Frania," he said, and helped her up. Then he embraced her for the first time in her life.

"Thank you," she whispered, tears rolling down her face. "Thank you for stopping him." She pressed her cheek to his chest.

"He wanted to rape you, didn't he?"

"Yes," she mumbled, embarrassed now, humiliated and feeling guilty.

But why should she feel guilty?

At the time of Frania's youth, the woman was always at fault when a man committed a sexual crime, and she knew her father shared that popular belief. He had warned her, many times, not to wiggle her hips when she walked in the field, not to wear thin blouses with low necklines, and told her to be careful when the wind blew so her knees wouldn't be exposed to the Kazakhs' eyes.

"I...I am sorry," she whispered, crying softly into her father's shirt, and waited for him to scold her.

His answer surprised Frania. "You have nothing to be sorry for, my daughter."

The next morning, two men from the secret police came to the schoolhouse and took Frania's father for questioning. That same day, without even letting him say one word in self-defense, they locked him in the local jail for beating the Kazakh. For weeks, they kept him in a hut with cracked glass in its tiny window, and furnished with a single bunk covered by a dirty, worn-out blanket, a pail serving as his toilet.

Frania never worked so hard ploughing, sowing, and weeding the rows of new crops that grew in the hot sun. She was responsible for supplying the soup she shared with Jozia and Helcia. Their care now fell solely upon her. One more time, death from starvation lurked around the corner. Frania could feel its cold breath on her back. In order not to let it come too close to what was left of her family, Frania kept exchanging more and more of her belongings, and her family's, too, for whatever food she could get.

When she finally realized that, if she wasn't careful, she could lose all her belongings and theirs, she went to visit Ivan B.

"Comrade, let my father go free," she asked the boss. "I can't manage without him anymore."

"You're asking the impossible, young woman."

"Why is it impossible to release an innocent man?" she said.

"Your father is a criminal."

"No, he isn't!"

"He almost killed one of my men."

"Father beat that man only to protect me, and you know it, Comrade."

"What happened that evening was unfortunate. As you know, I had that man sent away after the incident, but a crime is a crime."

"You're unfair and cruel, Comrade. Don't you know that my little sisters might die of starvation?"

He looked at her with his small, dark eyes and, after a pause, said, "They won't die, for they still have you."

"But I'm the only one working, and what I get is not even enough for me."

"Cheer up, woman. Soon we'll have harvest."

"Please, Comrade, give me at least an extra bowl of soup a day for my sisters."

He shook his head again and said, "Your sisters do not work. Haven't you heard our favorite saying?"

"Which one?"

"In Russia, the one who does not work, does not eat."

"This applies to children, too?"

"No. But your sisters are not Kazakh little girls," he said, and waved her away.

Plodding back to the shelter in the early morning, she was so angry and disappointed that she made up her mind not to go to the field. What was the use of trying to survive in this hellish place or help her sisters to survive? Nothing was going right. Nothing good was coming her way. She still had about a cupful of grain left under her pillow, and she would make soup in the late afternoon. But what about tomorrow and all the tomorrows after that? Tata looked so depressed, so dispirited. He reminded her of an eagle she had found once in a field back home. Its wing was broken, and it couldn't fly anymore. It looked at her with sad eyes before it died, just the way Tata had looked at her the day before.

"Mama," she whispered, glancing up at the sky, "if your soul exists in Heaven, and you can look down and see me, please help your family here on earth, in awful Kazakhstan." Lately, she had begun to pray to her dead parent instead of God.

"Frania, Frania," a voice called out to her. She halted on the road at the edge of the village and looked to her left. She smiled, seeing Kozachka standing on the doorstep of the hut she shared with her sister.

"You're not working today?" asked the widow.

"No." Frania shook her head and looked down. "And you?"

"I have the day off. Come in and visit me, my friend," Kozachka said.

Frania had never been inside a Kazakh dwelling before. She always did her exchanging outside, in front of a hut or on the road.

"Thank you. I will come in," she said, her voice eager.

She looked about the one-room home, spacious and furnished with two sets of double bunks leaning against the walls. In the middle of the wooden floor stood a square table embraced on two sides by low benches. In a corner near the entrance stood a built-in stove, a duplicate of the one in the shack underneath the hill, but not as old or as shabby. Next to the stove, there were wall shelves filled with wooden tableware and iron pots. Red curtains shaded two small windows in the hut. Throw rugs scattered all over the floor made a cheery-looking room. To Frania, Kozachka's home looked like Paradise.

"Beautiful—a charming room!" she said.

"Thank you," said Kozachka, and she smiled.

"Dear God, you should see the hole my sisters and I live in."

"I know. Sasha told me. He used to visit you often at one time," said Kozachka, staring at Frania with a strange light in her eyes.

"Please, my friend, don't look at me like that. I don't need your pity," said Frania.

"I…I have just come up with an idea."

"Idea?"

"Would you and your sisters like to move in with me?"

"What? We would love to, but where is your sister?"

"You don't know?"

"Know what?"

"She died, and we buried her just yesterday."

"I'm sorry."

"Don't be. She suffered so because of cancer."

"And Sasha? Where is he now? I haven't seen him in the field yet this year."

"He's working in the kitchen this spring," said Kozachka, pride in her voice.

"That's wonderful!" exclaimed Frania, knowing that families of cooks ate well, almost as well as Ivan's.

"So what do you say to my proposition?"

"Yes, yes, and yes again! But what if Ivan will not permit this?"

Kozachka winked at Frania. "Where there is a will, there is a way."

Frania and her sisters didn't move in with Kozachka until the following week, because of difficulty with Ivan B. At first, he wouldn't even hear of such a thing as a foreigner living with a Kazakh family. He had planned to place a young widow and her small daughter with Kozachka. But his pretty wife and his sisters pressured him so, he finally gave in.

The day of her dwelling relocation, Frania cried with joy. Her sisters' eyes shone like the forget-me-nots that dotted the meadow and basked in the sun. Frania and her sisters were happy. They would have been happier still, if their father had been with them.

Frania took over the upper bunk on the left side of the room, while the girls settled in the lower one. The bunks had once belonged to Kozachka's sister and her son, who had left long ago for the front lines. He died defending Moscow from the Nazis, and now the sister was dead, too. But life went on.

The new occupants' belongings fit just right under their bunks, including Frania's trunk. All she had left was her holy oil painting, a cracked jewelry box, a summer suit of Henio's, a set of Andrzej's fine linen handkerchiefs, and her mother's rosary made of crystal beads.

This spring, Frania, Jozia, and Helcia not only slept in comfortable beds, but also ate well. Soon, all three of them reached a normal weight and began to look pretty again. Frania performed her work more quickly in the field and pleased her overseer, who was a woman. Because of that, she gave Frania a double portion of bread each day and an additional two glasses of milk for her sisters. In addition to this, Sasha was bringing extra soups and bread for them on the sly.

One time, under the shadows of evening, he brought a sack of grain and presented it to Frania.

"Thank you, Sasha," she whispered, and placed a loud kiss on his cheek, close to his lips.

"You're welcome, Frania," he said, smiling happily. At that time, he had a girlfriend, pretty Marusia with smiling eyes, yet still he was pleased with every little word or gesture Frania made on his behalf.

The same evening, still shielded by semi-darkness, Frania sneaked out and walked over to the schoolhouse. She carried with her a large portion of the grain Sasha had given her.

In the dim light coming from the stove, she was barely recognizable to her former roommates. "Good evening my friends," she said.

"Hmm? Is that you, Frania?"

"What are you doing here?"

"Did they throw you out of Kozachka's house already?"

Frania shook her head and smiled in the swaying light. "I brought you all something."

"What?"

"Hope it's something to eat, for I don't remember when I have eaten last," said Ala, raising herself up on one elbow from where she lay on the floor.

Almost blindly, Frania walked over to the two stones that her mother and she had used and began crushing the grain. They all surrounded her and watched.

When she was done, she said to them, "I need a large pot or kettle."

"I have this one," said Kazia, lifting a pot above her head. It was black from cooking on the smoky fires.

Frania shook her head. "That's not big enough."

"How about mine?"

"I want a bigger one yet."

"This is my kettle," said another woman.

"That's it. This is perfect," cried out Frania, smiling. "Wash it, fill it with water, and then put it on the fire."

Soon, the soup was boiling on the stove, giving off an aroma that tickled the insides of their hungry stomachs. At this moment, nothing existed in the world for the Poles in the shelter but the coming meal that Frania was stirring with a wooden spoon. Grain soup, grain soup, soup, soup, soup. How soon was it going to be ready? They drooled and swallowed hard.

"Your supper is ready," finally sang out Frania. "Come close, everyone, and eat." The words rang out like crystal bells in the air and brought smiles to otherwise grim faces.

"Now make a line and step to the stove, one by one. I don't want to see any pushing or shoving."

Heads nodded in agreement, tongues licked lips eagerly, and throats gulped down saliva.

That night no one in the schoolhouse went to sleep without eating.

The next day, early in the morning and before leaving for the fields, Frania went to visit her father. She had done that every day since regaining her strength enough to walk about. "I brought you the cheese sandwiches you like so much," she said, pushing his breakfast through a hole in the glass window.

"Good, and thank you." In no time, he had devoured his food the way Frania's dog, Aza, used to eat her meals at the end of each day in Poland.

It broke Frania's heart to see her father withering away in the cell. He was a proud man, and being locked in a cage like an animal humiliated him more than the deportation itself. As the Chinese would say, his loss of face was causing him to lose the will to live.

The following week, he welcomed Frania with these words: "Frania, I'm not a killer. Why do they treat me as if I were?"

"Oh, Tata!" She swallowed her tears. "You know Communists. They are not always fair, even with their own kind." She glanced up at his haggard face and whispered, "I...I am sorry."

"Sorry for what?"

"It's because of me that you are here now."

"Stop that, my oldest child! I don't want you to feel guilty for something that was not your fault. I want you to remember that."

"Remember? Where are you going, Tata?"

"Nowhere, except maybe down into the ground."

"No, Tata! You stay alive, do you hear?" Now she scolded him. "Your daughters need you very much."

"Need me, huh? What can I do for any of you from inside these ugly walls?"

"They'll let you out. They have to," Frania said and went away. She could no longer stand looking at the pain spilling out of his eyes like hot, black lava.

The spring of 1944 was kind to Frania and her sisters. For the first time since they had come to Narod, Jozia and Helcia enjoyed picking flowers in the steppe. Only now, free at last of horrid hunger, were the girls able to admire what Nature had wrought in their midst: so many tulips, a whole carpet of them. Yellow, yellow, yellow.

This time, Frania paid more attention to the world's politics, especially the progression of WWII. So far, she knew just a little—that the Red Army had pushed the Nazis out of their country and that, by the end of 1943, it was approaching the Polish border. She wasn't happy about that, remembering how, in the early fall of 1939, Russians came from the east, not to save her country from Nazis, but to invade it.

Narodowians had one radio installed in such a way that it could blast the daily news onto the streets of the settlement. Mostly, the broadcasts bragged about how Batushka Stalin (Daddy), the hero and only savior of the world, was beating the Germans. Not a word was said about England and America fighting the enemy on other fronts. When, in February of 1943, the German Army retreated from Stalingrad, this historical fact was happily celebrated at Narod. Once or twice, the voice on the radio mentioned the Polish Army with its leader, Berling, fighting at the Soviets' side. Wanda Lewandowska's name came up, too. Frania guessed that these two persons were Polish Communists. Where was Anders' Army? Why wasn't it liberating Poland from the Nazis? Had the radio stuck to the truth, it would have told Frania that Anders and his soldiers—who fought on the British Army's side—captured Monte Cassino on May 18, 1944. It would have also announced that, when the Russians finally liberated Warsaw on January 17, 1945, the city lay in ruins because the Red Army didn't come in time to save it from Hitler's destruction.

Early one morning, Frania was ready for work. Jozia and Helcia were still sound asleep. Kozachka was getting breakfast, and Sasha stood in the doorway of their hut, saying goodbye to Frania.

"Take it easy in the field. Don't try to kill yourself harvesting."

"Goodbye, Sasha, and thank you for wanting to take care of my sisters while I'm away."

"You're welcome," he said, waving her off. "I like them. I'll visit your father in the jail now and then, too."

Frania smiled. "I appreciate your good heart, Sasha. God bless you." She threw him a kiss from a distance.

He caught it in the air with his fingers, brought it close to his lips, and gave his fingers a loud smack.

She turned around and quickly walked away, smiling. It felt good to finally have the luxury of being able to stay out in the field for days and nights. She was now to be one of the workers who lived in the fields among the crops throughout the whole hot season.

She and the others were to labor in the early morning, rest during the hot hours, and work again in the late afternoon. They were to rest and sleep in a temporary shelter, a hole dug in the ground and shaded by a thatched flat roof supported on four poles. Frania knew the floor of the shelter was covered with a thick layer of straw to sleep on. In one corner free of straw stood a stove for cooking meals, and next to it was a barrel of lukewarm water for drinking.

In the late fall, Ivan B. let Frania's father go free, and right away he sent him with heifers into the steppe. With him went Frania, her sisters, and the two old maids, Ala and Kazia.

Frania watched her father rise every morning and, when she saw how much effort it took him to do so, she began to worry about his health. For weeks, his legs dragging and his face sullen, he would dress in his outdoor clothes, eat whatever there was to eat in the shelter, and get up on his horse. He would then herd the heifers out to pasture and, later on, to the haystacks. He was weak and dispirited, yet he did his work throughout the fall and up to the middle of winter.

One blustery evening, they were all stuck, as usual, inside the hovel. Frania washed the wooden soup bowls—now badly cracked and chipped—after supper. As she did this chore, she listened to the wind wailing outside. Suddenly, she heard her father saying, "I think I'll go to bed."

She turned to look at him sitting in front of the fireplace. "Aren't you feeling well, Tata?" Usually, he was the last one to retire for the night.

He shrugged his shoulders.

"Your father had a hard day with the heifers," said Ala from across the room. She was washing her things in a washbowl underneath the window.

"Maybe I should have kept the animals in the barn today, but I felt sorry for them," he said, examining his worn-out shoes in the swaying firelight.

"You're a goodhearted man," said Kazia, getting ready for bed.

Frania put away the last bowl on a shelf fastened to the wall, and then went to stand by her father.

"I'm cold," he said, and lightly brushed Jozia aside in order to get closer to the burning manure. Jozia and Helcia sat near his feet.

"Hurry and get in bed," said Frania, helping him up.

"Yes, Frania, I'd better," he said, his teeth chattering against each other.

"I hope you aren't coming down with something bad."

"I told you, I'm just tired," he mumbled, and walked over to the blanket hanging in the corner, behind which he changed into his night-clothes.

After he had gotten up into his bunk, Frania covered him with an additional blanket she had taken off her own bunk. "Rest, Tata, rest. You'll be all right tomorrow."

But in the middle of the night he called out for a drink of water, for he was running a high fever.

While Tata stayed in bed, Frania, Ala, and Kazia did all the work. They prayed to God that he would get well before someone from Narod came checking on the young cattle. Too soon, as if to fulfill their worst fears, two Kazakhs came on one of the milder days. Right away, they discovered Father's illness. That day, they decided that another group of caretakers should replace him and his helpers for the rest of the season.

Chapter Sixteen

BACK TO THE OLD SCHOOLHOUSE WENT FRANIA WITH HER FAMILY AND their friends. Her sick father needed medical care, and her sisters looked at her as if they expected Frania to create miracles for them. What could she do to keep her family alive? She couldn't ask Kozachka for help because that situation had changed. Sasha had married a month before Frania returned to Narod. Now, not only his bride had moved in with him, but also her mother. What was unfortunate for everyone concerned was the fact that, for some reason, Sasha had lost his job in the kitchen. Now he was delivering heating fuel and water from the creek to the public buildings and to the upper crust of Narod.

Frania and her dear ones could find nothing to eat, and not much was left in the trunk to exchange for food. Were they destined now to starve to death?

One night, Frania dreamed of her mother, who appeared on the threshold of the shelter. "Mama!" exclaimed Frania, staring at the image across the room. "I'm so happy to see you."

The image said nothing, but stood there, staring at Frania. Tears flowed from her mother's eyes like silver raindrops. They rolled down the vision's cheeks and fell to the floor. The strange thing about the tears was that, the moment they hit the floor, they turned, one by one, into grain—nice, fat seeds of grain.

Frania looked at the grain and licked her lips.

"Come with me," the vision said.

Frania tried to move her legs and arms, but her body would not respond to her urging.

"Get up, Frania."

"I can't, Mama."

"Try again. Try harder."

Now she got up easily, with no effort. "Where are you taking me?"

"You will see."

Half walking and half flying, Frania followed her mother's spirit outside, all the way to the open fields. A sudden gust of wind rushed across the field and blotted out her mother's image. Frania waited for the view to clear again, and when it did she saw nothing but snowy fields and straw stacks scattered all over.

Her face wet with tears, she woke. It was early morning. Everyone was asleep. Because there was nothing for her to do, and she had no place to go to, Frania stayed snug under her bedding. For a while, she watched the ceiling as it emerged from darkness. As she stared at it, she thought of the tragic situation she and her family were in. The more she thought, the more frightened she became. Death grew ever closer, and there was nothing she could do to protect them all from it. Or was there something she could do? She thought about her dream. What did it mean? Was her mother's spirit trying to tell her something?

Suddenly, she understood. Yes, she knew!

Three hours later, when Frania returned from her trip carrying a pail, her father accosted her. "Where have you been, Frania?"

"We thought you had left us," said Jozia, tears moistening her eyes.

"Yes, we thought that," said Helcia, her misty blue eyes on Frania.

"Left you?" Frania called out. She came closer to her family's corner and squatted beside her father. "I have brought you something," she said, placing the pail near him.

He raised his head and looked into the pail. "Grain," he said.

"Grain?" repeated Jozia and Helcia. They both sat up. The mere thought of food made them want to move about.

"Where did you get it?" asked Tata.

Unwrapping herself from her heavy clothing, Frania smiled and said, "I picked it from the straw stacks in the field behind the kolchoz."

"You did?"

"You know, Tata, it's a good thing the workers here are so careless that they leave grain in the straw when threshing the crops. Otherwise, you, I, and my sisters would have nothing to put in our mouths until spring."

He lay flat on his back and stared at the ceiling. "People who don't own their own land don't give a damn how they work. I know they leave too many potatoes in the ground over the winter each year because they are late with the digging."

"Yes, so many things are wasted here, while people starve each winter and spring. The Communists' deliverance of the little guys didn't bring anyone prosperity, did it?"

"Hush, Frania. Don't you know they could arrest you for criticizing their system?"

"Do you think any jail could be worse than this life?"

"Anything is better than being locked in a small space," he said.

"I'm sorry. I forget you know what you're talking about, Tata. You were there."

The freshly made cake, baked on top of the iron stove, tasted delicious. Frania and her dear ones ate slowly, chewing each bite with care so it would last as long as possible. As usual, whenever they ate, they worried about whether or not they would have anything to fill their stomachs with the next day, and the day after that.

The following morning, Frania took Ala, Kazia, and whoever else wanted to go to the straw stacks. Thus, five women, carrying containers, went out into the blinding, bright new day spiked with frost sharp as a razorblade and capable of blistering their skin if they did not cover themselves carefully against it. Beneath their feet, the snow was hard, yet not hard enough to keep them from sinking deep, making their trip exhausting and slow, so slo-o-o-ow.

Like ancient warriors inside their shiny armor, the straw stacks glowed in the sunlight. They beckoned the walkers and seemed to call silently to them, *Come close, dear ladies. We will save you from your foe. We are your knights and your protectors.*

Their feet ploughed through until they made it to the field, where they disturbed crows pecking at the straw. "Caaw, caaw," the black-winged creatures cried angrily as they flew away.

"Vermin," said Ala.

"They are after the grain," said Kazia.

"Don't they have to live, too?" said Frania.

She stopped to listen. From far away came the howling of wolves. Yes, most certainly wolves. Then all was quiet.

The woman pounced on the straw stacks. They fingered the straw, combed it for every grain of wheat hiding in it. Pick, pick, went their fingers. Pick out one here, one over there, and yet another deeper in the stack. The grain was frozen and hard. Each morsel clinked as it fell to the bottom of the steel container. Clink, clink, clink. Clinks, enjoyable clinks, life-saving clinks. More clinks falling upon Frania's ears meant more grain was accumulating for today and for their tomorrows.

Winter was heedless of the fact that Frania and the other exiles at Narod had no food, nor enough warm clothing, or that the walls of the schoolhouse were not thick enough to keep cold air from seeping in. Nature was indifferent to their suffering. Snowstorms and harsh winds dominated the weather and kept them from going into the fields after grain. Once more, starvation visited the shelter, grinning its toothless grin, smelling of grave and corpses. At such times, Frania used whatever grain she had left sparingly and waited—waited for Tata to get well, for weather to get milder, for spring to come.

One day, after a bone-chilling trip to the straw stacks, Frania came down with pneumonia. Though her body lay on the floor of the schoolhouse, her spirit stood on the bank of a strange river. The blue water was crystal clear, and its color and movement seemed to have an extra dimension. On her side of the river, the land was cold, barren, enveloped in a thick gray fog. She lingered there, shivering and squirming in pain for days, until she felt numb from head to toe.

Across the water, the far shore basked in sunlight. Trees, bushes, and flowers—a shimmering rainbow of colors and hues—waved to her, inviting her to join their kingdom. She heard them whispering tales of eternal peace and happiness, and she smiled.

It would be so easy. A sturdy bridge lay across the river, and all she had to do was cross it. Yet she hesitated. Why? Something or someone would not let go of her. She heard thin trembling voices, as if from a far distance. Once or twice, the image of two sobbing girls and an older man came into her view. Their voices swelled and receded like the crest of a huge ocean wave.

When the wave subsided, she stepped onto the bridge and began to walk to the far riverbank. Somehow, she knew that, once she had crossed the bridge and allowed her feet to touch the strange land, she would never be able to return to the old world. But at the moment she didn't care. She didn't want to go back.

"Frania! Frania! Frania!" Three voices called out to her from the gray shore. She stopped in the middle of the bridge and looked back. In the thick fog, she saw three faces again, barely visible.

"Don't leave us here. Don't go, Frania. Without you, we won't survive. Please, please."

"It's my family calling me," she whispered to herself and turned around. She walked back into the fog, toward the barren shore.

She opened her eyes slowly and blinked at sunlight streaming down through the unshaded window below which she lay. For a while, all she saw was a blur, but then her father and her sisters came clearly into her sight. Tata was still shaking her by her shoulder. Helcia and Jozia stood behind him, and they were both crying.

"Why are you crying?" she asked. She closed her eyes again and fell at last into the deep sleep she needed in order to heal herself.

Dressed in rich, freshly greening gowns, spring arrived with life-giving sun to smile at the birds nesting in her golden hair. But why should this prolific lady care about Frania and her dear ones, who had gone for days with no food?

Frania was happy. She was in a warm, bright family room in Poland. It was Christmas Eve, and she sat at a table covered with various dishes that filled the air with the aromas of boiled mushrooms, eggs, and fried onion. A bowl of steaming barszcz (sour soup) stood in the center of the table. On a large platter lay stuffed, baked fish sprinkled with herbs and spices. Pierogies (pies) were filled with potato, cheese, or sauerkraut. Two wicker baskets overflowed with bread and sweet pastries.

Frania was about to reach out for pierogies, when suddenly she awoke in the schoolhouse at Narod. She wanted to go back to her dreamland, but Jozia, on her left, smacked her lips as if eating something delicious. Helcia, on Frania's right, kept muttering, "Mama, Mama." Under his covers, Tata snored softly. Across the room, someone cursed the fate that had brought him to Northern Kazakhstan.

If only it would bring Henio and Mama back to life, Frania would curse, too. She would shout out all the profanities she knew if it would chase away starvation from Tata and her sisters. She would scream and yell at the top of her lungs, if that would take her back to Poland.

The time for each human spirit to come live in its bodily shell, and when and how it is to leave it, is written across the heavens. Therefore, it is very important that each of us serves our full time of living, no matter what we have to overcome to make it to the finish line. Frania knew this universal truth instinctively, for it was imprinted upon her very soul. During the war and throughout her exile, she was determined to pass the tests Stalin put before her. She had fought and won many battles with death, but now, for the second time in Russia, she felt different. Was she finally to lay down the sword with which she had, so far, successfully fought off the cold angel?

Very carefully, so as not to wake anyone, she got up, changed into her daytime clothes, and stepped outside. The young day gleamed white and pink above the Kazakhs' huts with their narrow doors and small windows. Wobbling, she took several steps. The fresh air revived her from her lethargy and helped her to think more clearly. Was there anything else she could do that she had not already done to save herself and her family from dying? Last week, she had tried to plough, but after only five minutes she had collapsed in the field. The following day, she had visited Ivan B., but he had no food to give them.

"What else can I do now?" she whispered to the air. Nothing, she decided, and sighed, recalling how it was when her mother was alive and her father well enough to work. When they all worked, the family managed to pull through the difficult seasons. In addition to what their labor earned them, the exchanging of articles from the family's belongings helped. But now, no one worked, and most of what they owned had already been traded away. Frania's trunk was empty of linen and lace. The holy picture was the only thing left.

A voice whispered inside Frania's head: *Why don't you sell it to Ivan's wife?*

"Sell Matka Boska Chestochowska? Never. I wish that woman had never heard of the picture. She wants it not only for its beauty, but also for the magic she thinks it possesses."

Sell it, the voice repeated.

"No, no, no, I will not," she cried out.

Somewhere in the depths of Narod, a dog barked. A voice called out. Frania's eyes widened. So the Kazakhs were waking up. Frania turned around and looked at the huts, their glass windows reflecting hopeful sunlight. She smiled faintly, thinking of Sasha and his mother, living in the group of dwellings to her left. Maybe she should visit them? No, no, she couldn't bring herself to do it now, when Kozachka was ill, and Sasha's wife had given birth to a daughter.

What then? What was she to do next?

Suddenly, she had an idea, although she hated the very thought of it. "Could you spare a piece of bread or a potato?" she asked the first woman who answered Frania's knock at her door.

The woman held a glassy-eyed infant in her arms. She shook her head. She and her child stared at Frania with eyes that were burning with pain.

"Please give me something, just a little for my sisters to eat," she begged a middle-aged man who came out to talk to her. "My father is ill, and my little sisters and I haven't eaten since last week."

Shaking his head, he pointed to the inside of the hut, where someone lay quietly in one of four bunks. Frania strained her eyes and saw an old woman, probably the man's mother.

Frania knocked on more than two dozen doors before giving up. It was a bad year, and all the natives were sorry, she could see that on their sad faces, but they didn't have enough to feed their own families, and she believed them.

She walked out of Narod into the wilderness. "Our Father, who art in Heaven..." she prayed. The bright sun blinded her eyes, but she didn't mind. The steppe bloomed yellow at this time of year. She hated yellow now. Water was not yellow, and water was what her body screamed for. Water and food. It also demanded rest. Rest! Rest! But she kept plodding, plodding, plodding until she was out of the yellow land.

"Poland." Her parched mouth formed the word over and over again. She kept licking her lips, wondering why she couldn't moisten them.

She looked ahead, expecting to see her beloved village or the golden gates of Heaven somewhere at the end of the horizon. When would she reach the line connecting the yellow earth to the blue sky? She walked and walked, seemingly forever, never getting any closer to it, for the magic line was just an illusion. The earth and the sky were made of entirely different matter, and they could never meet, never touch each other. Frania could touch the dirt under her feet, but not the air she inhaled or the limitless blue of the sky, which seemed a vast, intangible space in the universe. If the sky was just an illusion, then she was fooling herself that a Heaven existed after death.

Her face grew even sadder. But then her mood changed. "Sweet Jesus!" she sang out next, for she saw a two-story wooden house with happy windows. It stood apart from the nearby silo and the barn where cows mooed. A white picket fence with a black iron gate cut into it embraced this farmstead. Why was the gate shut tightly against her? Why? Why? Where was her still young and energetic mother? What had happened to her father and her many sisters, always noisy and demanding attention from Mama?

"Please, someone, tell me…where did everyone go?" she said. She folded her hands and prayed. "Holy Mary, Mother of God…" The sound of her own voice kicked her back to the steppe. She stared at the horizon, and it seemed farther away now than ever before. She blinked, and blinked again.

Another scene from her past flashed across her mind. In it, she saw herself as a little girl, playing in the young potato field while her mother hoed it.

"Frania, I love you," the woman said.

"I love you, too, Mama."

Her face smiling and glowing in the sunlight, Mama said, "I will teach you to make soups, to hem dresses, and to spin thread out of flax before you are six."

"Yes, Mama. Teach me to do all these things."

"Frania, you will have a sister."

"When?"

"Soon."

But the picture of Mama and the beloved field disappeared in the yellow fog. And then she was looking at Julek, her school friend. He wasn't the most handsome youth in the village, but he had thick wavy hair, and his dark, shiny eyes were kind and understanding. Why hadn't she married him? Instead, she said her wedding vows to Andrzej, the handsome and sophisticated teacher.

Horror fogged her face. "Stalin, Hitler, you are evil men, and I hate you!" she shouted, beating the air with her hands as if she were caught in a tornado. "No, no, don't kill my baby!"

A cool breeze came from the east. Its delicate fingers caressed her face. Gently, she was brought back to the present time. She looked about, listening. All around her in the yellow grasses, birds twittered and insects buzzed. In the distant field, men cursed their animals.

"I should be ploughing for soups," she muttered.

It was getting warm, and Frania felt dizzy. Now and then, the yellow and blue world blurred into green. She strayed off the road and struggled onward, fighting the vegetation that seized her ankles.

Julek, something said in the thickness of the yellow fog.

"Julek," she repeated, her voice rasping in her throat. "He is not at Narod. For all I know, he may be dead."

He's not dead.

"Even so, it's too late for us. Too late."

What about your father? What about Helena and Jozia? Don't you think you should go back to them?

"I can't do that."

Why not?

"I can't stand to look into their eyes, begging me to save them."

Are you sure there is nothing else you can do to help them and help yourself?

"Nothing," she muttered, and tripped over a clump of grass under her feet. She fell down, but got up again.

You still have the oil painting, Frania.

"So what? I can't sell it. I just can't."

The sun rose above the steppe. Frania stood still. What was she doing in the steppe? She couldn't even remember how she got there. She only recalled trying to walk away from her pain, the same way she had walked away from Polish Village that day in the long ago past. Back then, she wanted to kill herself, and only Julek had saved her.

Today, he was nowhere near. He would not be able to interfere with her plans to meet her end. She would drag her feet across the yellow earth for as long as it took to exhaust her weak body. She would let this land—her foe since the day she entered it—suck out the last drop of her strength. She would let the air dry all moisture from her flesh. Frania wanted to die, but not under the roof of some miserable shelter. No, she would leave this life under the open sky, exposed to the universe. Let God see her swollen belly. Maybe then the Almighty would do something to end her people's suffering. All over Russia, bellies were swelling from starvation.

Death, why don't you come with your scythe and do your stuff right now? Hadn't she reached the finish line? Did she deserve to feel this awful burning in her throat and chest? Yes, this was the end; she was sure of that. Her father and sisters would reach it soon. It was all over for her roommates, all over for the exiles suffering throughout Russia. All over...all over...all over...

"All over," she repeated, gasping. Something strange was happening. The sky was falling downward in front of her, as if someone had drawn a blanket over her face.

She heard a bird screaming up above. When she opened her eyes, she saw a crane beating the air with its wings. It was telling her to get up. Frania sat up and scanned the grasses near her. Wild onion and sourgrass grew abundantly here. Why hadn't she seen them before? Within arms' reach, she found two baby cranes with their beaks wide open. She stared at the featherless creatures, who looked like tiny chickens plucked and washed for a pot. What if? No, no, she couldn't be that cruel. Was she not raised to admire birds and respect their right to live and multiply? But then, why not? Wasn't this world arranged so that the fittest would survive?

Later on, she moved back onto the road that went west, leading her back to the schoolhouse. Tied in the kerchief taken from her head were edible grasses. Nesting in their softness were the baby cranes, their tiny necks broken.

The soup Frania made that day was nourishing. It was like the first stepping-stone up the ladder of life for her and her dear ones. The next day, she took the holy picture to Ivan's wife, Nina.

"Do you still want it?" she asked the young woman, standing outside her home's doorway. Frania raised the picture up so the sun hit it just right to make it glow. She wanted Nina to be even more dazzled by its beauty.

"So finally you decided to part with your holy thing?" Nina said, her eyes fixed on Holy Mary's face.

Frania nodded, thinking that the young woman wasn't a bad sort. So far, she had always acted fairly in their exchanges.

"Name your price, Frania."

"Price. I—" Frania faltered.

"What do you want for the picture?" Nina's voice was spiked with impatience.

"I want you to know that this is an expensive painting, and very dear to my heart."

"So what is it going to cost me?"

"How about three sacks of grain, four pails of potatoes, and some onions."

Nina snatched the image of Holy Mary from Frania's hands. Pressing it tight to her chest the way a little girl holds her new doll, she smiled at Frania.

But Frania now stared at her departing treasure with regret. She couldn't bear the thought of parting with it after all. She just could not.

As if reading her mind, Nina stepped back and rushed to say, "I will give you six sacks of grain, seven pails of potatoes, some onions, and a whole loaf of cheese."

Frania's mouth opened wide and hung there. She couldn't believe what she was hearing. All that food, a mountain of it, she was being offered in exchange for the picture of Matka Boska Chestochowska. How many meals could she make from that? Hundreds of good, life-prolonging soups and cakes. She still stared at the picture in Nina's arms, but all she saw was Tata, Jozia, and Helcia eating and eating, gaining weight and the strength to move about again.

"Is it a deal?" said Nina, backing away a little farther from Frania and pressing the picture to her chest.

"What?"

"I will add two glasses of milk a day to the price."

"It's a deal!" cried out Frania, smiling in a way she had never imagined she could smile again when she wandered the steppe just yesterday.

Right there and then, Frania made an arrangement with Nina that she would take the purchased goods, not all at once, but in weekly installments, for both their safety.

From thence forward, she made breakfasts, lunches, and suppers on the hot stones outside the schoolhouse. She fed these meals to her family and shared them with other roommates too weak to work. She baked little cakes. Her thick soups were mysteriously flavored with meat. What were these tiny specks of meat floating on top of the pot? And the other bits that looked like egg curds. Where was she getting all this stuff? Only her father knew the answer. To others who questioned her, she would say, "I have my ways."

Several days later, Jozia and Helcia were already playing happily in the back yard. As soon as Tata got up and started to move about, he wanted to go to the fields, but Frania stopped him.

"Not yet, Tata. Take it easy for another week or so. You were sick for too long."

"But you're the only one working now to feed us, and I want to help, too."

"You will, in time. You will."

"I hate being useless," he said.

"You're not useless. You're helping me to keep going just by staying alive."

He looked down at his feet and frowned.

"Hey, Tata, why don't you come with me on my daily trips to the steppe," she said, and winked at him.

He lifted his head and smiled. "I'll come. Yes."

Chapter Seventeen

ONE GLORIOUS DAY, FRANIA AND TATA WALKED OUT OF NAROD AND headed eastward toward the bend of the creek where the brush was tallest and thickest with wildlife nesting in its foliage. This was Frania's secret discovery, the place where she found bird's eggs to add to her soups.

"I've been so busy lately that I lost track of time. Is it the end of April, Tata, or the beginning of May?"

"The beginning of May."

"May 1945," said Frania thoughtfully, realizing that three long years had passed since Julek went away. Why hadn't he come back to her?

"People are saying that the war with Germany is practically over."

"Hmmm? What did you say, Tata?"

Patiently, he repeated himself.

"Yes, I've heard that. I wonder how this victory over Hitler will affect our lives, if at all."

"You never know. Maybe things will get better for us."

"I don't see how. We can't even think of going back home."

"Why not?"

"We haven't the strength to walk thousands of miles, and we've no other means of transportation," Frania said. Looking ahead, she spotted a dark object far down the road.

"But unexpected things have happened to us before in exile," Tata said.

Frania strained to see what was approaching them. "You mean, like Stalin giving us the amnesty in 1941?"

"Yes, and our meeting soldiers of Anders' Army in Buzuluk."

"Yes, that too," she said, but then her voice changed. "Is that a cart coming to Narod?"

"It looks like a cart. Probably a new Kazakh family moving into the settlement."

Frania quickened her steps, eager to see who was riding in the crude vehicle pulled by a horse. "Is that a young girl sitting by the driver?"

Her father lengthened his steps to keep up with her. "Yes, it is."

"She doesn't look like a Kazakh woman, Tata."

"No, she doesn't."

"Is it—oh, God—can that be Basia?"

"Julek's sister? I don't know."

"Oh, yes, it is!" Frania started to run now. "Basia. Basia. Basia!"

The thin and ragged girl looked hard at Frania. Suddenly, she waved her arms wildly in the air. But why wasn't she smiling? Something was wrong. Basia said something to the Kazakh driver, and he halted the cart right beside Frania and Tata.

"Where is Julek? Basia, where is he?"

Basia turned around and pointed behind her to the floor of the cart. "Frania..."

She heard a feeble voice, and saw Julek trying to lift his head, but failing. "Dear Lord! You are sick, Julek."

He looked up at her with glassy eyes, while his mouth formed words she couldn't hear.

She reached down for his hand and, holding it in both of hers, whispered, "Hold on, my love. I will take care of you from now on."

This time, Ivan B. let Julek and Basia move into the schoolhouse, and Frania was glad. She could hover over her beloved man like an angel of mercy. He responded to her care by getting a little better each day. Soon, he was eating more and more of her special soups, and one day he got up.

The following week, Frania, Basia, and Tata went back to work. Julek was still recovering from the malaria that nearly killed him.

"Why did you stay away from Narod—and me—for so long?" Frania had wanted to ask that question the day she saw Julek lying on the bottom of the cart, and again when he was strong enough to talk, but she waited until today, when they were both out in the steppe in the late afternoon.

"Why?" he said, half sitting and half lying on the grass beside her.

"Why? Why?" she said, sitting with her hands embracing her knees. "You stayed away for years." Something in the tone of her voice implied he should have been with her in crucial times.

"I…I stayed away because I love you too much."

"What? That doesn't make sense to me, Julek."

He rose to a sitting position and stared into space. "You see, Frania, you were still married, and it hurt too much to see you in the fields every day and not be able to hold you in my arms."

"It wasn't easy for me, either, to keep away from you. But then, a year later, I wasn't married anymore."

"And how was I to know that?"

"You would have known had you bothered to check."

He said nothing.

Frania sat silently rocking, rocking, rocking herself back and forth, not looking at him. Her eyes were on the golden red sunset that was turning pale all too quickly. "Julek, tell me something about…about that Natasha Ivaniewiczowa of whom Basia talks so much," she finally said, choosing her words carefully.

"Ivaniewiczowa?" he said, as if just awakened from a nap.

"Yes, that one. The boss of Mroczno," she said, and leaned over to look into his face.

He didn't turn to meet her eyes, but sat staring down at his legs spread out in front of him. "Natasha was not bad."

"So you called her by her first name, Julek?"

"Everyone in that kolchoz called her that."

"Was she as fair with her people as Basia says she was?"

Julek nodded, still not looking at Frania. "Under this woman's management, not only the Kazakhs, but we Poles, too, had enough soup and bread to keep us alive even through spring. She never left any crops in the fields."

"Was Natasha young and pretty?" Frania asked, and bit her lips hard.

Julek glanced sideways at Frania. "Some said she was a good looker. Why do you ask?"

"I just wanted to know," muttered Frania, her eyes fixed on the grass that swayed in the evening breeze.

"You know, Frania, after Ivaniewiczowa left, things changed drastically," Julek continued. "We Poles were the last ones to get work and the last to get food. Hunger visited Mroczno then. That's why everyone was sad that the good woman was gone."

"I've heard that Natasha was especially good to you, Julek," said Frania. "And you must have been the one who missed her most."

"It's just as I told you—everyone missed her."

Suddenly, Frania blurted out in an angry voice, "Were you in love with Natasha?"

He turned to look at Frania. "What did you say?"

"You heard me."

"Are you accusing me of being unfaithful to you, Frania?" he said, his voice spiked with hurt.

Unfaithful, unfaithful, unfaithful, hummed the insects in the greenery. *Unfaithful, unfaithful, unfaithful,* hissed the wind-whipped grasses. "I will ask you again, Julek. Were you in love with Natasha Ivaniewiczowa?"

"Of course not! Ask Basia."

"Then why did you come back to Narod only after she had left you?"

"But Frania…we stayed at Mroczno a whole year after that."

"A whole year? Why didn't you tell me that?"

"You didn't ask."

"Tell me the truth, now. Why did you finally come back?"

For a long time, they sat together in silence. Frania waited and waited, expecting to hear words that would crush her, cut her heart into pieces and make it bleed. "Why don't you tell me?" she said. "Do tell me, please."

Tell, tell, tell, the insects buzzed.

"Frania, you hurt me badly by questioning my love for you." Julek turned and looked at her. "Would you like to know why I really returned to Narod?" He said these last words in a strange voice she had never heard him use before.

"Why did you?" she asked, looking into his eyes.

"It was because of one thing only."

"And what was that?"

"I...I wanted to see your beautiful face again before closing my eyes forever." Tears glistened in his eyes.

"Oh, Julek, my darling," she whispered. "Can you forgive me for doubting you?" She laid her head down on her knees and cried.

Julek put his arms about her shoulders and rocked her the way a mother rocks her crying baby to sleep.

She cried and cried, and Julek let her. She cried not only because she had falsely accused her beloved of betraying her with Natasha, but also because of the war that had broken out in the early fall of 1939. This war changed her life so completely, turning everything bright to dark. She sobbed for Henio, Andrzej, and Mama, the loved ones she had lost to death, that powerful monster whose black mouth and sharp fangs cut human throats and sucked the breath out of them. She cried remembering the horrid deportation, the hard labor in the taiga, the walk to Nieznajdowka, and the train rides to Buzuluk and back north to Kazakhstan. She cried to think how she and her dear ones had suffered hunger, cold, and heat while in exile. She cried because of Marysia and Aniela, whose whereabouts she still didn't know. But she shook with violent sobs knowing that Julek and she couldn't marry or make love until they were back in the village of their birth.

Would they ever return to Poland? So much depended on answering "yes" to that question. Their happiness went hand in hand with their personal freedom to live where they wanted, and it was not to be found at Narod, Mroczno, or Bialy Jar, but only in Poland. They both grew angry and determined not to join in matrimony while in Russia. If their fate was to keep them in exile, they were ready to defy it and Mother Nature by staying away from each other, so as not bring new life into this world of poverty, hardship, and misery.

The Second World War ended with Germany's complete defeat. Stalin not only acquired eastern Poland, but also was free to dictate to western Poland that it must accept Communism.

The Poles were crushed by the outcome of the war. They hadn't fought side by side with the Allies for nothing. They fought both inside and outside Poland in order to regain freedom for their motherland—the freedom to govern their country in a democratic way.

Thousands of Polish soldiers fought in France, Italy, and Germany. Churchill praised their bravery in *Triumph and Tragedy*. On page 652, vol. 6, he wrote:

"There were about 30,000 in Germany, and a Polish corps of three divisions in Italy (right after the war)...This army totaling, from front to rear, more than 180,000 men had fought with great bravery and good discipline, both in Germany and, on a larger scale, in Italy. There they had suffered severe losses, and had held their positions as steadfastly as any troops on the Italian front. These troops had fought gallantly side by side with ours, at a time when trained troops had been scarce..."

When Nazis threatened to overrun Europe, and when Hitler rose above the lands like the giant head of a cobra ready to strike at the whole world, the Allies' collective military forces got together and fought the enemy. The Poles were with them, and they deserved better now. These people protested against the Yalta agreement under which Poland was sold to Russia, but the Western powers didn't listen. Many Polish soldiers disarmed after the war outside their country, and civilians refused to go back home from their exile. Their land was to be under the foot of Communism, which they hated and wanted no part of. Therefore, many of them sought refuge in Canada, New Zealand, England, and, later on, America.

While the world celebrated the victory over evil Hitler and his helpers, the Poles at Narod weren't jumping up and down in joy. They didn't even want to contemplate how this historical event might change their fate for the better, because they didn't want to be disappointed again. Were they really to be forgotten by the West and their own people, who were busy recovering from the war? Were they to be the forgotten ones, doomed to stay in Kazakhstan for the rest of their lives?

Even so, down deep in their hearts they felt a spark of hope. Their hope was the size of a pinprick, but it was a spark just the same. They passed the days in silence, without communicating this thought to one another as they waited...waited...waited.

The rest of May passed, then June, July, and August, but nothing changed. The same labor awaited those exiles who were still strong enough to work. By now, about one-third of those in the schoolhouse had died, including Kazia. Her sister, Ala, would also have died if Frania hadn't taken care of her friend.

This summer, Frania, Tata, Julek, and Basia were to go to the field farthest from Narod, located about ten miles away, and stay out there until the harvesting was done. They could sleep and eat in the temporary collective shelter put up for the workers in the field. Because of the heat, these men and women would rise at the crack of dawn each day, eat breakfast, and work until eleven o'clock in the morning. Then they would eat their lunch in the shade of the shelter, where they would rest until five in the evening. Then it was back to the fields, where they would labor until dark.

Staying in the field for weeks meant leaving behind Jozia and Helcia, who were still too young to be on their own. Walking back and forth at the end of each day was out of the question, for it would use too much of the precious energy desperately needed by the workers to harvest the crops.

Frania and her dear ones were faced with a dilemma. She thought and thought about the problem, trying to find a solution. She asked everyone in her group to think about it, too, and think hard to see what answers they could come up with. Then, one day, she suggested that everyone, including Ala, gather outside behind the shelter for a family meeting. They sat in a half circle on the ground.

"Since you act like the head of the family lately, Frania, you take over our talks," said Tata.

"I will," she said, and sat in front, facing everyone as if she were a teacher, and they, her students. "My dear ones, you know why we have to talk."

Heads nodded.

"I know," said Helcia.

"Me, too," said Jozia. "Everyone was supposed to figure out what to do with Helcia and me over the summer."

"And what do you think, Helcia?"

"Do I have to stand up to say it?"

"No. You can sit."

"I think that Jozia and I should go with you to the fields."

"Wish we could take you, but children aren't allowed to live out there."

"Frania, you could ask Ivan B. for permission," said Jozia.

"I already did," said Tata.

"And?" asked Frania.

"He said no."

Jozia's head went down.

"That figures," said Frania. "But, Tata, what else did you come up with?"

"Why don't we take a chance on Jozia and Helcia being big enough girls to stay here by themselves?"

"All that time?"

"We can visit them on Saturdays."

The girls glanced at their father, and then both cried out at the same time, "No, no. Don't leave us here alone!"

"Tata, I'm afraid your idea won't work," said Frania. "What do you have to say, Basia?"

"What if we take turns and commute to work on foot?"

"Each of us would have to come visit the girls every fourth day, you mean?"

"Yes."

"That's not good, Basia. Ten miles of walking would use too much energy."

"I would like to say something," said Julek.

"Yes?"

"I was thinking that maybe we could afford to have one member of our family stay with your sisters, Frania."

"No, Julek, all four of us must work."

"Then what can we do about the girls?" said Basia. "What?"

Frania turned to look at Ala, who was silently listening to the family's discussion. "I want to find someone outside my family to stay with my sisters."

"But who can we find? Most of our people work, and those who don't are too weak to even take care of themselves."

Ala raised her hand. "How about me?"

"I've been waiting for you to say that, my friend," Frania said, smiling.

All eyes turned toward Ala. Neither Jozia nor Helcia objected to the idea of having Ala stay with them.

Frania's father thoughtfully scratched his forehead and said, "I know Ala can look out for my daughters, but what are they all to live on?"

"Yes, Frania, we have to eat, too," Ala said.

"Don't worry, Ala. I have that all figured out." Frania fixed her eyes on the older woman. "Ivan's wife still owes me some grain."

"She does? How much?"

"Two large sacks. She promised to deliver them to me."

"Two sacks! That should last you and the girls for quite some time," said Julek.

"Make meals twice a day for Jozia, Helcia, and yourself."

"I will do that, Frania. You can trust me."

"I know."

"But, Frania, there's one thing that bothers me."

"What is it?"

"How am I to communicate with you when you're away?"

"You can write notes and send them to us through Ivan's helpers."

"Then that's what I'll do."

Frania smiled and shook hands with her friend.

Lately, the days were always hot. The door of the schoolhouse was left open to invite in any slight breeze. Unfortunately, the only ones to visit were flies, and they came to stay.

One afternoon, Jozia was playing on the floor with pebbles. Helcia had been ill and bedridden since Monday. She refused to eat or drink or to get up in the mornings, although she had no fever. When asked why she lay about day and night, she said it was because she was sleepy.

Caaw, caaw, caaw. Jozia heard the sound coming from outside, and she tossed the biggest pebble into the pile at her feet. She liked to see the tiny stones scatter all about.

Caaw, caaw, caaw. Ala also heard the crows cawing and she listened with fear growing in her heart. Something bad was going to happen. But what? She was reading a book and, when she heard that hateful sound, she lifted her eyes from the page and glanced at Helcia, who looked peaceful, her eyes closed.

"I wonder if your family has received my message?" she said to Jozia.

"Message?" Jozia repeated, gathering her stones to make a new pile.

"They have to know about Helcia."

Jozia said nothing. She was getting bored with the pebbles, and her attention was drawn to the flies that buzzed all about. Some rested on the glass windows, others hovered over the sticky spots on the floor. Newcomers flew straight at the walls, hitting and then bouncing off them like tiny rubber balls. Jozia wondered why none of the pesky creatures ever died. She would hurt herself badly if she rammed into the wall with such speed.

One fly landed on Helcia's face. "Shoo, shoo, fly away," Jozia said, and waved her hand in the air. It flew to Ala's head where two old timers had already made themselves at home.

Ala sat still, reading, reading, reading.

"Miss Ala."

"Yes, Jozia?"

"Please read aloud to me."

"Not again!"

"Please, please, please."

"All right, then. I will read you one of the chapters."

"Read the whole page."

Ala sighed and said, "Move closer so you can hear me better."

Ala had a beautiful reading voice, fitting for a former teacher. The words she read were strange, but sounded melodious, something like the Latin used by priests to say a holy Mass in Poland. Jozia listened as if hypnotized, wishing she could read, too. Because of the war, she hadn't been to school yet. What Jozia didn't know was that she was hearing a story written in French.

"Mama? Mama?" Helcia's voice came to Ala's ear. The woman stopped reading.

"Where are you, Mama?" The voice came from up above.

"What are you doing up on the window sill, Helcia?"

"Mama? Mama, I want you."

"She's looking for Mama," said Jozia to Ala. "Doesn't she know that Mama is—"

"Shush," Ala said to Jozia, placing her fingers to her lips. "Your Mama is not here, Helcia. Let me help you down before you fall."

"I want my tiny cross," mumbled Helcia, letting Ala pull her down.

"It's under your pillow, dummy," said Jozia and giggled.

Ala helped Helcia down and put her back on the bedding. "Here is your cross, dear little girl," she said, thinking how attached she had become to Helcia and her sister. By now, these two girls seemed very close to her heart, as close as if they were her own children.

"Good," whispered Helcia. She clutched the cross as if it were a relic. "Now I'll be all right."

Ala and Jozia watched Helcia kiss the cross, and then place it on her chest. Pressing it to her, she smiled a happy smile and closed her eyes.

"She's asleep again," said Jozia. "Read me another page, Miss Ala."

"I will read," Ala rushed to say in a strange, choked-up voice. She was the one who noticed how Helcia's head dropped suddenly to one side.

An hour later, Frania showed up in the shelter.

"Your message came this afternoon, Ala," Frania greeted her friend. "I came as soon as I could."

"Did you walk in that heat?"

"No, Kazakhs gave me a ride in their cart."

"Good for you."

"How is Helcia?"

"She's asleep," said Jozia, eyeing the brown package Frania held under her arm.

"And how are you, Jozia?" Frania handed her sister the package.

"I'm okay," said Jozia, and then, "Bread! Frania, you brought us real bread."

Frania ignored Jozia's happy outcry. Her eyes on Ala, she asked again, "How is my baby sister? She looks all right lying there."

Ala said nothing.

"She's very, very sick?"

"No, not any longer, Frania."

"What do you mean?"

"I think…Helcia is dead."

"Oh, Lord, not her, too," moaned Frania, her heart sinking deep into a well of sorrow.

Frania stayed at Narod two nights and a day to witness Helcia's body being lowered into the freshly dug hole next to her mother's grave. She and Ala cried hard at the burial. Jozia sobbed herself almost to unconsciousness out of grief. That night, she kept waking up screaming and mumbling words no one understood.

The next morning, Jozia was up very early and silently watched Frania getting ready for work. Everyone in the schoolhouse was still sleeping, putting the finishing touches on their dreams. The sun wasn't up yet, but daylight had already half chased away the night shadows. In the neighboring yards, chickens pecked the ground contentedly, but dogs still lay curled up by the front doors.

"Have to go," Frania said, squatting down. She stretched out her arms toward Jozia. "Come here and give me a hug."

Jozia leaped at Frania. She put her sisterly arms about Frania's neck and whispered into Frania's neck. "Don't go."

"I have to," said Frania, hugging the girl to her bosom. Then she pushed Jozia away from her.

"Don't leave me here all alone, Frania." The thin arms clutched tighter.

"You won't be alone, dear; you'll be with Ala. We'll be in touch. Let me know if you need me." Frania tried in vain to pry Jozia's arms from around her neck.

"I won't stay here without you! I just won't!" Jozia said, tears brimming in her eyes.

"Why not?"

Jozia's chest heaved. "Be…because I…I'm scared."

"Of what?"

"If I stay here, I will die, too. Just like Helcia."

Frania hugged her sister again, but then she quickly freed herself. "You won't die, Jozia. I promise you that."

Jozia collapsed to the floor, and her body shook from crying. "Don't go," she sobbed.

"Bye, bye, Jozia. I have to hurry to the field," Frania said, and rushed out. She closed the door behind her. When she was outside, she sighed with relief, thinking that she was free to go now.

Suddenly, she heard Jozia shrieking behind her. "Take me with you! Fra—aaa—nia!"

Frania didn't look back, but quickened her steps, and then she ran and ran and ran, wanting to be far away from Narod.

But Jozia didn't stop screaming. She screamed harder yet. She screamed as if someone were beating her or even skinning her alive. Her screaming disturbed the chickens, who clucked and flapped about the yard. It also woke the dogs, who began to howl, raising their snouts to the sky.

Her screaming brought out Kazakh women and their children, still sleepy-eyed.

"Why is this Polish girl carrying on so? Has she gone mad?" they asked, glancing questioningly at one another, and then staring at Frania, who was trying to walk down the road with Jozia holding onto her skirt and pulling her backward.

Her screaming also made Ivan B. come out of his house.

"What's going on?" he asked, looking at Jozia lying on the ground. Her skinny hands were wrapped around Frania's left ankle, and she was being dragged along the road by her big sister.

"My sister doesn't want to stay here without Helcia," Frania called out to him from a little distance.

"Why not?"

"She's terrified of dying and wants me to take her to the fields with me."

At that moment, Nina came out to stand by her husband. She said something to him, and Ivan answered her, nodding.

And so Jozia got her wish.

Chapter Eighteen

IN THE MIDDLE OF THE SUMMER A KAZAKH WOMAN WHO COOKED FOR the field workers became ill. So the workers choose Frania for their cook, and she happily accepted the position. Right away they were impressed by Frania's cleanliness, her thick soups, and the portions of bread she served. How did she manage to make her soup so thick? The answer was simple: unlike cooks before her, she had no heart to steal food from others.

All the grain she received daily (whether it be wheat, oats, or rye) she crushed between two stones before boiling it on the iron stove, three times a day. She cooked in the corner of the shelter free of the straw that covered the rest of the floor. Sometimes, she crushed the grain only halfway and made a thick mass whitened with milk. Delicious. Sometimes, she crushed it into a fine powder and made dumplings one could sink one's teeth into. Ach, they were good and nourishing.

The only thing she felt guilty about doing was feeding Jozia as much food as the child wanted. She did that knowing her sister needed nourishment to grow and to stay alive.

Jozia was quite contented to live outdoors. In cooler hours, she played in the shade of the shelter or on the shore of a man-made canal that fed the fields with its water. She was up early each morning to help Frania serve breakfast. This blue-eyed child with rosy cheeks, handing out slices of bread, was a bright sight for the workers. Jozia represented goodness, innocence, and charm, parts of Nature they had no time to enjoy and admire while harvesting. Her smile brought forth smiles from them in spite of the hardships they endured. Their labor was exhausting, their sleeping arrangements uncomfortable. Crowding against one another on a bed of straw kept them from a good night's rest.

Pound, pound, crush, crush. Today, as always, Frania crushed her grain for the next day's breakfast at sunset. Pound, pound, pound. She pounded the wheat inside a sack, a little bit at a time, so as not to lose any grain. Precious, precious grain, life-sustaining grain. She made meals out of it, meals everyone waited for and looked forward to. She made meals for Julek, Tata, Hasia, Jozia, herself, and all the other Poles working in the fields. She made them for those Kazakhs who believed in her enough to trust her with the preparation of their meals.

While resting between pounding and crushing, she listened to voices calling from the field, and the singing of a lonely watcher of cows grazing in the distant steppe. To her ears, Kazakh singing sounded harsh and sad, but she still enjoyed listening to it. Pound, pound, pound, crush, crush, crush. Rest. This was the rhythm of her life.

Suddenly, she stopped. Jozia—where was she? It dawned on Frania that at this time of day—it was already turning gray out—Jozia was usually back and safe at the shelter. Why wasn't she in yet today? Frania went out and stood under the sky, which was quickly paling on the low western horizon. "Jozia? Jozia! Jozia!" she called.

No answer.

"That child," muttered Frania, running toward the road that led to the canal. "Just wait till I get my hands on her. Jozia! Jozia! Jozia!"

Still, she heard no answer. Oh, God, don't let anything bad happen to Jozia. Let Frania find her before darkness enveloped the steppe, fields, and shelter.

"Jozia! Jozia!"

"Frania!" A thin voice broke the evening air. It seemed to come from behind the young willows, or beneath them.

"Jozia?"

"Here, Frania. Help me!"

Frania ran to the edge of the canal and stopped. "What are you doing down in the canal, Jozia?"

"I…I got in to wash up," sobbed the child, "and I can't get out by myself."

"Dear Lord," moaned Frania, squatting down. She reached out her hand toward Jozia. "How long have you been down there?"

"Long," said Jozia, climbing up. "I called out, but no one came."

From that time on, Frania forbade Jozia to venture out too far from the shelter and her caring sight.

This happy season ended too soon for Frania and her dear ones, the way all good things do. They returned to Narod to wait for potato digging to begin. But before work started, something unusual happened at the settlement.

One day, all Poles were told to meet in front of the new school. Up until now, no one had bothered checking on non-working exiles at the kolchoz. The sick, the weak, and the starving were left alone. No one cared if death was breathing down their necks. Today was different. All those who could make it were asked to show up at the meeting place. And they did come. Some moved slowly, shuffling their feet. Many staggered along, supported by someone stronger.

Ivan B. greeted them. "You're going home."

"Home?" they queried.

"Yes, you are going back to your homeland. Do you understand what I'm saying to you?"

"Poland, you mean?"

"That's right, Poland."

"Oh! Oh!! Oh!!! But how are we to get there, Comrade? We can't walk and have no money to buy train tickets."

"We will take you in carts to the railway station, and then put you on the train."

"When? When are we to go?"

"Next week."

"Next week! That's good."

These words passed so quickly between the boss of Narod and the exiles that at first their meaning didn't fully sink into their minds. But when it did, the Poles went insane, rejoicing at the wonderful news.

Anyone who could still jump and dance about did just that. Others sat on the ground, embraced one another, and kissed in a brotherly fashion. All faces were bathed by happy tears. Still others knelt down and gratefully praised God, whom they believed had performed this miracle for them.

Ivan B. left as quickly as he could. As always, he was indifferent to the feelings of the Poles: indifferent to their suffering in the past, and now indifferent to their happiness. He didn't hide the fact that he would be glad to be rid of them. He didn't bother to share the news that, in delivering them to the station, he could wash his hands of them forever.

And that was what he did. After giving a small portion of bread to each person, he drove them all away one rainy day in a cart pulled by camels. He drove them for two days, and then left them to wait outside the station, though he knew how bad the train service was in Kazakhstan.

One day, one of the clerks working at the railway station was overheard talking to someone on the phone. "Why aren't you sending a train for the Poles? But, Pavel Pietrowicz, about one-third of them sleep outside in the rain. No, I don't blame you for the bad situation here, but I don't want to be responsible for any of them dying. Food? I haven't seen any of them eating."

Similar conversations occurred nearly every day somewhere in the depths of the room behind the ticket window. Frania heard them, and so did Basia, Ala, Jozia, and Julek. They sat underneath the window on the floor. Each day, Frania repeated what she heard to others packed into the room. These were the same passengers—or what was left of them—who, three years earlier, had ridden in four wagons from Uzbekistan to Kazakhstan to be dropped off at different kolchozes. Among them, Frania recognized the bearded man with a good singing voice who'd had the berth across from hers, and the grandfather she had helped to walk that day in the steppe while looking for a settlement with food. The grandfather's hair was all silver now, and his grandson was older, but not much taller, because he lacked proper nourishment.

"Send them back to their kolchozes?" said the clerk today. His last words hit Frania hard. She strained her ears to catch every word.

"I...I don't think they will want to go, Comrade. Why? Because they will fear missing their train when it finally comes to pick them up."

"Did you hear that, Basia and Ala?" whispered Frania.

"Yes, we did."

"They want to send us back."

"We won't go," said Basia.

"Of course not," said Frania. "Now pass the bad news to everyone. We must warn our people."

In no time, all who were inside, and then all who were outside, knew what was coming their way, maybe even late this afternoon. Their jaws set hard, and their eyes dark with the determination to fight for the right to stay, they waited. And that day they fought with words and won.

"Something has to be done for the exiles starving here," another clerk was heard to say on the phone the next day. "Maybe you could send them some soup now and then?"

Frania's eyes lit up with hope.

"No? Can't send anything, huh? That's too bad. Yes, I do feel for them. Wish you could see these women and their children sitting and staring ahead of them. My God, I have a son and a daughter the same age as some of them."

"I can't believe this man actually feels for us," said Ala.

"Shush," Frania said, her ear touching the wall just beneath the window. "Listen."

"You came up with an idea, Comrade? Tell me," the clerk said. "Ask them if they want to work for potatoes?"

"Work?" whispered Frania, turning her eyes to Basia now. "I would work for potatoes."

"I would, too," said Basia.

The next morning, Julek, Frania, Tata, Basia, and many other Poles were on their way to the nearest potato field, about seven kilometers from the station.

"It's good to see the sun and be warm again," said Julek, walking beside Frania.

"You poor thing," she said, and reached for his hand. "I worry so about you and Tata because you have to sleep outside at night."

He squeezed her fingers. "Don't worry, Frania. We're both all right."

"I hope so, Julek. I know how it is to sleep under wet covers. I wish there was enough room for us all inside."

"We keep dry lately."

"You do? How?"

"We found an old beat-up canvas by the tracks and cleaned it as best as we could."

"And that protects you from rain?"

"Yes, it does."

"That's good." Frania sighed, and felt as if a huge burden had fallen from her shoulders.

After a whole month of waiting and struggling to survive hunger and cold, a train finally arrived to pick up the exiles. This time, they occupied two wagons instead of four at the tail end of the train. But that day they all cried out for happiness.

Would this be the end of their suffering? They had lived in misery for so many years and learned what there was to learn from the tragic experiences of the past, and to draw from them what they could to use in their future lives. War and deportation had made these humans more aware of how precious their homeland was, how dear their freedom. Now they knew what it was to die of starvation, for they had already touched the bare bones of this horrifying fate. They also knew how it was to fall into the pit of despair at the death of loved ones. From these experiences, they learned to care more for those who still survived, and for themselves, as well.

Their past life in Poland seemed so far away. Polish mountains, forests, rivers, lakes, fields, meadows, and Polish cities, towns, villages— these images flashed across their minds, often. It seemed a wonderful land, pure paradise. Had this other life and this other place ever really existed? Or was it all just a figment of the imagination brought on by dreams at night and days filled with longing for something better?

Poland must be real, because each of them had memories of it. Over there, everything was better. The sky and the sun were friendly. Flowers, grasses, and crops were more beautiful. Seasons passed away quickly and held all sorts of joys. Even exhausting labor in the fields was not as bad in Poland as in Kazakhstan. After each workout back home, one could look forward to a well-deserved rest. After each loss of energy, one replenished it with a fresh intake of good food.

Only death seemed less frightening in Kazakhstan than in Poland, because it visited the Poles so often it lost the ability to shock them by its presence. This terrifying presence, a skeleton wearing a black, flowing gown with a hood covering its skull, came to cut the life cord of those who suffered too much. Snip, snip, snip. Death cut one cord after another, and cut them with a scythe. It came to those who wanted to be taken out of their misery and pain. It came to those who yearned to cross the river dividing the two worlds, one a world of physical senses, the other beyond the senses.

Death harvested too many lives, but also left many survivors, who learned that the ability to breathe in and out was a precious thing, no matter what, and still worth struggling for.

But hunger, that awful monster, followed the passengers riding the train as they headed for the Polish border. It followed them as if to strip them of every last drop of strength. Why did it not stay behind in Kazakhstan?

"So, we are going home," said Frania, the first day of their ride. She often repeated this sentence.

"Yes, we are," said Julek, sitting next to her. "Wish my parents and our missing sisters were riding this train with us."

"And my mother, too, and my son, and the others," she said. "Why did they have to die?"

"It's God's will."

"No, Julek, God had nothing to do with this. We lost our loved ones because of the war and the Russians. They are the ones who killed them."

He sighed, but said nothing.

"They are responsible for our sisters being separated from us, too."

"Veronka, Marysia, and Aniela," he said, staring into space. "I wonder where they are now?"

"Maybe back home already," Frania said, suddenly excited. "Can you imagine how they will welcome us?"

"Yes, I can almost see them running, their arms outstretched toward us."

"They will have tearful smiles on their faces," Frania said, and smiled herself.

"Our beloved Poland."

"Our precious home. Do you think our farmsteads have survived?"

"I pray to God they have."

"Ach, to be living under the protection of our forest again! It's like a dream."

"A dream," he repeated, and glanced at her.

"Have you thought about our future, Julek?"

"Yes, I have. We'll be living together for the rest of our lives as man and wife."

"Is this a proposal?" she asked.

Pro-po-sal, pro-po-sal, repeated the wheels of the train.

"Are you surprised?"

"Yes, I am."

"Why?"

"You haven't said anything about our getting married for such a long time."

"There was no use."

"No use?"

"Would you have married me and had our child in Kazakhstan?"

"No."

No, no, no, the wheels clattered.

"Are we engaged now, beloved?" he whispered into her ear.

"Engaged?"

"That's what couples do before they marry, don't they?"

"I guess so."

"Will you marry me, Frania?"

"Let me think about that," she said teasingly, and grinned.

"Frania!"

"Yes, I will. I will be your wife."

"Thank you, Frania. I love you so much, it hurts." He slipped his arm about her waist and pulled her close.

"I love you, too," she whispered, resting her head on his shoulder. After a pause, she said dreamily, "You know, Julek, I would be completely happy just to sit by you if only I wasn't so hungry."

"Hungry," said Julek, as if to himself.

Hun-gry, hun-gry, hun-gry, said the wheels.

"Frania, you will never be hungry in Poland. I promise you that."

She looked up at his handsome face and smiled through the mist of tears. "I know, Julek, I know."

Stoo-koo, poo-koo, stoo-koo, poo-koo, the train sounded out as it rolled forward. It spat plumes of smoke out its chimney and whistled *woo, woo, woo* now and then. But it was a finicky thing, for it moved only when it wanted to, and rested too often and for too long.

Wheels, be good. Please keep going fast, faster. Don't stop in the steppe. If you have to rest, do it by a field, please. Roll, roll, roll forward and take your poor passengers home before they die of starvation.

That fall it rained and rained, as if the sky couldn't stop sobbing for the exiles traveling in misery. How did they survive? Not all did. The ones who remained lived on potatoes, cabbages, and sugar beets found when the train stopped near a field. Mud everywhere covered the plains with its chocolate slush. It streaked down the hills. It lay in the form of puddles on fields and roads. It colored the railway tracks brown.

Rain wet the cities, towns, and villages that they passed, most of them ugly and scarred after the war. The closer the exiles got to the Ukraine Republic, the more lush vegetation they saw. Here, the fields grew practically everything. But they also saw machinery rusting in the rain, and crops rotting. If only they could get their hands on some of the crops that were passing by, they would eat them boiled or even raw— all but the bitter sugar beets that left an awful aftertaste that lasted for hours. Uncooked beets also caused stomachaches.

"I am very hungry," Jozia moaned one day.

Frania reached into her skirt pocket and pulled out a cold boiled potato. "Sit up and eat," she said to her sister, handing the food to the child. Why did Jozia lie on the berth so much of the time lately? Why did she nap so often? Was it because she had no energy? Or was she getting ill?

The girl rose with effort. She ate, taking small bites and chewing carefully, as if treating herself to a chocolate bar. She smacked her lips and licked her fingers.

Frania turned away and swallowed hard. She suddenly had too much saliva in her mouth. She also swallowed tears provoked by the sad sight of her hungry little sister. She swallowed more tears, thinking that it was the last potato she could give to Jozia that day.

Food, food, food, the train's wheels clattered.

"Food," Frania whispered back. "When and how are we to get more of it?"

You...won't...get...any, said the wheels.

"In that case, we'll die before we reach the border."

Die, die, die, die, the wheels mocked.

All around Frania, people were dying. The sick and weak went first. One morning, Basia died, too, after only a short illness. Strangers took her corpse away, with Julek crying hard as he said his goodbye. Horrified, Frania stared at the body, thinking it could have been Julek lying stiff and cold on the stretcher.

Chapter Nineteen

One Thursday was gloomy, but dry. In late morning, the two wagons carrying the exiles were detached from the train and left standing on the sidetracks for a long time. When the doors opened, those passengers who could walk stepped down onto the ground, but those who couldn't, stayed inside.

Frania glanced up to the sky and said to Julek, "Look at these clouds! They're moving southward. And over there I see a break in them."

"Isn't this a good sign?"

"Yes, it is. We may have a nice day, after all."

"Wish there was a field nearby with some vegetables left in it."

"Isn't that just like the Communists to leave us in the woods?"

"It's like them, all right. At least there's a river nearby."

"Frania! Frania!" Jozia called out from a distance.

"Yes, Jozia?"

"I can't find any berries or mushrooms in these woods."

"We should be that lucky," Frania said to Julek, but in a different voice she called out to her sister, "Jozia, don't go too far into the forest, or you'll get lost."

"I won't, Frania."

"Can't find anything around here to eat," a voice behind Frania moaned.

Only now, she looked about and saw that the trees and bushes were crowned with flaming red foliage. A beautiful sight. Under her feet, fallen leaves made a thick carpet that crunched under her steps. Fall here was lovely, just like the ones she remembered back home in Poland. Her

eyes searched the floor of the woods and found grasses, withering flowers, and ferns. She loved the greenery, but couldn't eat it.

Suddenly, the sun flashed a generous smile at the earth. For a minute, the vegetation gleamed in sunlight and the river glistened. A glim-
mer of hope for a better future stirred in Frania's heart.

Now she noticed that her people were starting small fires, and so
was her father. She knew how few vegetables they had left on the train, if
any. Her family had six large beets in its possession. If they all brought
out bits of their treasure and put it in one container, it would make up a
good soup; she was certain of that. Past experiences had taught Frania
how to make others cooperate for the good of all in crucial times. Today,
she found it easier than she thought to persuade these starving exiles to
collectively work on making a meal for everyone.

Men and children eagerly gathered stones and firewood. Frania's
father piled up the stones and made an outdoor stove. He formed two
walls several inches high with a good space between for twigs, branches
and pieces of logs. One of the older men expertly arranged the wood and
in no time started a gorgeous fire. Someone brought out a large metal
basin. They scrubbed it carefully with sand, cleaned it in the river and
placed it on the top of the stove. Into it went water, pieces of potato, onions, beets, and even grain someone had managed to save from Narod.
To everyone's surprise, an older lady came up with a piece of salted pork,
which she dropped into the soup for flavor.

In no time, the fire was blazing, giving off a golden warmth that
caressed the exiles surrounding it. The fire crackled merrily, smoked a
little, and furiously licked the washbasin. Delicious aromas of boiling
vegetables, and especially of pork, drifted out of the basin, lacing the air.
When would the meal be ready? It was much too hard to wait. All eyes
were glued to the steam, and noses twitched, sniffing the air. Stomachs
churned and gurgled more viciously than ever before, demanding nourishment. Throats ached from swallowing too often, and lips dried out
from constant licking.

"Hey, everyone, look!" A boy's voice called out from the edge of the
forest. "See what I found."

Heads turned to the left. "What is that you're carrying? What?"

The boy came closer to the fire. "I found this." And he smiled the brightest smile as he hugged something to his chest.

"What is it?"

"Look and see."

"A hare!"

"I spotted it sitting under a bush over there," he pointed with his chin toward the thickest part of the woods. "It has a broken leg and couldn't hop away."

"What are you going to do with it?"

The boy looked at the animal with pity on his face, but he handed it to one of the women. Tears gleamed in his eyes.

The poor hare was killed, skinned, and cut into pieces, washed, and thrown into the washbasin. Now the soup was even more nourishing because of the meat.

Just like everyone else, Frania sat on the ground, holding a bowl on her lap and waiting for the soup to be ready. Now and then, she glanced down the tracks where the train had disappeared an hour earlier and worried that it might return too early, snatching her and the others away from their meal. But luck was with them today.

She looked about, scanning faces around the fire. "Where is that little girl who sometimes comes up to our berth to play with you, Jozia?"

"Wandzia? I think she is still inside the wagon."

"Why didn't she come out?"

Jozia shrugged and stared at the washbasin. "Her mother is very sick," she said.

"Why didn't you tell me about your friend sooner?"

Jozia shrugged again and said nothing.

"Julek, keep my spot for me here, and I'll go check on the child."

With effort, Frania climbed into the boxcar, and what she saw on one of the berths broke her heart. There sat Wandzia, tugging at her mother's sleeve, tears running down her hollow cheeks. One look at the woman's face told Frania that she was looking at a corpse.

"Wandzia," Frania whispered, and went to the child's side.

Dark, expressive eyes lifted to Frania's face. "Mama doesn't want to wake up," the girl said, her lips trembling.

"Let her sleep then, honey, and come outside with me."
Wandzia shook her head vigorously.
"Aren't you hungry, Wandzia?"
"Yes."
"We're making a delicious soup on the fire out there."
"Soup?" Wandzia said, pressing both hands against her stomach.
"Do you have a bowl or tin can, Wandzia?"
"We have two soup cans."
"Take yours with you so you can eat."
"But...but Mama is hungry, too."
"Take your Mama's can. You can bring her portion to her later on."
"I will bring Mama's soup," said the child, and smiled wanly.

Frania sipped her soup slowly and chewed the solid pieces very carefully in spite of a strong urge to gulp them down. At that moment, no one and nothing existed or mattered to her but the steaming mixture on her lap. In it, there was a tiny portion of meat on the bone. Meat, delicious meat! If only it could last longer, for the rest of her life, if possible. Chew and swallow, chew and swallow. Down, down, the soup wound its way into her stomach, but it was like a handful of sand thrown into a well.

And then it was all gone. All that was left was the bone. She couldn't believe she had already emptied her container. For a while, she chewed on the bone, sucked on it until it tasted like straw. Then she tossed it away on the fallen leaves and stared at it. Did she expect it to turn back into a hare?

Later, through her window, she watched the wet land speeding backward with her usual sad fascination, knowing that each passing mile brought her closer to Poland. She would never relax until she had crossed the border. She didn't trust the Russian officials. They were as bad as the Nazis, who had persecuted the Jews and killed thousands of her people. Both Hitler and Stalin were cruel, she knew. Both leaders were dictators who tortured and murdered the human beings who dared to oppose them. At least, Germany was defeated now, and Hitler was dead. But Russia, with her powerful Stalin, was in her glory.

On Friday, it rained harder than ever. The train sped across the Ukrainian Republic, and Frania was glad. She was close to touching the old border of her birth land, so why didn't her fate seem to improve? Time, the lord of change, stayed the same, slow and unfriendly. Time plodded, shuffled, and dragged its feet instead of strolling briskly across the face of the sunless sky that hovered above the still unfamiliar earth.

She turned away from the view to glance at Jozia and Wandzia, lying side by side, and wondered which one of them would die first. After her mother's death, Frania had taken the orphan under her caring wing. The little girl was now a part of their family and thought of herself as Jozia's sister. Jozia was very attached to her friend and playmate. The two girls acted and even looked like sisters, though they were of a different age and size.

"Julek, are you napping?" Frania whispered, nudging her fiancé, who was sitting by her side, as usual, his head down on his chest.

"No, I'm just thinking," he said, straightening up.

"These two," she pointed with her chin at the little girls, "are getting weaker and weaker."

"Is there anything left of the potatoes and cabbage we picked in the field three days ago?"

"Nothing," she said, and sighed. She glanced at Julek's profile, and now she was amazed at how good he still looked in spite of everything. He looked self-confident, and that made her love him even more, if it were possible.

"Aren't you worried about your father?" he said, looking at the older man, who was napping. "He looks so old and beaten down."

"Tata isn't complaining of any pain or anything. He lies there because there is nothing for him to do."

Julek looked away.

Without another word, Frania turned to look out the window and thought about how much she feared for her family's health and life.

An hour later she felt the train slowing down.

"Are we stopping here?" asked fearful voices in the wagon.

"It's so cold and miserable outside, and we won't be able go to looking for vegetables."

Wooo, wooo, wooo, the locomotive signaled its arrival at a lonely building in a deserted area.

The rain was still pouring down when the train came to a halt. Half an hour later, the passengers were still sitting on their berths. Frania's father opened his eyes but didn't rise. Jozia and Wandzia sat up and kept watching Frania. In their sunken eyes, she read, "We are hungry, so hungry."

"We're all going to die," Frania whispered to the window.

"Hold on, beloved," said Julek, who had heard her words. "Poland is not so far from here." He embraced her lovingly.

Now the exiles' sensitive ears picked up a new sound. What was going on outside? Then they recognized human voices. Had someone come to visit the Poles? All the way from Kazakhstan to the Ukrainian Republic, no one had shown any interest in them, or cared about their hunger or discomfort.

"I see Russian soldiers out there!" someone called out from the berth opposite Frania's.

Frania strained her eyes to see through the rain, and then she herself spotted three uniformed men coming toward the entrance of her wagon.

"Sweet Jesus, what now?" she muttered, a sudden fright squeezing her heart.

As if in answer to her question, the door slid open and a voice shouted out in Russian, "People, get off the train!"

The exiles looked at each other, unable to speak.

"Get down right now!"

"But we're not in Poland yet," someone cried out. "Why do you want us to get off here?"

"We have orders, and we obey them."

"We refuse to budge!"

"Then you'll be taken off by force!"

Silence.

"We're waiting!" shouted the same voice.

The silence was heavy now in both wagons.

"I repeat, come down, all of you Poles!" The voice was laden with threat.

More silence. But then someone cried out, "You can wait, you Russians, until the sky turns green, but we're not getting off!"

Six soldiers climbed into the wagon. Four of them were armed. They paired off, a gun pointing at each berth.

The leader called from outside. "Now start moving!"

The people sat stubbornly on their berths, staring at the Russians and their guns.

"Kill us now! Kill us all and here!" Frania screamed in fury.

"Isn't this what you were planning all along?" shouted Julek.

One soldier raised his gun until the muzzle was on a level with Julek's eyes.

"Shoot us inside, not out there in the cold rain," someone pleaded from the opposite berth.

Jozia and Wandzia began to cry. Tata put his arms about them both and held them close to him.

Frania closed her eyes and prayed to God to forgive her sins. She didn't want to go to Hell when she died, but up to Heaven. She prayed that she would be shot first so she would not have to listen to the pain and anguish of others being killed, especially her dear ones. Pressing her body hard against Julek, she waited. She braced herself for what was to come, expecting any second to be hit with a bullet. If only she could die instantly, without pain. If her destiny was to die now, today, there was nothing she could do to save herself. Some part of her looked forward to an end of suffering. Soon she would be reunited with Mama and Henio. She felt resigned to her fate, but then why was she shaking so?

However, it soon became evident that the soldiers had no intention of killing the stubborn exiles. Instead, they pulled, pushed, and dragged the passengers down and out into the rain and wind.

Dear God, it was cold and wet out there! The poor Poles huddled together for warmth, of which there was none in the drenching chill that surrounded them. Their teeth clattered so hard, their jaws began to ache. Was it only rain wetting Frania's face, or was it mixed with her own tears? She had never been as cold, wet, or miserable in her life as she was at this moment.

"Carts! Pulling up by the station!" someone cried out in surprise.

"They are coming for us? Oh, good. Good."

It never stopped raining that day. A layer of mud lay on fields, pastures, and countryside. This dark mush, picked up by horses' hooves and cart wheels, splashed in all directions. In these carts rode the Poles. Their faces, their blanketed heads and shoulders, were soon covered with mud. The sky tried to wash them clean, but all it managed to do was soak them through and through.

"I wonder where the Russians are taking us now?" Frania asked Julek. She sat between him and her father. On her lap sat Wandzia, and on Tata's, Jozia. There was little space in the carts, so families had to pile on top of one another.

"I don't know," said Julek. With the back of his hand he wiped a fresh splash of mud from his face. "We're probably going to the nearest village."

"It's getting dark, but I see no settlement yet," she said.

"The most we can expect at the end of this ride is to be brought into some old building," said Tata.

"At least, we can hope to have a roof over our heads," said Frania.

"Maybe they'll make a fire for us," said Jozia, shaking as if in a malarial fit.

"What I wouldn't do for a warm, dry corner somewhere," whispered Frania.

"I'm thirsty," said Wandzia.

"Hold out your hand and catch some rain," said Frania.

"Drink rain?" said the child.

"Dear Wandzia, this is the cleanest water you can find in the world, for it falls straight from Heaven," said Tata.

Wandzia held out her palm.

"Wish it was all over for us, either way," mumbled Frania.

"Don't talk like that," said Julek.

"And don't give up hope," said her father.

"What hope?" she asked, and shrugged her shoulders.

"Frania, don't be so gloomy," said Julek. "God will help us outlive these bad times, and someday we'll return home."

"Home…precious home and a dry, warm bed." Frania breathed her words into the back of Wandzia's head.

At that moment, a cart in front of Frania's tipped over and sent its passengers into a bed of mud. The caravan stopped. When it was determined that no one was hurt, the cart was turned upright and set back on the road. The people climbed back into it, and the carts continued traveling.

The awful mud seemed to have overtaken the whole world. Horses and carts were sinking into it. The animals moved so slowly, and darkness was enveloping the land much too quickly. How long were the shivering exiles and the poor horses to continue traveling? The animals might collapse from exhaustion, and the people could catch colds or pneumonia or worse. Was there no one to show mercy to these men, women, children, and horses?

Then, as if on a signal from Heaven above, the rain eased up to a drizzle. Next, golden dots appeared, twinkling before the caravan. Was it a village, town, or city they were seeing? Soon, they could see a large village made up of wooden houses with large windows and thatched roofs. Please, God, make the soldiers stop here for the night.

And to everyone's joy, the carts stopped before a large structure, probably the biggest in the settlement. Out of its door came women to greet the newcomers. And one by one they led the exiles away in small groups. In spite of their loud objections, Frania's family was separated. Julek and Tata were taken away by one of the soldiers and a woman. Frania, Jozia, and Wandzia were told to follow a teenage girl wearing a yellow trench coat, a red scarf on her head, and they obeyed.

"Frania, where is she taking us?" asked Jozia holding onto Frania's left hand.

"Yes, where?" Wandzia echoed, holding onto Frania's right hand.

"That's a good question, girls," said Frania, trying to stop her teeth from chattering. The mud was up to her ankles, and it was still drizzling. Why did it not stop? At least, the wind had died down.

Wandzia! Where was she? She wasn't holding onto Frania anymore. "Wandzia? Wandzia?"

"I...I fell into a puddle," came a feeble voice from behind.

Frania rushed back to help the orphan up. She wiped the child's face with her own sleeve, for it was dripping with mud. Meanwhile, the

Russian girl had turned onto a path leading to a house cheerful with bright lights. She pounded at its front door.

Frania and her little companions walked up the path, too. They waited, thinking the young woman was just stopping in for a moment to give the dwellers a message.

The door opened, and Frania stepped forward to see what was inside the house. She saw a spacious room, nicely furnished, and then a heavenly fire blazing in the stove. She already felt warmer just looking at it. A stocky, handsome woman appeared on the threshold, a young woman standing behind her.

"I brought you your guests," the girl in the trench coat said to the woman.

"Good. Tell Comrade Misha that I will take care of them."

Frania heard the conversation, and she wondered who was being talked about.

The girl in the coat went away.

"Come in," the woman said, and smiled at Frania and the girls.

But Frania didn't move, for she couldn't. She could only stare at the two women, who smiled at her.

"Please, do come in, all three of you," said the woman, motioning them into her abode.

Frania took several steps forward. Pushing Jozia and Wandzia in front of her, she shyly stepped into the house, dripping mud on the hardwood floor, which was clean and shiny.

"Get close to the fire and warm up."

Warmth, warmth, merciful warmth coming from the stove. It caressed Frania's face, her hands, her front, and her back. Her body began to tingle and shiver with joy. Her clothes grew warm and started to steam. Jozia, Wandzia, you're crowding me, she thought. It would be good not to have to share this fire with you, with anyone. Fire, fire, golden flames, she wanted them all to herself, just to look at and to feel their heat and brightness. Ah, she wished she could stay forever within the fire's radiant glow. She sniffed the aroma of good food. What was it? Fried meat, boiling dough, and vegetables. No, this wasn't real. She was only imagining the heavenly aroma because she was so hungry.

Jozia and Wandzia were sniffing, too, and licking their lips. Maybe the kind hostess would give them some bread? They would appreciate even a thin slice for each of them. Maybe the woman would give them a bowl of soup?

It was hard to swallow all the saliva accumulating in her mouth. Frania pressed her arms against her stomach, which painfully cried out to be filled. Were those pierogies she smelled? And meat? Holy Mary, who could bear this hunger, knowing that food was being prepared in the next room? The cruelty of it. Frania's stomach churned and bubbled so that she felt nauseated. She was nearly doubled up with pain when the hostess appeared in the doorway of the room.

"My dear guests," she said, smiling. "Please come into my kitchen."

Frania walked into the next room and gasped. Before her was a table laden with various dishes: a large basket filled with bread, a platter of chicken, pierogies (pies) stuffed with mashed potatoes, cabbage, cheese, beans, beets, and other things. A tall bottle of vodka towered above the food.

"Sit down and eat," said Tasha, the daughter of the house.

As if in one of her dreams, Frania slid down onto a bench and reached out for a piece of chicken. Would she awaken before she had a chance to sink her teeth into it? No, this meat was too hot and delicious not to be real. She burned her lips with it and, when vodka was offered, she took a sip and swallowed it. Soon she felt warm all over. She took another sip between huge bites of food and relaxed.

The hostess and her daughter settled on the bench across the table from them, but they didn't eat.

"What are your names?" the mother asked.

Frania gulped down what she had in her mouth and said, "I'm Frania. Next to me is Jozia, and next to her is Wandzia." Then she took another sip of vodka.

"Where are you coming from, and where are you going?"

"From Kazakhstan to Poland," said Frania. "But tell me, my good lady, why did they not take us all the way there?"

"You should not ask us questions like that," said Tasha.

"I'm sorry," said Frania. "I understand."

"We had nothing to eat on the train," Jozia suddenly said, and almost choked on a pierogie.

"You poor, poor people," said the mother. "How long have you traveled from Kazakhstan?"

"Seventeen long days."

"That's a long time to go without food."

"We ate sometimes."

"Ate what?"

"Whatever we could find in the fields." Frania finished her shot of vodka, and suddenly she was happy. "Why are you so good to us?" she asked the woman.

The hostess and her daughter smiled, but said nothing.

"Want some more?" the mother said, picking up the bottle.

Frania nodded.

"Vodka will help you forget your misery for awhile," the mother said, refilling Frania's glass.

"Thank you," muttered Frania. She took two sips instead of one and felt light as a feather. Was she floating up in the air, near the ceiling? "Am I dead and in Heaven?" she asked, looking at her plate still loaded with food.

"No, you are alive," said Jozia, and she giggled into her fist the way she had in the wagon when Marysia said she was dead.

"Are you two angels?" Frania asked the good hostesses.

They both shook their heads. From the expressions on their faces, it was easy to see they were trying hard not to laugh.

"Yes, yes, you're angels. You're good and beautiful. So beautiful, both of you."

"No, no," said Tasha. "We are just two Russian women who were told to feed and shelter you."

"And you, Frania, are drunk," said the mother.

"Drunk?" Frania stifled a hiccup.

"You're funny, Frania," said Wandzia, and she laughed.

Jozia laughed, too, and the daughter and her mother laughed.

"Stop laughing at me," mumbled Frania, closing her eyes. She tried to stop hiccupping. Her head went to her chest, and then to the table.

"You girls must be tired," said Tasha to Jozia and Wandzia, who were still stuffing themselves.

"I'm sleepy," said Wandzia, her cheek puffed out like a hamster's, but her eyes half-closed.

"After you're done eating, I'll help you wash up and change into something dry."

"Can we sleep on the floor by the fire, please?" said Jozia.

"No. You'll sleep on cots under warm covers," smiled the older woman.

The girls smiled. Good food to fill their shrunken stomachs, alcohol to help them forget their misery, dry beds to sleep in overnight. All this human kindness suddenly poured upon the Poles. What was the reason for the change of the Russian authority's heart? The answer to the question was a mystery to Frania, but she soon discovered the reason. The stubborn survivors of the deportation were to be fattened up before returning to their friends and relatives in Poland.

The next morning, Frania woke up with a terrible headache. She winced at the dazzling sunlight flooding the small room in which she lay with Jozia and Wandzia. Soon, her eyes adjusted to the brightness, and she sat up. Next to her cot, she saw the girls were still asleep in theirs. They were dressed in clean nightgowns, and so was Frania. Why couldn't she remember getting out of her wet clothes? Oh, yes, now she knew. She drank too much vodka and blacked out.

She looked carefully at the girls' faces. They looked unusually pale. Were they ill? Later on, she found out that her sister and Wandzia ate so much, they were both throwing up all night and had to run outside often.

"How are you, Frania?" asked the older woman, as she piled scrambled eggs on Frania's plate for breakfast.

"Not too well," moaned Frania, holding her head in her hands and massaging her temples with the tips of her fingers.

"Eat and you'll feel better."

"Strange, but I don't feel hungry," said Frania, and pushed the plate away.

The Russian woman shook her head. "Drink your tea then."

Frania reached for the cup, but before she took a sip of the hot liquid, she looked up at the hostess and asked, "Can you tell me what happened to the rest of my people last night? Where did they go?"

"They were all placed in private homes just like you and your sisters were."

"That's good. They are all well and alive then?"

"No," said the mother, glancing at her daughter, who was adding logs to the stove in the front room.

"Oh?"

"My Tasha tells me that two persons died last night from overeating."

"Dear God! Who were they?" Frania asked. Her heart pounded hard enough to leave her chest.

"I don't know their names," called Tasha from the stove.

"Were they men, women, or children?" Frania called to the girl.

"It was an older woman and a teenage boy, they told me."

"Thank you—oh, God, it wasn't my father or my fiancé."

"I'm glad for you," said the mother, and she pushed the plate with the eggs toward Frania again.

This time, Frania started to eat.

A human being is like a meadow, for both need nourishment and sunlight to live. A meadow slips into a dormant state in wintertime, when the sun backs deep into space, far away from the earth. A human being can barely exist in poverty of the lowest kind, without some ray of hope for a better future. Each year, spring revives the meadow, which sprouts new growth. A person returns to a full life when he or she starts eating well and goes back to a comfortable living. Just as new greenery covers the bare earth after the cold and snow have left, the intake of rich food covers a human body with fat. The new fat obscures most of the marks a human wore on his or her body during a time of starvation and harsh living.

This was the case with the Polish exiles, who spent the whole winter in the Ukrainian Republic. Here, they were well fed, and lived with Russian families in exchange for their work, which was never too difficult or exhausting. Women knitted sweaters, socks, and mittens. They mended clothes and cleaned houses. Men fixed things and did odd jobs. Because they were treated well and lived a normal life, they began to look happier. With time, most of them grew fat again, even Frania.

Chapter Twenty

FRANIA AND HER GROUP WERE TRAVELING AGAIN, BUT THIS TIME ON A train, in third class, and it was springtime.

"We'll be crossing the border soon," said Frania to Julek. "We'll be arriving in Lwow today. Aren't you excited?"

"Yes and no."

"Why not?"

"I'm happy to be on the way home, but have you forgotten that Eastern Poland belongs to Russia now?"

"And that Lwow won't be ours anymore?" asked Frania's father, crowding Julek on the bench from the left side.

"No, I have not forgotten about that, but I just don't want to think about anything sad right now."

"Why do we have to get off at that—that city, Frania?" asked Jozia, biting her fingernails. "I want to go to our village right away."

"We have to pick up special papers there," said Frania. She slapped her sister's hand. "Will you stop that biting!"

"Ouch! I don't want to sit by you anymore. Tata, can we switch places?"

"All right."

Jozia moved to a seat between Julek and her father. "Tata, tell me something," she said.

"Tell you what?"

"Are we going straight home after we get these papers Frania is talking about?"

"I hope so," he said, gently moving Jozia's elbow, which was poking him in the side.

"Where am I to go?" cried out Wandzia, who up until now had sat quietly by the window.

Everyone turned to look at the orphan.

"What do you mean, Wandzia?" asked Frania.

"I...I got no place to go," the child said, her lips curving downward.

"Sweet girl," Frania sang out, and held out her arms. "Turn around and give me a hug. So that's why you look so sad."

Wandzia wrapped her small arms about Frania's waist and pressed her face against her chest.

"You have no place to go, you say, Wandzia." Frania hugged the orphan.

Wandzia nodded, her face buried in Frania's blouse.

"Don't you know you're part of our family? You will come home with us."

"And you'll be my mama?" said Wandzia with a smile.

"Well, I thought of myself as your big sister, but if that's what you want, I can be your mama." Frania smiled and kissed the top of Wandzia's head. Frania realized with a jolt that the girl was about the same age Henio would be, had he lived.

"Mama," repeated Wandzia.

Two weeks later, they arrived at the station near Jaroslav, the same station they had left from on the cold, horrid morning of their deportation to Russia, many years ago. Today was warm and dry, but their faces were wet with joyful tears. At last, they were stepping down onto Polish soil, their soil, the land they loved as much as life itself. The sky above was clear and blue and matched the forget-me-nots that dotted the green meadows. The precious countryside ran northward from the station for several kilometers before meeting the wall of the forest they remembered so well. Under the shadow of that wall sat the village where Frania, Julek, and Jozia were born.

They had to walk the rest of the way, but that was just fine with them. Each step they took brought them closer to the beloved place they had longed to see for so long. This was the place they kept seeing in their dreams all the while they were in exile. This place caught and held a large part of their past, their happiest memories. This place could never change the way other places had. It was their home; it had no right to change.

The sun moved to the far side of noon, and the land gleamed in its light. Birds sang familiar songs, melting the returnees' hearts. Up above their heads, a skylark hung suspended in midair, spilling forth Frania's favorite merry tunes. She had loved to listen to its trilling while working in her parents' fields before the war.

These were dear sights Frania was seeing now—friendly and familiar, yet somehow unfamiliar. Something was missing from the old picture. But what? She pondered the question for some time, and then turned to Julek. "Where are all the farmers who should be tilling their fields at this time of year?"

He shook his head, and so did Tata, who strolled alongside her.

She gave herself a shake, as if to chase away her terrible suspicions. No! She refused to consider that the reality might not match her expectations.

"Look, Frania! Look to your far left. Isn't that Zapalov, our neighboring village?" cried Julek with excitement.

"It must be," she said, straining her eyes. "I see some rooftops and chimneys."

"I do, too, but where is the church steeple? Maybe we're lost," said Tata.

"No, we're going in the right direction, because there is our river. See?" said Julek.

"Yes, it's our river!" said Frania. "Look at the line of willows running all the way in both directions."

"Can we go swimming in it, Frania? Can we?"

"No, we can't. Jozia, you're thirteen now, but sometimes you act like a two-year-old child," Frania said, trying to sound cross, but at the moment there was no room for anger in her heart.

Soon they were all running, with Frania ahead of her father and Julek and the girls, too. Somewhere, just before the curve in the river, there was a walkway without any rails to hold onto. She was determined to get to it before anyone else, and cross the river first. This was the walkway they had always used on Sundays on their way to the church, the one now missing its steeple.

Frania and the girls crossed the river before the men did. When they gazed upon their birth land for the first time, they blinked and rubbed their eyes. Had they come to the wrong place? What they were seeing now was not a settlement, but a young forest that seemed to be an extension of the old one. What had happened to the beloved image the returnees carried in their memories? It had been broken into tiny pieces and burned.

Who or what had wiped out Surmaczowka? Even a child could guess it was the war that was the culprit here, the villain responsible. But what they couldn't understand at first was how Mother Nature had tried to conceal all evidence of these criminal acts by covering the place with new vegetation. Maybe Nature was just like any human mother, who would do anything to conceal the wrongdoing of her wicked sons.

But even Mother Nature couldn't hide what had happened to Frania's village. She looked around and found signs that easily pointed out that her village once had existed here. Underneath the thickest and tallest weeds lay piles of ashes, from which poked the ends of charred boards laced with nails bleeding rust. The first three piles she discovered were all that was left of what once had been her parents' homestead. In the house that used to be, but was no longer, she and her sisters had laughed, cried, played, and worked while growing up. Here, they had enjoyed their summers and borne the hardships of winter. Here they had all rejoiced at the return of Easters and Christmases. Over there to the left was a pile that said, *I was a barn, once upon a time. I sheltered cows, horses, and pigs that complained through the winter of being cooped up inside for too long.*

Seven years ago, this place would have been filled with the sounds of singing, laughing, crying, teasing, dominated by Mama's scolding. Mooing, neighing, quacking, a rooster's crowing would have filled the air around the farm. Today—how sad, oh God!—a grave silence hung above the ruins.

That healthy fruit trees, bushes, and flowers had once grown about Frania's home and all the others wasn't hard to prove. Broken tree trunks, some only half burned, rose above the ground like the fingers of giant skeletons. Frania's favorite apple tree, crippled and barely alive, gazed at the sky as if pleading with God to wreak revenge on whoever had destroyed its companions. Bold and pushy weeds had overgrown the flower gardens. Still, here and there a lovely blossom of some rightful old resident broke through to smile at Frania.

All was painfully quiet for Frania now, all that had been precious and dear flooded away on the wave of time. Her energetic mother was no longer around to make delicious meals or to hug her oldest daughter when she was sad. Marysia and Aniela weren't here to whisper secrets to. If they were still alive, they were grown up by now. Had they come back to this place and then left again? Or had they ended up someplace else altogether? And the farm animals, which were a great part of the family's past? Frania was sure they had all been slaughtered and eaten.

Frania walked up to the apple tree, slid down to the ground, and slumped against its trunk. She broke down sobbing. She cried because, finally, she realized there was no turning back to some happier past, not when all she had loved and cherished as a young girl, and all she dreamed of during her exile, existed no longer. Yes, everything was gone, disappeared as if devoured by the new growth that sprang from the old wall of the forest. Not one friendly or familiar thing remained intact. The forest had spread greedily over the fields where lupine or potatoes usually grew. It covered the demolished farmstead, slowing down only a little when it came to the main fields, which used to produce wheat, buckwheat, millet, cabbage, carrots, corn, sugar beets, flax, and other crops. This part of the land now lay uncultivated, lush with tall weeds and short, shy bushes. This wilderness wasn't the Surmaczowka she remembered, with dreamy chimneys smoking their pipes. If only Frania's room had survived, with the window through which she had once crept to dance at a party, she would feel better. If only she could find her school still standing at the other end of the village, where Julek had leaned over a classroom desk and confessed his love. Her heart fluttered just thinking how fantastic it would be to see the front door of the building. Through it, Andrzej had approached to talk to her, as if by accident, when she was passing by.

Until now, she had believed that, once she saw the village and her birthplace, she would forget the awful exile. She thought that, somehow, the past years could disappear as if by magic, and she would make up the lost time to Julek. Enveloped by her reveries, she hoped to see her mother as she was seven years ago, and everyone else unchanged, untouched by past events.

"Frania," she whispered, as she cried even harder now under the apple tree, "you foolish woman! Why did you let yourself fall into such daydreaming? You're not a little girl anymore."

A gentle breeze rustled the leaves of a healthy new linden growing on the spot where the old one used to be. *Hush-hush-hush*, it whispered in Frania's ear. But how could she not cry over the graveyard of Surmaczowka? It hurt so very much to see the ruins of the settlement where her family, her neighbors, and her friends once had lived.

In Russia, Frania had struggled with death itself. She fought the Black Angel with her bare hands and won the right to live. Many times, she did that just so she could find her way back to Poland and see Surmaczowka as it was before the war. Today, she was back, but there was nothing left and no one to greet her return.

A tap on her shoulder startled her. She looked up and saw Julek leaning over her.

"Frania," he said in a soft voice, squatting down before her.

"Julek," she whispered, "tell me—where did everything and everyone go?"

"I don't know," he said, wiping her cheeks with the tips of his warm fingers.

"What are we to do now? What?" she cried.

He took her in his arms and held her tight. "We'll think of something."

For a while, they sat comforting each other.

"Where is Tata?" She suddenly remembered the older man.

"I saw him going through the barn rubble as if he were looking for something," said Julek.

"Jozia and Wandzia. Where are they?"

"They're picking wildflowers to make you stop crying."

"They are? God bless them. I was so absorbed in my own sorrow that I forgot about them—about everybody," she moaned.

"It's all right, Frania. We all need time to mourn over Surmaczowka."

Several minutes later, the family grouped together. Frania's father was the first to speak.

"Have to start farming right away."

"First we have to find a place to stay," said Julek.

"But where can we go?" asked Frania, looking at Julek. At that moment, she decided he should be the one to make decisions, for she was tired of relying on herself.

"Let's go to Zapalov," her father suggested.

"We have no relatives there," said Julek. "We'll walk to Jaroslav instead."

"Yes, we can do that," smiled Frania. "Andrzej's parents can help."

Julek shook his head vigorously. "No. I don't want their charity. Remember how high and mighty they acted at your wedding, Frania?"

"It's only Andrzej's mother who acts that way. His father is a very decent man."

"Still, I don't want to go there."

"Then where?" asked Tata.

"To my Uncle Jan."

'That handsome bachelor who owns a brick house?" asked Frania.

"The same one. He and my mother were very close, and I was his favorite nephew."

That afternoon, the weary travelers walked toward the city. By the time they reached it, the sun was withdrawing its light as if trying to hide the ugly ruins that ruthlessly mocked them. Julek found his uncle's house half burned and empty except for rats. He then knocked at the door of his uncle's neighbor.

"Jan was a stubborn man and a humanitarian," said the neighbor.

"Was?" said Julek.

"He knew it wasn't healthy for him to be hiding Jews, but he took chances."

"Nazis killed him?" asked Julek, his voice suddenly choked up.

"Yes, they did."

"Dear God!"

"I told him over and over again that someday his luck would run out. And one day they found two young Jews in his attic. They shot Jan and the Jews too, the same day."

"Why did he have to be so goodhearted!" shouted Julek. He raised his hands and pressed them hard against his temples. Tears ran down his cheeks.

Frania rushed to his side. She slid her arm about Julek's waist. "I'm sorry, my darling."

"I know, I know," he said, lowering his arms so one of them was free to wrap around her shoulders.

"If you people have nowhere to go, you're welcome to stay here overnight," Jan's old neighbor said.

Frania smiled a thank you through her tears.

Frania pressed the doorbell of the home that had once been hers and Henio's, and waited in the semidarkness of the fast-approaching night. She was about to turn away when the door finally opened.

"Yes, young lady? Can I help you?" said a ghost of what once had been Andrzej's father. He came out carrying a kerosene lamp.

"Father," Frania said in surprise. "Don't you recognize me?"

"No," he said, and brought the lamp close to her face.

"It's Frania, your daughter-in-law."

His mouth fell open. "You don't look like her."

"I know. I've come back from Russia."

He blinked, then stepped to her right side and raised the lamp, the better to see the companions standing behind her. "Andrzej? Henio?"

"They are both dead, Father."

The old man took two steps back. For a split second, his figure swayed, but then he steadied himself on the steps. "She...she...his mother died, too," he said, his voice hoarse.

"Oh, Father," Frania said, and stretched out her arms. She wanted this man to forgive her for not dying, too.

He put down the lantern and took her into his arms. She sighed with relief. They hugged each other, both of them crying.

"Did Andrzej suffer much?" the old man whispered into her hair.

"No, he passed away peacefully," she answered. She couldn't tell this poor man that his son had starved to death, whereas she herself stood before him now looking fat. Of course, she would tell him later on about how they had all starved, and how the Russians were told to fatten them before sending them home.

"His mother worried so much about Andrzej that she couldn't sleep or eat."

"I understand. I also lost Henio, my son."

"Where did he die?"

"The first year, in Siberia."

The old man let go of Frania and said in a voice that tried to be cheerful, "Forgive me, Frania. I don't know why I let you stand in the doorway instead of asking you all inside."

"We could use some coffee," she said.

"Please, do come in, all of you."

Frania introduced her co-survivors to the old man, and he repeated their names and smiled at each of them.

"And—and Julek—he's my fiancé," she said, watching for some change of expression in the old man's face.

But he smiled back at her, a small smile, and said, "God bless you both."

They were hungry, and he gave them ham sandwiches and coffee without milk for their supper. After the meal, the grownups talked until past midnight. Jozia and Wandzia went to sleep on the bed that had once belonged to Frania and Andrzej.

When the newcomers told the old man about finding their village in complete ruins, he nodded knowingly and said, "What you don't know is that the war alone was not responsible for the fires that destroyed yours and other people's properties."

"What else?" asked Frania's father.

"Bandits. They kept coming out of the forest to loot, rob, and kill innocent families who were lucky enough to avoid deportation."

Frania could not believe her ears. "Dear Heaven! Is there no end to the bad news we're to hear?"

"Hope you aren't planning to go back there right away," the good host said.

"We were hoping to," said Julek.

"You can't do that—not just yet."

"Why not?"

"Because bad gangs still exist, and they prowl the countryside around Surmachowka."

"So that's why we saw no farmers working in the fields," said Frania's father.

"They were not all killed, God forbid?" said Frania.

"No. Most of them escaped to the cities."

"That's good."

"And I suggest that you, Frania, and your dear ones play it safe and stay here for a while."

"Stay here?"

"Yes, with me."

"I don't know. We don't want to impose."

"Nonsense. You would be doing me a favor. I'm lonely," said their host.

"It would feel good to have a roof over our heads again," said Julek.

"Then it's settled. My store is gone, but I have enough room for you here, and a supply of food left in the pantry."

"Thank you, Father," said Frania humbly. She was very tired suddenly, and the thought of sleeping in a real bed sounded like luxury to her.

"Thank you," said Julek and Tata together.

Thus, the returnees stayed in Jaroslav and lived on what they found in the pantry: stale flour, withering potatoes, a large slab of bacon. These meager provisions would run out too fast, they all knew. Would the survivors wait until the pantry was completely empty? No, it wasn't in their nature to do so.

The following week, Frania and Julek began to look around and ask many questions. Soon they discovered something they could do to replenish the food supply, not only for themselves, but also for their good host.

Chapter Twenty-one

SUSPENDED HIGH IN MIDAIR, A SKYLARK SANG BEAUTIFUL NOTES, AND Frania listened, her heart melting with joy. She was weeding and hoeing rows of young potatoes in a field located on the other side of Jaroslav, just three kilometers outside of town. Because they lived far from the forest where bandits hid, these farmers felt safe enough to stay home and work their soil, just like they did before the war. The sun was bright and warm, the air clean and permeated by a special scent that only the Polish countryside held in its bosom. For a moment, Frania forgot that the farm she was working wasn't her parents' or her own, but one belonging to strangers.

As noon grew near, she felt hungry and thirsty, just as she often had at this time of day when living with her parents. She grinned as she hoed, imagining her mother or one of her younger sisters bringing bread, cheese, salted pork, and milk for lunch. Nice, cold, delicious milk, chilled in the cellar. Her stomach rumbled in anticipation.

She straightened up, looked northward and wrinkled her forehead. It wasn't her home she was seeing, but the edge of Jaroslav, its broken chimneys slowly being replaced by new ones. A tear squeezed from under her eyelid and rolled down her cheek. Her eyes scanned the land and fell on Julek and her father, plowing the adjoining field for crops to be planted later. Julek was no longer a boy with an easy smile. He was a mature, sober-faced man now.

"And you, Tata," she said softly to the air. "You don't look as strong as you once did."

As she glanced toward the road that led to the village, where the owner of the fields lived, Frania noticed a woman walking in her direction. She carried a large basket filled with food for the field workers—her husband and son, Frania and her co-workers.

Once again, Frania and her dear ones were working for food the way they had in Kazakhstan. The difference now was that they labored for six days a week and rested deliciously on Sundays. Most importantly, they currently earned generous quantities of freshly baked bread, sweet pastry, eggs, ham, cabbage, onions, potatoes, and other goodies. They had already accumulated more than enough to last them not only through the summer, but over the wintertime, too. Through the fall, they worked for money to buy new clothes and badly needed shoes.

In the early fall, Julek and Frania were married with the blessing of both fathers, hers and Andrzej's. The wedding was held in the church that was being rebuilt. By this time, Frania's weight was down to normal. She looked beautiful in the light blue dress her bridesmaid sewed for her. Julek looked handsome in a suit he had purchased in the thrift shop on the corner. That day, the newlyweds were happy, and their happiness radiated all around them.

As a wedding gift, Andrzej's father gave them a spacious room in the west wing of his house for privacy.

Finally, Julek and Frania made love. For the first time, Frania knew what it was to be fully loved by the one man who was right for her. They fit into each other's arms so well and made unhurried love, which satisfied them both. They didn't need special sex classes or the advice of older folks, for they followed their instincts and the beat of their two hearts.

On Christmas Eve morning, Frania and Julek rose at the crack of dawn. He started a fire in the stove in the front room, which served the family as a kitchen, recreation place, and dining room. She prepared dough for rising, from which she would bake sweet pastries. Then she made coffee, and the aroma woke up Jozia, Wandzia, and the two fathers. One by one they came in, greeting Frania and Julek with smiles and thirsting after the strong black liquid. When they saw the blazing fireplace, their eyes lit up like sparkling firecrackers.

"Dziendobry," sang out the old man, who came in last.

"Dziendobry," they all greeted him with a smile, admiring the way he looked lately. He had grown a snowy-white beard and looked just like

Father Christmas in the book Jozia had brought from school. She and Wandzia were now attending classes at the Convent.

"Frania, you and your husband are up so early this morning. I heard you moving about in the kitchen," he said, sitting down for breakfast beside Frania's father.

"There's so much to do, Father Number Two," said Frania, filling the old man's cup with coffee.

"Let me help," he said, glancing up at her. Raising his hand, he signaled her to stop pouring.

"Let us all help you," said her father, just before he sank his teeth into a fat piece of buttered bread.

"What can I do?" asked Jozia, her cheek stuffed with homemade cheese.

"And I?" sang Wandzia.

Frania said nothing. She was busy putting the coffee pot back on the stove with care, for there were so many things crowding it. In one corner, the dough was rising. Next to it stood a large pot half-filled with dried mixed fruit, soaking. On the biggest burner, now shut off, a large kettle waited to be filled with water to boil the pierogies.

"Since you're all willing to do things," she finally said, as she sat down by Julek at the table, "I will gladly give each of you a task."

They all perked up their ears.

"I need more firewood to be brought in from the shed."

"I'll take care of that," said Father Number Two, "and tend the fire."

"Good." Frania nodded. "Someone has to sweep and wash the floor before supper."

"I can do that," said Tata.

"And there is a big beautiful tree to be bought at the market," Frania said, grinning at her husband.

"Of course, my beloved. I will get that."

"Frania, you didn't tell us what to do," said Jozia, pouting. "Wandzia and I might as well be at the Convent. At least there, we'd be needed."

"Oh, come on, you two, don't sulk! You can make up the beds, wash the dishes, and then—"

"Can we decorate the tree?" sang out Wandzia, her dark eyes shining like two deep pools.

"Of course. This work is yours, too, Jozia and Wandzia. What else can you do with all the paper chains you made yesterday?"

It snowed that day, but there was no wind, and the temperature kept its head above zero. Inside, Frania, rosy-cheeked and happy, baked two baskets of fresh white bread, some sweet pastry, and cookies for the tree. She also made pierogies filled with prunes, potatoes, and cheese sweetened with sugar. She prepared her mother's favorite dish, a mushroom soup, and made hot cereal topped with honey. Her fruit compote was the hit of the evening.

The family consumed their meal while gathered around the crackling fireplace, just as they had years earlier. Afterwards, they all stood around the tree. There were no candles or electric bulbs to light the branches, but that was all right. Right away, the family started to sing carols. These were beloved tunes they had learned in early childhood. The songs flooded the front room like ocean waves that washed away debris left lying on the shore. The caroling filled Frania's heart with happy memories, which slowly were cracking the hardened layer of her tragic past. The harsh years had to be chipped away bit by bit and flushed from her head and her heart so she could be free to start her life anew, with no more nightmares, no more jumping with fright every time she heard a knock at the door.

Shortly after the holiday, Jozia and Wandzia expressed the desire to become nuns. Frania didn't object. Soon, they both moved into the Convent.

During the cold months, Frania, Julek, and her father made friends with their new neighbors and the people they worked for. They did odd jobs: cleaning houses, fixing things, taking care of the old and sick. They listened to what was said about politics on the radio and read the newsletter printed by their new government. They learned that people who had left their properties in the eastern part of Poland, which now belonged to Russia, could claim new land in the far west, territories taken from the Germans. Frania's father and Julek had lost their farms to the forest. Maybe they could fill out a claim for new land to take the place of the old?

To find out, Julek and Frania visited an official in Jaroslaw. Shortly before spring of the next year, they were informed that a large piece of good land between the river and Zapalov was theirs to take. The property had belonged to two Ukranian families, who were deported to Russia during the last year of the war and were not expected ever to return.

As soon as the weather grew warm, Julek and Tata threw themselves into building their own house on the opposite bank of the river across from the old place. By the middle of April, they had managed to make a cellar good enough to shelter the family.

On the day she was packing to move, Frania said to the old man, "Father Number Two, you're welcome to come with us."

"Thank you, dear, but no," said he, tears moistening his eyes.

"Why not?"

"I…I prefer to die in my own corner," he said, and lowered his head to his chest.

"And who's talking about dying? You're still strong and young enough to be useful."

He shook his head. "You are good people, all of you, but I want to stay here."

She bent over him, kissed his forehead, and whispered, "I understand. You love this place."

"Yes, I do."

"We'll visit you as often as we can, and we thank you for your hospitality."

There were no words to describe what Frania felt to be working again on land that belonged to her and her family. A well-deserved pride and joy flooded her heart, and she felt as if she stood on top of the world.

"We've made it!" she wanted to shout for the Russians to hear her on the other side of the border. "Five of us have survived your war and your exile, and we want you to know…" she looked toward the east and then toward the west, "…that we'll raise great crops, multiply in numbers, and we will never again go hungry or live in poverty. Do you hear me? Do you?"

On the day of beet planting, a strange man came to the fields. He strolled out from Zapalov and handed something to Frania's father.

"What have you got, Tata? What?" called out Frania, as she rushed to his side.

"A letter," he said, turning an envelope in his hands. It was yellow with age, all wrinkled and smudged.

"Who is it from?"

He gave her the letter. "I don't know. Can't read without glasses."

"This came from—I can't believe it! It came from East Africa."

"Who could be writing from that hot country?"

"The name of the addressee is smudged, Tata."

"Open the envelope and read the letter, Frania," he said impatiently.

"It's...it's from Marysia! Oh, Tata!"

"Marysia?"

"Yes. She's alive, and Aniela, too. And...and Veronka."

"My daughters are alive! Thank you, God," exclaimed Tata.

"Julek! Come here," Frania shouted across to the next field, where her husband was working. When he came near, she said, "Veronka didn't die in Russia."

"How do you know?" Julek asked.

She handed him the letter. He read it and smiled. Hugging his wife, he sang out with happiness, "I still have one sister alive!"

"When was the letter written?" Only now, Frania's father thought of asking.

"Let's see," said Julek. "Oh, here it is. January of 1944."

"So this letter is old. It probably traveled all over before it finally came to us."

"We have to thank the stranger for bringing it to us," said Frania.

"Yes, we'll go to Zapalov on Sunday to find him," said her father.

Marysia's letter was very informative. In it, she told her father that, after leaving the hospital in the year of their separation, she, Aniela, and Veronka wandered about Kagan streets for a week. Then they hopped a train to Bukhara in hopes of finding the family there. In both cities, the girls had nothing to eat. They slept on the pavement even in the rain. In Bukhara, they met some Polish soldiers. One of them was especially interested in Veronka and helped them to get the papers they needed to be evacuated.

We crossed the Caspian Sea in the summer, wrote Marysia. *And I want to tell you, Tata, that the day of our crossing was the happiest day of our lives!*

The minute we left Russia, we ate better and slept on cots, not on the ground. We were still sick for a while, because we brought our diseases with us. The sad fact is that too many of our people died in Iran, in spite of the medical care we received there from friendly nations. But thousands survived.

We traveled by land and across the Indian Ocean and came to Tengeru, a freshly made settlement near Arusha. They gave us comfortable houses to live in, with regular beds and other furniture. We eat well here and enjoy a normal life while waiting for the war to end and our Poland to be freed from its enemies.

As soon as schools opened, Aniela and I went to advanced classes to learn to read and write better. I know, I know—we are both too old to be going to school, but there's nothing for us to do here but be educated, and we are trying to be just that...

That evening, right after supper, Frania wrote to her sisters. From that day forward, they kept in touch with each other through correspondence.

Three years had passed since the war ended, but still the girls didn't return home. When Tengeru was dissolved, Marysia and Aniela signed up as textile factory workers and went to England. Veronka preferred to settle in Australia with a former Polish soldier, who arrived there a year before her. She had been writing to the young man for years, while he was fighting the Nazis outside Poland. After he reached Australia, he proposed to her in one of his long letters, and she accepted.

Marysia and Aniela married, too, several months after arriving in England. Marysia's husband was like Veronka's, a man who had served well in the Second Polish Corps. Aniela wedded an Englishman, the manager of the factory where she worked.

In 1951, Marysia emigrated to America. She was then six months pregnant and gave birth to a healthy son, who, to the utter joy of his parents, automatically became an American citizen.

Both Marysia and Aniela kept asking Frania to leave Poland and come either to America or England. But Frania refused to budge. She loved her country and her new farm. Her world began and ended with

Poland. Nowhere else produced richer or fatter grain. Here, the lindens' white blossoms gave off the aroma of warm honey. Here, and only here, wild strawberries were as sweet as candies. She loved to pick them in the forest on Sundays.

While reading her sister's letters, Frania saw that the girls' lives had turned for the better. With time, they both enjoyed their own homes in their respective cities. They also had cars to drive around in, automatic washing machines, gas stoves, and indoor plumbing with hot and cold running water. Frania still hauled water from a well and washed her clothes by hand. She walked to Zapalov and Jaroslav to do her shopping. Her men had constructed a spacious house modeled on the old one, but it was still heated by logs burning in the stove.

Secretly, Frania envied the material things her sisters had, especially the beautiful clothes they wore in their photos. Still, she felt more fortunate than they, because she breathed Polish air. But one thing she had learned was that change is inevitable.

When she and Julek started to farm their land after the war, they had no idea the new government would someday try to force them and all the other farmers to give up their soil to collective farming.

"Collective farming?" she shouted, when two students from Jaroslaw came to her field and tried to brainwash her. "Just like in Russia? No! No! You two youngsters get off our land."

Julek and Tata reacted the same way she did to this plan for collective farming. All the Polish farmers resisted the government. Luckily, in time the plans fell through. But then the government revenged itself by inflicting high taxes on the landowners.

After that, Frania lived in fear of Russians, especially when she saw red troops stationed in Jaroslav. What was to stop them from deporting her and her dear ones to Siberia again?

Fearing an uncertain future, she didn't want to have another child. And when, one day, she realized she was pregnant, she was shocked. For as long as she could, she kept the news a secret from Julek. But then she began having nightmares again. In them, she saw herself and her new child back in the wilds of Russia. It was a daughter this time, suffering from cold and starvation on a wintry night.

She and Julek were sleeping, cuddling up close to each other. Through a half-shaded window, a stream of moonlight fell upon the floor, and then slowly traveled up their bed. When it touched Frania's face, she stirred and turned away from Julek. For a while, she lay quietly, then her eyelids began to move rapidly, and she started mumbling. The mumbling rose to a scream: "No! No! That cannot be!"

A gentle slap on her cheek woke her. She opened her eyes and saw Julek bending over her.

"What's the matter with you, Frania?"

She blinked at him, a dark light of horror in her eyes.

"You had a nightmare again," he guessed.

She nodded.

"I'll light the lamp to help you forget the bad dreams."

"Please do," she managed to whisper.

Silently, he slid to the floor and stumbled over to a box of matches. "What did you dream about this time?" he said, and struck a match that flared up brightly.

She waited until he had lighted the lamp and climbed back into bed.

"Oh, Julek, my beloved, it was awful." She reached for his hand and held it close to her cheek.

"What was awful? Tell me about it," he said, hovering over her like a mother hen.

"I was in Russia."

"Oh, no! Frania. You have to forget the past."

"Wish I could," she said. She sat up in bed.

"Did you dream about Henio?" Julek asked, embracing her.

"Yes. He...he's lying in a coffin, about to be lowered into the grave. When my father was about to pull on the rope, I asked him to wait. Then I came close to the coffin and lifted the lid. And...and what I saw then made me scream."

"What did you see?" he asked, tightening his arm about her.

"It was—oh, Julek. I...I don't want to talk about it now."

"You have to talk. You have to."

Frania shivered all over.

"Tell me, Frania."

"It wasn't Henio. It was our child."

"Our what?"

"Our child," she repeated.

He pushed her gently from him and turned her so he could look into her face. "Frania, you are pregnant?"

"Yes."

"Why didn't you tell me?"

"Because I…I'm terrified!"

"Terrified?"

"I would die if the same thing happened to her that happened to Henio."

He kissed her forehead and said, "Nothing like that is going to happen to him, trust me."

"Her," she said, then gave him a small smile.

Each person should live life to the full, and human life should go hand in hand with happiness. Unfortunately, happiness flies away when confronted with fear. Frania knew she had the power to free herself from her fears, but she didn't know how. For days, she moved about the house, thinking and struggling within herself. Then one day she knew. Yes, she woke early one morning and knew what to do even before she opened her eyes to the snowy day.

"Julek," she said, and listened for a response, but all she heard was his steady breathing. She sat up. The cold air of the unheated bedroom hit her shoulders and made her shiver. She pulled the covers up her chin and looked at her husband, who lay there peacefully. But what was this deep line between his eyebrows? The line told her that her dear man was worrying, too, about the future of their unborn child.

She withdrew her hand from under the quilt. With the tips of her fingers, she gently tapped his cheek. "Darling, wake up," she said in a soft voice, careful not to startle him.

He opened his eyes wide and smiled up at her. "Dziendobry, my beautiful wife," he said, and moved to take her in his arms.

"No, no. Not now, Julek," she said, and pushed his arms away.

He looked up into her eyes and said, "Something is wrong."

She shook her head. "We have to talk."

"Oh?" he said and yawned. "Is that all?"

"Let's go to America!" she blurted out.

Her sentence struck him the same way his words had surprised her that long ago day back in Siberia by the Irtish River, when he suggested they go for a picnic together in the taiga.

"Please, Julek. I really want to go."

He stared up into her face as if seeing a stranger.

"Why don't you speak up?" she said in a harsh voice.

"I...I don't know what to say," he finally mumbled, and rose to a sitting position.

She pulled the covers up to his chin and waited. "Marysia can help us, you know."

He still said nothing, but tiny lines on his forehead showed that he was thinking hard.

"I can write to my sister today."

He raised his hand and said, "Frania, think about what you want do."

"I've been thinking for the past two weeks, Julek."

"Can you really leave our homestead and our country that you love so much?"

"It's going to be hard, but we have to do it for the sake of our daughter."

"Our son," he corrected her.

"Whatever," she said, and waved her hand in the air.

"How about your father?"

"He'll go with us."

"Do I have to give you my answer this morning, Frania?"

"Yes, I need to know," she said, and then her words came so fast, they began to tumble over each other. "You see, darling, you can work in a factory like Marysia's husband does and earn good money. We'll have to rent out a small room at first, but then we can buy a house near my sister's, and—"

"Whoa! Stop! You're going too fast!"

"Sorry," she said, but kept right on chattering. "And…and we can buy ourselves a car, a washing machine, a gas stove, a television, and… and…and…" she slowed down suddenly, but then added, "In America, we will be safe from the Russians."

"Yes, we will. It would be good to know that our child can grow up happy and free of the kind of fears we have had to face."

"Oh, Julek! Does this mean, yes? Yes? Yes?"

"Yes, it does," he said, staring out the window as if he were already seeing himself and his family traveling to America.

About the Author

JANE BORUSZEWSKI was born in Eastern Poland in 1926. In 1940 she was deported with her family to Siberia. After amnesty, they left the place of their imprisonment. While traveling by train, she and her sister and brother, suffering from typhoid, were put in hospital somewhere near Bukhara. They survived, but following their release from the hospital were homeless and separated from their family.

Jane crossed the Caspian Sea in 1942 and was brought to East Africa, where she attended school in Tengeru, near Arusha, and graduated from high school. After WWII ended, she refused to go back to Poland and signed up for work in a textile factory in England, where she met and married her husband, Walt. They emigrated to America in 1950, where their three daughters, Teresa, Linda, and Irene, were born.

Eventually, Jane went back to school and graduated from Onondaga Community College with highest honors.

CPSIA information can be obtained
at www.ICGtesting.com
Printed in the USA
LVOW12s1500051117

555096LV00001B/25/P